AND HOUSE OF PAIN!

"*House of Pain* is horror at its best."
—*The Midwest Book Review*

"A powerful and unflinching novel."
—Peter Atkins, author of *Wishmaster*

"If Poppy Z. Brite and Nancy Kilpatrick turn your cold blood to hot, then welcome Sèphera Girón to the short list of dark mistresses of terror truly worthy of that title."
—Stanley Wiater, author of *Dark Dreamers*

"Girón's prose is smooth as silk; the pacing is dead on. I devoured this book in a single sitting."
—*Horror World*

"*House of Pain* is a perfect—if far from safe—place to lose yourself on a stormy fall night."
—*Fangoria*

"Genuinely creepy."
—*Cemetery Dance*

"*House of Pain* rocks with good old-fashioned creepiness."
—Edo van Belkom, author of *Teeth*

THE BOOKSHELF
NEW BOOKS • USED BOOKS
101 N. Walnut
Batesville, IN 47006
812-934-5800

Rd-2004 - Judy Gray

THE SWARM

A thick fog coated the country road. He put his high beams on and squinted his eyes. He had drunk just a bit too much tonight, partly because Katey drove him to it. Dumb bitch. Why couldn't she just deal with shit as it happened? Why was she in such a hurry to get tied down? She should enjoy the fact that they had some good times and just leave it at that.

Ahead, it looked like there was something at the side of the road. He slowed, hoping it wasn't a deer or some other animal that would just spontaneously leap out in front of the car.

No, it must be a hitchhiker. Someone just standing there. He got closer and the front of his windshield darkened.

"Holy goddamn!" he cried out as he saw that the darkness was a swarm of bugs. Of bees.

"What the fuck . . ." He slammed on his brakes, unable to see the road. He was glad his windows were up, and started the wipers. Dozens of bees smeared across the glass as the wipers went back and forth. Where the bodies were squished, more swooped in to take their place. . . .

Other *Leisure* books by Sèphera Girón:
HOUSE OF PAIN

SÈPHERA GIRÓN

THE BIRDS
AND
THE BEES

LEISURE BOOKS   NEW YORK CITY

For Derek

A LEISURE BOOK®

November 2002

Published by

Dorchester Publishing Co., Inc.
276 Fifth Avenue
New York, NY 10001

If you purchased this book without a cover you should be aware that this book is stolen property. It was reported as "unsold and destroyed" to the publisher and neither the author nor the publisher has received any payment for this "stripped book."

Copyright © 2002 by Sèphera Girón

All rights reserved. No part of this book may be reproduced or transmitted in any form or by any electronic or mechanical means, including photocopying, recording or by any information storage and retrieval system, without the written permission of the publisher, except where permitted by law.

ISBN 0-8439-5085-4

The name "Leisure Books" and the stylized "L" with design are trademarks of Dorchester Publishing Co., Inc.

Printed in the United States of America.

Visit us on the web at www.dorchesterpub.com.

ACKNOWLEDGMENTS

Books are never written in a vacuum. Friends and acquaintances are a wonderful inspiration, especially when tragedy strikes.

This past year was a painful, difficult year on so many levels. The events of September 11 affected everyone so differently. On first impulse, for me, it was the bell tolling the beginning of the end. As of this writing, it is unclear as to what will really happen and how the world will transform to absorb the continuing onslaught of war.

This wake-up call became a chance to examine what was near and dear to me and I appreciate even more the generosity and kindness of so many people.

In the past few months, I felt like I was living out the final scene in *It's a Wonderful Life*, where so many people have rallied around to throw me a lifeline.

I owe Cathy Smith a huge thank you as well as her mother, Shirley. Others who have pulled me from the depths of hell include: Julie Finlay, Nancy Kilpatrick, Yvonne Navarro and Weston Osche, Cecile Phillips, Tina Jens and the entire staff of World Horror Convention 2002, Caro Soles, Rain Graves and Dr. Crystal and her staff.

People who have helped me forge ahead with my career are many, but I'd like to thank Peter Atkins, Michael Rowe, Stanley Wiater, F. Paul Wilson, Edo van Belkom, Karen E. Taylor, Rick Hautala, David Nordhaus and Keith Herber.

Also, I would like to thank so many friends and fans who have listened to me and inspired me. Sandra Kasturi and Brett Savory, Sara Newman and Jill Cross, Heather and David Edwards, Julian Grant and Leslie Anne Coles.

Thank you to my agent, Lori Perkins.

A big thank you to my family—Adrian and Dorian, Patricia and Arsenio, Aunt Ruth—who have been very supportive. And especially to Derek for hanging in there through a most difficult time of my life and repairing that disastrous bathroom in my southwest corner.

Thank you, Don D'Auria, for your belief in me!

THE BIRDS
AND
THE BEES

Chapter One

It stared at her with cold, black button eyes. She held its gaze as long as she could, until she felt as though she might asphyxiate. Her legs trembled.

She closed her eyes and turned her head.
Counting.
1-2-3.
It would be gone when she looked back. It had to be.
4-5-6.
She slowly turned her head back and winked open her eyes.
It still sat there, staring at her.
Watching.
Waiting.
Waiting for what?

She couldn't take it anymore.

Even as she walked away, she knew it was still watching her, could feel the blinkless penetration of that glare beaming up her back, worming its way into her brain.

She shook her head and quickened her step.

After half a block or so, she stopped and turned around.

It was still there, perched on that bike rack, staring in her direction.

Staring at *her*.

No. It's not staring at me, she told herself.

But she looked back, could swear that they met eye-to-eye, even from half a city block.

It cawed once, then spread its coal-black wings and flew away.

Gabrielle sucked in a deep breath, watched the crow circle once, then disappear.

It was ridiculous. It was just a bird. It was only watching her because she was watching it. Nothing more. Nothing less.

She tried to smile.

That was all.

And that would be it too, except that she seemed to be seeing birds a lot the past few years. Much more than she ever remembered before, even as a child spending long lazy days in the country at her grandmother's house.

It seemed like every day, no matter where she went, there would be a large black bird, maybe two, maybe ten, perched somewhere, staring

The Birds and the Bees

with those beady black button eyes, following her every move. They almost always felt compelled to speak to her, to caw or screech or shriek.

She wondered if other people had this, if other people noticed birds as much as she did. If other people were as disturbed by these birds that stared and screamed.

Gabrielle entered the coffee shop and stood in line. It was nearly nine o'clock and she had a deadline to meet. Birds and their mysteries would just have to wait.

After what seemed like the edge of forever, she was handed her double mochachino, and she continued on down the busy street. She watched the blur of people walk by as she sipped on the frothy sweetness of the whipped cream topping her coffee. It was always interesting to see the differences in people, the first thing in the morning, on the few days that she went into the office, and in the evening, at the bars and clubs.

She found herself watching people, wondering if that woman in the expensive three-piece suit carrying the leather briefcase didn't throw on garish disco clothes and go boogying till the wee hours of the night on the weekend. Did she spike up her short-cropped hair and plaster it with sparkles? Or did she live in a big house, with three kids, two cars, and spend her evenings on the computer, working away, trying to stay ahead of the mortgage?

She wondered what people saw when they looked at *her*.

What did they see?

Gabrielle caught a glimpse of herself in a store window and stopped.

What did they see?

She knew what *she* saw, but what did others see?

What did the birds see?

Her reflection stared back at her, eyes dark with scrutiny, forehead furrowed, long hair blowing in the gentle breeze. She wasn't a businesswoman, anyone could see that, with her knapsack and baggy clothes. Maybe they thought she was an old college student, for the lines around her eyes and mouth showed that she was far from her twenties.

Did they see the pain she had been through in this life?

Certainly she made no claim to more pain than anyone else, but her pain was her own, rolled up tight and tucked away in the stone that thumped against her chest with steady persistence. The stone that she wished would just suddenly stop, so that she could be done with it all.

But it still beat.

Minute by minute, it pumped the blood

The Birds and the Bees

through her body, whether she wanted it to or not.

Every morning she woke up in her small apartment, feeling the ache for children that were no longer there, stroking the side of the bed that had lain empty for more than four years now. And she wondered how she could bear to go on for one more day, how could she drag herself out of bed and into the world for one more day.

Yet somehow she did.

Somehow she found the strength to pull herself out of bed and do what she needed to do to pay the rent, to get through the day.

She knew that the divorce had been for the best. There was no point in hanging onto a marriage just because there were children. No child should have to feel the contempt and disdain that two adults held for each other. No child should feel that they had to take sides, that they had to hide while voices were raised, that they had to watch Mommy cry quietly in the bedroom while Daddy chain-smoked in the kitchen.

That was no life for any of them. They had done the right thing. For the children.

How she wished it had been different, though. That she really had found her Prince Charming, that they could have been a family, with birthday parties and weddings and vacations.

Sèphera Girón

How she wished that she could see her children more often than the weekends—and sometimes she didn't even see them that that often.

But it had been for the best. He had taken custody a couple years ago. After all, he had a good income and a new wife with her own kids, and a house. A home.

She, Gabrielle, was still finding herself, still struggling to understand who she was and trying to scrape up a living. Her hours were so crazy at the magazine that baby-sitters ate up all her income, and the kids were at that weird in-between stage. Too old for baby-sitters, too young to truly be left alone for more than a few hours. So they had agreed that he would take them.

And the stone had grown colder and harder in her chest.

Yet staring at her reflection in the store window, she saw that no one could see that much about her. No one could really tell how she ached.

And who cared really?

Everyone had something that hurt them. Everyone accumulated grief and burdens. She was just the same as everyone else.

She turned away from her reflection and wondered what her job held in store for her today.

* * *

The Birds and the Bees

The darkness swallowed her as she walked deeper into the cave. She had been walking for hours, so she knew she must be close. There were so many curves and splits in this underground maze, no one would ever be able to find her. She herself didn't know where she was going, she was only following some internal instinct, the same instinct that had forced her from her bed at an ungodly hour and proclaimed that *this was the day. This was the day of all days, when it all would begin.*

The cool air tickled her skin, and it was getting harder to breathe. She didn't worry about it, though, barely even noticed it as she continued on, led by the strange pull in her belly.

How long had she been preparing for this time? Or had time been preparing for her?

Even as a child, she had known she was special, had known that she would walk the path of greatness one day. That her name would be perched on the tip of the tongues of millions, as familiar as Cleopatra, Pandora, Joan of Arc, Lilith . . . Eve.

The new millennium had come and gone with no great apocalypse. That was because the prophets were wrong. The prophets were all men. How could they predict the actions of a woman, a woman guiding Mother Nature on beloved Mother Earth? A woman anonymously born with no star in the sky, no angels to sing or kings to worship her. The power was there

Sèphera Girón

for the taking, anyone could have done it. Any woman with enough sense to feel the ebb and flow of the cycles, to study the patterns of the planets, knew that when the earth was in its own chaos, that was man's time to panic. Once the planets settled back down and humans resumed their clockwork lives, working, sleeping, and fucking, then that was the time to insidiously take control.

Her training had been from the gut as well. And dreams. Lots of dreams. There were shadowy figures that trained her, that taught her how to harness her energy, how to walk unnoticed in a throng of people, tug at another's thoughts, pop into another's skin. Those were mere tricks, though, and didn't prove anything or benefit in any real way, except to help her understand just how many people walked through life on automatic pilot.

It was amazing how many people took the easy way out. Instead of facing life's challenges, going that tiny bit extra distance, they would throw their hands up in despair.

It's too hard. It's too expensive. Or the best one, the one that filled her with the most contempt, that popular New Age chant, *It wasn't meant to be*.

She could walk down the city street and pinpoint with a glance those who were lazy. Not by their clothes or their hair. Not by their faces or their shoes. But by their very souls. People who

The Birds and the Bees

stayed in dead-end jobs for fear of carving a new path. People who stayed in dead marriages, since building a new relationship would take work, and why bother doing that when at least you knew what to expect from the same old nightmare that droned on day after day after day? People who had babies, to prove a point somehow, instead of sharing their love. People dulling their senses with drugs or booze or sex to the point where they couldn't feel the truth of life.

She had named herself Armina, after thinking long and hard about a name for her new life. Being Amy Brown just wasn't important enough for the work she had ahead of her.

Her gut ached with excitement; she knew she had nearly found her new home.

The power she had could be anybody's. Anybody who had half a mind to hear it and half the discipline to hone it. She was a big believer in the spark that burned within all humans, at least as children.

But when it came to adults, the spark had burned out in most. In some, it lay dormant. And, of course, there were those that reached for the highest heights of what society had to offer, and their fire burned bright.

She thought about the work she had to do over the next few months. How grueling and challenging it would be. She would never be the same again, in mind, body, or spirit.

Sèphera Girón

Her mind hummed and her gut buzzed like an electrical charge as the winding tunnel spilled into a huge cavernous room.

This was it . . . this was the perfect place.

Her eyes glowed as she lit a candle that she pulled from the heavy knapsack on her back, holding it up so that she could see how big this place really was.

She was not a pretty girl. She had shoulder-length red hair and was bordering on obese. Her face was freckled, her eyes a pale blue. Armina was glad she was nothing special; it was easier to do her work this way.

The humming in her mind echoed around the cavern. She held up her candle and to her delight, found a giant bees' nest clinging to the wall.

"Ah, my pretties, you have made it," she said happily.

As if in response, the insects poured forth from the nest and flew toward her. They covered her face, her arms, her legs. She welcomed the cloak, thriving on the tiny legs dancing along her flesh, relishing sting after sting as their venom sank into her bloodstream. She laughed, a hollow victorious sound that echoed along the cavernous chamber.

Mary Anne hung the clothes on the line, carefully fixing each corner with a wooden peg. The sun was shining although the air was a little

The Birds and the Bees

cool. Summer was fading fast already.

The sheet she was hanging flickered in the light wind and she nearly lost her grip on it. However, years of hanging clothes had given her the knack for anticipating the teasing wind, and she clamped the errant corner tightly with the peg.

Over by the house, little Jimmy and Deedee were digging in the rocks of the driveway. It wouldn't be long before they would be taking the big yellow school bus just like their brother, Eric, down the country roads and off to the little school several miles away.

Her heart skipped a beat as she thought of it. The tiny house empty all day as her children went to school and her husband worked. She wondered how she would stand the loneliness. Maybe she would learn how to drive.

Her heart now raced at the thought of sitting in the driver's seat, hands clutching the wheel, her feet trying to remember which pedal was for the brake, which was to make it go faster.

No, she didn't take to the idea of driving at all. As lonely as she was, the idea of driving a heavy piece of metal was too much for her to bear. She would just wait for John to come home and drive her on her errands. She didn't need much anyway. She had the chores and the kids, and a TV that almost worked and if you tilted the ears just right, could pick up a couple of channels.

Sèphera Girón

Sometimes she wondered, but only sometimes, why if John was off all day working, they were so poor. It seemed like every day was a struggle for food and cigarettes. He managed to pick up the odd bottle of whiskey, but they had no fancy clothes, no fancy lifestyle, and were poor as poor could be. If John's grandparents hadn't left this land and the broken-down shack that they used for a home to Eric, Jimmy, and Deedee, they would be really out of luck.

Sometimes Mary Anne wondered if she wasn't just born under a bad star. It seemed most of the kids she had grown up with had moved away from this tiny town, moved to nice big homes and drove fancy cars. They had husbands that washed and shaved and wore clean clothes. Some of them had those portable phones. Even her old girlfriends would be yammering on those phones while stuck in traffic, the few times they would think to call her.

But the calls became less and less frequent as the years went on.

And she supposed she knew why.

They all thought she was a loser. Had married a loser. And would never move on or grow. She was still a teenager when she had Eric, and she knew that a lot of the girls had looked down on her for that. But John had married her and they had lived with first one set of parents, then the other, until they ended up here. She was the first of all her friends to have her own home,

The Birds and the Bees

and while her friends were off at university or working, she would keep it washed and dusted as best she could, just in case they would stop by to see her and the baby. They used to come by before, one by one, they moved out of town.

Now, the little piles of clutter were growing into mountains. Toys, magazines, this and that . . . she found it nearly impossible to stay on top of it all. The living room was a precarious mountain, the couch ringed by teetering piles of God knows what. Pop cans and beer cans rolled underfoot and collected under the sagging couch.

She found that often she just didn't care.

But now, in the sunshine, hanging the soggy sheets, she felt an urge to clean up her home, to clean up her life. There had to be more to life than raising children and being a wife. There had to be something she was put on the earth for . . . but she couldn't decide what that might be.

It wasn't often that she felt a nagging sensation that there had to be something more. Most of the time, the days just passed, one melding into the other, babies born, babies grown . . . and she would have had more babies too, if only . . .

She stopped and rubbed her belly.

The last pregnancy had been a nightmare. It was two years ago, but it felt like yesterday.

She could still imagine her swollen belly,

could still feel phantom kicking where there was none.

She remembered how happy she had been, pregnant with their fourth child. At the time, she hadn't care that they had little money or that John came home from work later and later smelling like booze. She had her hands full with three children, and spent her few spare minutes feeling the kicks of the fourth. Then one day, the kicks just stopped.

After two days, she was able to convince John that something was terribly wrong, so he drove her to the doctor. An ultrasound showed that the baby had died inside her. There was nothing to do but wait for her body to go into labor.

Another week passed while she carried the dead baby. She would talk to it, trying to will it to move, trying to convince herself that it was all just a terrible mistake, that the baby was fine, was just sleeping.

But it was to no avail.

When a week had passed, the familiar cramps had started in the night. She had woken John, who packed up the sleepy children and drove her to the hospital. He and the children sat in the waiting room while she underwent her private agony. His reasoning was that the baby was dead, so he saw no reason to go into the labor room with her.

In a wash of blood and pain, she gave birth to little Nigel. Perfectly formed and blue. She

The Birds and the Bees

held him for a while before handing him over to the doctor. They didn't have the money for a grave, and so the baby was disposed of by the hospital.

Thinking about Nigel brought tears to her eyes, but she pushed them away. She wasn't a big believer in God, yet she found comfort in the thought that God had wanted this little soul with Him, that Nigel wasn't meant for this earth, there was a bigger Plan for him.

Not many people knew about the fourth baby; most of her friends were amazed that she'd had three at such a young age. She was just twenty-five, and sometimes felt as if she had the soul of a woman who was eighty.

After she had Nigel, they'd told her she could have no more children, that there was something wrong inside her, and had persuaded her to have her tubes tied. In a daze of pain and drugs, she had agreed.

But on this sunny cool day, she pushed all thoughts of Nigel aside and focused on the task at hand, hanging out the sheets to dry, since they couldn't afford to run the dryer year round.

She was so lost in her thoughts, it took a moment to register that the children were crying.

"Mommy! Mommeeee . . . !" they shouted. She shoved the last peg on and ran over to them.

"What is wrong?" she asked, though she didn't need to ask as she drew nearer.

Jimmy and Deedee sat paralyzed with fear as

a cloud of bees swarmed around them.

Dammit, they must have disturbed a nest, she thought.

She grabbed the outdoor broom that was leaning against the porch step and swung at the bees.

"Run," she screamed. The children stared up at her with big teary eyes. Bees were crawling all over them.

"Run!" She swatted at the bees on Deedeee's face, tried to brush them off her arms as she scooped Deedee up in one arm and Jimmy in the other. The children were heavy and the bees were thick. She didn't know where to go, until her glance landed on the little duck pond in the middle of the lawn. The angry buzzing grew louder, and she felt tiny legs landing on her own arms, crawling along her own face. She ran, the toddlers screaming and crying as the bees stung them. She felt a few barbed points entering her own flesh as she dove into the muddy water with the children in tow.

The pond wasn't very deep and she put her face under, hating the murky water on her flesh, but hating the bees even more. The children gulped and splashed, but at least the dunking seemed to do the trick. The bees flew off, a dark cloud that darkened the bright sky. She watched them go, across the lawn, and disappear across the field.

She pulled the sputtering children from the

The Birds and the Bees

pond. They were covered with bee stings wherever their skin was exposed. She felt her own flesh throbbing with pain, and knew that they must be in agony.

Deedee's eyes were rolling back in her head as she gulped in air.

Oh, God, I hope she's not allergic....

Mary Anne lay them on the grass beside the pond, where they lay crying. Soon, Deedee started to regain her senses, and sat up.

"Where am I?" she asked, looking around herself in a daze.

"Oh, Deedee..." Mary Anne hugged the four-year-old. "How do you feel? Are you all right?"

"It hurts, Mommy... make it stop." Deedee sobbed. She scratched at her arms.

"I know, honey... I know... we all hurt."

Jimmy was crying, staring at the welts on his arms. Mary Anne crawled over to him.

"Come on, let's go take care of these bee stings," she said, trying to get them to their feet.

She didn't know what she was going to do, but figured a long warm bath with baking soda might take down the swelling. It was hard, but soon she got the children stumbling toward the house.

As they passed by the spot where the children had been playing, Mary Anne looked at it. There was no sign that there had been any bees there at all.

She wondered what had provoked the attack, then led the children into the house.

Chapter Two

It was a breezy evening, but still warm enough to count as summer, as Gabrielle, Lisa, and Marie scored the last table on the patio.

"I'm in the mood for beer, and lots of it!" Lisa laughed, flipping her short, burgundy bob as she sank into one of the steel chairs.

"Here, here," echoed Marie, her face red from the heat.

"Beer sounds good to me," said Gabrielle, already positioning her chair so she could see the tiny stage where a microphone was set up.

The women dug through their purses, hunting for cigarettes and lighters. Lisa lit everyone's cigarette while Marie looked for a waitress.

Sèphera Girón

"So who is it we're seeing tonight?" Lisa asked.

"Let's see . . ." Gabrielle pulled a piece of paper from her purse and studied it. "Tommy. Huh . . . just goes by Tommy. He's in town for a couple nights. Supposed to be good. Does a mix of covers and originals."

"Hmmm . . ." Lisa said. "Well, I hope he's better then that last clown you dragged us off to see."

"I'm just sent out to review them, I don't pick 'em!"

The waitress returned with their beer.

"Ah, yes, this is just what the doctor ordered," Lisa said, reaching for her glass. She raised it in a toast.

"To girls' night out!"

"Hear, hear!" said Marie.

"To the divorcées of the world," Gabrielle said.

They touched their glasses.

"Oh, my!" Marie said, looking toward the stage. The women followed her gaze to see a young curly-haired man holding a guitar, fiddling with the mike.

"What a cutie." Lisa smiled. "Hey, Gabrielle, he's got that long-haired-guitar-player thing going on that you like."

Gabrielle smiled, staring at the young man . . . Tommy. He was a cutie, no doubt about it. Tommy finished adjusting the mike and

The Birds and the Bees

strummed the acoustic, singing a slow bluesy song. The women watched in silence as he performed.

Gabrielle felt her heart skip a beat as she listened to his voice wash over her. She stared at his hands, how they tickled the strings effortlessly. For a moment, she thought of them running along her body, and then stopped herself. He wore a wedding band.

She pulled out her notepad and pen and made notes as one song blended into the next. By the end of the first set, she knew what her review would be.

Tommy left the platform and made his way over to the bar that was set up on the edge of the patio. Gabrielle watched him as he sat alone on a bar stool, sipping on a beer, staring out across the street.

"I'll be right back," she said to her friends. Clutching her notepad, she approached Tommy.

"Hi," she said. Tommy nodded.

"Hi."

"I'm a reporter from *CitySites* magazine. Gabrielle Light." Gabrielle held out her hand.

"Tommy," he said, taking her hand. They shook, the grip lasting a bit longer than a mere business shake should. Gabrielle flushed and pulled her hand away.

"I really liked the set," she said. "I haven't heard you before."

Sèphera Girón

"Thanks."

"I'm hoping to give you a bit of a review in my column. I see you are playing here once a month for the next couple of months."

"Yeah, I managed to score a couple gigs here. I guess the patio is a draw," Tommy said, staring at the platform stage.

"It's nice to hear your kind of music out here on the patio. The weather is perfect for it." Gabrielle wondered why she was babbling like an idiot. She talked to musicians all the time, ones even cuter than Tommy. There was something. Something she couldn't quite put her finger on.

Tommy nodded. "So far so good." Gabrielle had nearly forgotten what she had said, but she smiled. They looked at each other, their eyes locking as they each searched for something more to talk about. Gabrielle looked at Tommy's beer.

"Can I buy you another drink?" she asked. Tommy held up his bottle, examining it.

"Sure, thanks," he said.

Gabrielle signaled to the bartender to bring over two more bottles. Beyond the patio, the street was getting busy as people cruised up and down the strip. Car horns blared and people walked by, some dressed to the nines, others hurrying home from work, still others aimlessly wandering with no real place to go. The bartender handed them two bottles, which they took.

The Birds and the Bees

"A toast..." Gabrielle smiled, holding her bottle out. "To good tunes on a lovely night."

Tommy touched his bottle to hers. Gabrielle was about to take a sip, when she noticed a hornet clinging to the neck.

"Christ," she said, putting it down.

"What's wrong?" Tommy asked.

"Damn bee," she said, staring at the yellow and black insect.

"They seem to be worse this year than usual," he said.

Tommy picked up one of the coasters and flicked gently at the bee. Gabrielle cringed, sliding off the bar stool and stepping back. The bee clung stubbornly until at last, Tommy dislodged it. It soared off with an angry buzz.

"Sheesh..." Gabrielle sighed. "Who needs that?"

She picked up her bottle and held it up.

"As I said, cheers!"

"Cheers."

Tommy looked at his watch. "Guess I'd better get back up there."

"Break a leg," Gabrielle said as she got up to rejoin her friends.

John looked at his watch.

"Shit, better get home to the missus," he groaned, and sat up. Lolling beside him was a skinny young girl that he liked to bang now and again. She was a bit of a whiner, but she would

Sèphera Girón

do. After all, women were born to complain and nag. Nothing any man did was good enough or smart enough. He felt that all the time. More so in recent years, especially with Mary Anne.

"You hafta go so soon?" Katey pouted.

John reached over for the whiskey bottle. It was a cheap brand, but it did the trick. He knocked back a few swallows and wiped his lips.

"You know the deal," he said. "Gotta go."

He pulled his jeans back on and looked for his boots. Katey sat staring at him.

"When are you gonna leave her?" she asked.

"I told ya, I'm not leaving her." John was irritated. It was the same old shit, every few days. The dumb bitch couldn't get it through her thick little pea brain that she was just a fuck and nothing more.

Katey wrapped her arms around his neck while he tied his boot laces. She nibbled at his ear.

"You know if you came to me, I'd take good care of you. No kids to worry about. Jest you an' me."

"I know that, kiddo, but I ain't going nowhere. Child support alone would kill me."

"But I work. You could pay child support an' I'd take care of both of us."

"It's not that easy. Not by a long shot." John leaned over her and reached for the bottle again. "Ya know, in a different time and place,

The Birds and the Bees

yeah, maybe we could have worked something out. But not now. Not the way things are."

Katey frowned. "You said you get along better with me than her."

"Sure I do. Don't mean I'm gonna leave her, though."

Katey slipped off the bed and pulled on an oversized T-shirt.

"One day you'll realize what I mean to you, and by then it'll be too late," she said coldly.

"You say that all the time. But in the meantime, you just be my fun-time gal, okay? Don't make anything more of it than what it is."

"Sure," she said sulkily. John took one last slug of the whiskey and lit a cigarette.

"See ya round, kiddo," he said as he kissed her.

"Think of me . . ." she said, but he was already out of the bedroom and out the front door of the apartment.

Katey wandered out of the bedroom, went into the tiny kitchen, and turned on the gas under the teakettle. Tears came to her eyes, and she wondered for the millionth time just what she was doing.

He wasn't that great a lover; he was barely attentive to her half the time. She knew he just liked to come over and hang out, watch TV for a bit, and fuck her. She knew he just liked to have a place away from all the kids, that any woman who would put up with him would do.

She thought about Mary Anne. She wondered if she suspected what a cheating dog her husband was. She wondered if it was time for her to find out that for the past year he hadn't been working overtime at all.

The kettle whistled, and she poured steaming water over a tea bag. Were all men dogs? she wondered. It seemed like that was the case these days. When she went out to the bars with her girlfriends, the guys that hit on them almost always had a girl waiting for them at home. Sometimes she dragged one home and got fucked good and proper. There was something about John that never quite satisfied her. Maybe it was because he never really tried to please her. He was more interested in getting himself off and that was it.

Yet there was something about him that she was drawn to. Maybe it was the way his eyes sparkled sometimes when he saw her. She was sure he did feel something for her, or why did he keep coming back?

However, the whole deal was beginning to annoy and depress her. She wondered how long it would be before she would break it off.

John weaved his way home. Damn but that Katey was really beginning to annoy the hell out of him. He was going to have to break it off soon. Maybe find an older woman who wouldn't ask so many questions, a woman who would

The Birds and the Bees

just accept the situation for what it was. He wasn't sure. But it was so much work, finding someone, sweet-talking them, getting things set up so that they were workable.

A thick fog coated the country road. He put his high beams on and squinted his eyes. He had drunk just a bit too much tonight, partly because Katey drove him to it. Dumb bitch. Why couldn't she just deal with shit as it happened? Why was she in such a hurry to get tied down? She should enjoy the fact that they had some good times and just leave it at that.

Ahead, there looked like there was something at the side of the road. He slowed, hoping it wasn't a deer or some other animal that would just spontaneously leap out in front of the car.

No, it must be a hitchhiker. Someone just standing there. He got closer, and the front of his windshield darkened.

"Holy goddamn!" he cried out as he saw that the darkness was a swarm of bugs. Of bees.

"What the fuck..." He slammed on his brakes, unable to see the road. He was glad his windows were up, and started the wipers. Dozens of bees smeared across the glass as the wipers went back and forth. Where the bodies were squished, more swooped in to take their place. He hit the gas again, setting the wipers higher. There was no goddamn way he was going to stop if there was a swarm around.

What the fuck were bees doing out at night anyway?

The truck crawled along, the wipers relentlessly sliming them back and forth, back and forth. The swarm seemed to be thinning, and at last, he seemed to drive out of it.

His heart was pounding as he drove on. What the hell was that all about?

He thought about how Mary Anne had told him about the random attack on the kids the other day. There was definitely something going on. He was only a mile from home.

As he drove up the driveway, he thought he'd better figure out someone to call about the damn bees and get that hive, or whatever it was, exterminated.

He saw Mary Anne peering out the window as he drove up.

Goddammit. Now he would have to play twenty questions with her. It never ended. The hounding. The relentless hounding from woman to woman. Why couldn't they all just shut up and leave him alone?

As he devised his latest excuse for being so late, he had already forgotten about the bees. He stumbled up the driveway, and made his way into the house.

Tommy lay on his hotel room bed. If you could call this dive a hotel. The room was tiny and grotty, with garish black and pink wallpaper

The Birds and the Bees

coming unglued in the corners. At least the little television was color and got a few channels.

He lay clicking the remote, pausing now and again to catch a moment or two of a sitcom or infomercial. He pulled out a smoke and lit it. The smoke curled around his face as he stared thoughtfully. He had a bit of Jack left in the bottle, and chugged it down.

Damn but was he lonely. He had only been on the road a week, and already he yearned for home. Well, a home. He didn't really yearn for the home that he had at this point.

He wasn't sure when it had turned, when the joy and fun had begun to slowly drain away. It was inevitable that as life went on, marriage wasn't the fun and games that it used to be. He fully expected that. But he hadn't expected to feel so empty so young. He didn't *dislike* his wife, but she wasn't the exuberant girl he once knew. Life had taken its toll on her already, and she was often snappy and curt with him. Of course, most of their issues revolved around money. What else was new? That was how it was for everyone, wasn't it?

Their daughter, Wendy, was turning into a pretty young girl. Her marks at school weren't the greatest, but he had never been a high achiever himself, so he wasn't too concerned. As long as she held her own, kept that bare-minimum thing going on, he didn't bug her about it much.

But Sheila . . . well, Sheila was a whole other deal. She just wasn't happy these days, and it was mostly with him. It seemed like he could never do anything right anymore. The smallest details escalated into all-out screaming matches, and heaven forbid he forget to do something like pick up bread at the store. Over and over again she would complain about how he was thirty now and should have a real job, a real income.

Hell, he had been a musician when she married him; it wasn't like he'd changed or something. She knew the deal when she first saw him play. That had been fine for her then, but now suddenly, it was a problem.

He admitted to himself that maybe he hadn't worked quite as hard as he should have. Maybe if he had been a bit more aggressive, he would have hit the big time by now. Most rock bands came and went while their members were in their twenties. Hell, look at the teen bands, the boy bands. Those were mere kids.

He figured at thirty, he was nearly past his prime.

But maybe not.

After all, with age comes experience, and he had over twenty years of practicing under his belt. And when he wasn't depressed, he could pick away for hours, perfecting his technique, uncovering new songs from the layers of riffs and rhythms locked in his head. He had more

The Birds and the Bees

then enough for a CD; it was just a matter of getting the equipment together. And the money for a studio. Maybe his agent could find a sponsor or something. He could always pull together some guys he had worked with before. That part of it wouldn't be too hard.

The idea of a CD had haunted him for years. In the beginning, he'd felt he was too inexperienced to have anything meaningful to say. Now, he had things to say and even his technique wasn't too bad, but he had no money. Every dime he made went toward the wife and kid. And the dimes hadn't been coming in much at all.

Sheila had harped at him all spring, so much so that he could barely think, could barely practice, and certainly no muse came to him during that time. She figured that he should go out and get a day job. She was sick of shopping at Goodwill, and their old worn furniture and her jeans were older than her daughter. She wanted more then a few bucks for food and cigarettes.

Tommy had considered all that she said and knew that she was right to an extent. She had been a good sport for many years, hanging in there for him while he suffered through the crippling angst and depression that grips many a creative soul. There were days, even weeks, where he couldn't even so much as take his guitar out of his case, the idea of playing tormented him, his muse had left the building. Of course, there was pressure from all sides, family, friends, suggesting he get a real job and maybe the muse would return. But he knew better. He had to sit and think, wait it out, entice it back as if he were setting a trap for the most clever fox.

His "spells," as he called them, came more frequently as the years went on. He got so that he would take to his bed or the couch and just stare up at the ceiling, willing the music back into his head, urging his fingers to touch the strings. In those times of darkness, he couldn't practice, couldn't bear to lift that guitar out of the case. So he would sit, and think, while the world turned without him.

It was during one of these episodes that he'd had the epiphany. He would get his fingers back into shape and get out on the road again. Only this time, instead of struggling in small-time bands, he would venture out solo. He had some cover tunes, had a few original pieces, and knew that his voice was pretty good. He would hit a few of the cities where he had played years before, and get some money together. Enough to pay the rent for a couple of months, with some left over to cut a CD.

It was a perfect plan and the time was right.

He could feel it in his bones. There was a shift happening. This idea felt too good, too right for it to collapse. His head was filled with visions of power; his body seemed fueled by the desire

The Birds and the Bees

to leap out of bed in the morning and grab his guitar and play and play. He felt his muse creeping back into his bones, inspiration filling him with a joie de vivre he hadn't felt in a long, long time.

Sheila tried to rain on his parade, but it was expected. She didn't like the idea of him leaving for days at a time at all.

He had called up his old agent, who seemed genuinely surprised to hear from him after so long. Well, he hadn't played in bands for a couple of years. Tommy was actually surprised to realize that it was closer to three. How time certainly slips by. But he was an *artist*, and prone to temperamental moments, and it wasn't like he hadn't worked at all. He had picked up a few gigs here and there through friends, without telling the agent.

So now, here he was, on his little mini-tour. Him and his guitar and a new crappy hotel room every couple of nights.

The money wasn't great either, but it was better than nothing. He wasn't sure if he *would* even make enough to cut a CD. But he would get exposure, and that counted a lot. And not only would people hear him play, he was getting write-ups too. He thought about that reporter he had met. Gabrielle.

She'd seemed like a nice enough woman. The type of woman he would like to get to know, actually, if he weren't married.

He thought about his wife again. And his marriage.

Was it really working? Was what he had really it?

He lit a cigarette and pondered for a while. He just wasn't sure at all about anything anymore.

He had thought he loved Sheila, wanted to spend his life with her. But there were so many more days of unhappiness than happiness. Was that normal? Was that what he really wanted?

Maybe there was more to life. More to see. More to explore. He had been so devoted to her for so long, he hadn't noticed the slide into monotony, until recently.

Until now.

Chapter Three

She was surrounded by feathers.

No, buried in them.

Huge, black feathers that stank like death. They clung to her arms and legs, they tickled her face, and she cringed resentfully. There was no escape from them, she couldn't climb out or back up. Leaning to the side, stretching as far as she could go, nothing was working.

Wherever she was, it was dark.

Total darkness.

It was as if she were in a world contaminated by feathers. Sky, ground, everywhere in between.

If she couldn't climb out, maybe she could tunnel through, maybe swim through the feathers like a giant black pond. She flailed her arms

Sèphera Girón

and legs, clawing, reaching, gasping. But try as she might, she was getting nowhere.

Above her, there was a horrible screeching sound. Louder than the most obnoxious truck scraping concrete at a construction site. She covered her ears, trying to protect them from the painful shriek. A wind brushed her face and the sound came again. Instinctively, she started to run. Running in feathers, with no traction, no forward, no backward. Running in the stink with that hideous noise coming closer and closer.

Gabrielle tossed and turned, her sheets slick with sweat. She gasped, pulling at the sheets, her legs kicking against the bed.

Suddenly, she opened her eyes.

She blinked, and realized she was in her own bed.

She had been running and running.

From something or toward something else?

She couldn't remember.

She sat up, rubbing her temples, trying to focus on the floor in front of her.

Wherever she had been, she was no longer there. She was here, right here, rooted in the present. The foggy haze of the dream stayed with her, disturbance niggling at her mind just below the surface. She looked around her small bedroom. Her existence was minimal, reflected in the sparse furnishings. The bare walls. The bed that had no headboard. The dresser piled

The Birds and the Bees

with a few books, makeup, some clothes. And her night table with the lamp and more books.

It was Saturday today. The kids would be here soon and she had to pull herself together.

She went into the bathroom and took a long look at herself. She had stayed out far too late, watching the singer, giggling with her friends, drinking far too much beer.

No wonder there were dark circles under her eyes and her head felt like a large wad of cotton.

Gabrielle jumped into the shower, enjoying the warm water blast on her body. She thought about what she should do with the kids today. Where should they go? They were growing up so fast, she could see that it wouldn't be long before they would rather spend their precious weekend days with their buddies than with their old boring mom.

Well, at least they still liked to go to the movies, so she figured taking them to a show would give them something to talk about at the dinner afterward.

She toweled off and searched for something to wear. Something casual but warm enough for a chilly movie theater, cool enough for the schizophrenic weather.

She found a plain T-shirt and some jeans and slipped them on.

By the time she had dried her hair and thrown on some makeup, she felt almost human again.

Sèphera Girón

She wandered out into the living room, clicking on her computer as she walked by it on her way to the kitchen. While the computer booted up, she made a pot of coffee and some toast.

When the coffee was ready, she settled back in front of the computer and read through her e-mail. She checked her horoscope and the news. There wasn't much in the way of personal correspondence, and she dealt with that quickly and efficiently.

She pulled out her notes from the night before and set to work constructing her column. She did an Internet search on Tommy's name, and found a couple of other news articles on him. Just little write-ups here and there. There were no Web pages or lists, no help for her research.

As she wrote her column, she thought about the evening before, about how good it had felt to be out with friends for once, at a place that wasn't too crowded and smoky, where they could just relax and be themselves. They would have to do that sort of thing more often instead of carousing the dance clubs where the crowd was getting younger as they grew older.

They had even ended up talking to a few men as the evening went on. Lisa had exchanged a phone number with one guy. He'd seemed nice enough.

Gabrielle thought about Tommy's playing. He really was very good, and his selection of

The Birds and the Bees

music was perfect for the place. She thought about his hair, how it curled down to his shoulders. About his eyes. How they looked right into hers when she was talking, as if he knew something or was finding something deep within her that she didn't even know she had.

She shook her head. Enough of that. Fascinating or not, the man was married and that was that. After all, her own marriage had fallen apart because some chickie had the hots for her husband, so she knew all about that. She wouldn't wish that pain on any other woman.

The article done, she e-mailed it off and finished getting ready for the kids.

She wondered how was it that some people managed to pick up the pieces of a shattered marriage and plow forward with no looking back, no regrets. She thought about her ex, how after all these years and children, they spoke to each other like they were strangers meeting for the first time on the street. All the intimate hopes and dreams once shared, forgotten, as if they had never existed at all. It made her feel that secrets and goals shared in the marriage bed were as fragile as a spiderweb freshly spun in the morning. Any moment, some bug would be along to screw up the intricate pattern and nothing would ever be the same.

And if a marriage could fall apart with such ease, what hope was there for dating or a casual relationship? How could she get past the feeling that a big black bug was going to come along at any moment and upset the balance? Sure, the bug was food, fuel to design the next web. Yet the pattern was never the same. The perspective changed, and there was another notch of experience, another web to weave.

The intercom rang and she pressed the buzzer to let her ex and the kids in.

She got to be a mom for the next few hours, and she was looking forward to it.

Mary Anne was watching the children playing outside while she washed up the lunch dishes. She kept a worried eye on them, hoping that there would be no more incidents with bees or hornets or wasps or any of those creepy, crawling flying pinpricks from hell.

She didn't want to ban the kids outright from playing outside. That would be just nuts. Besides, she had searched all over for a nest or hive and found nothing. Nothing under the stairs, or in the bushes, under the eaves, in the troughs. Absolutely nothing.

So if there was no home for the insects nearby, chances were that they wouldn't come back again.

Her thoughts drifted from the children to John. She wondered what she was going to do about him. His drinking was pretty much out of control these days. He had been obviously wasted when he staggered in the night before,

The Birds and the Bees

but that didn't stop him from settling in front of the television with a few more beers in hand. Not only that, she wondered just who it was he'd been drinking with. He never told her stories from the bar like he used to. He never said so-and-so was playing pool, or that some asshole biker came in, or anything like that. For a man who liked to ramble on with stories, he certainly didn't have any to account for his longer and longer workdays.

There was a presence behind her, and before she could turn around, she felt the familiar grip of his large strong hand wrapped in her hair. She used to love the feeling, that sense of his dominance over her, the realization that he would take her, often forcibly, and in her younger days, that had filled her with a keen sense of excitement. Now, that same touch filled her with dread. She knew she had to follow his lead exactly, or there would be hell to pay.

"Gimme a kiss..." John said, his voice hoarse, his breath rancid with cigarettes and stale booze. Mary Anne pressed her lips gingerly to his. His other hand slid down her back and cupped her ass.

"Let's go to the bedroom," he said.

"The kids... I have to watch..." Mary Anne stammered.

"You have to watch your husband." He tight-

Sèphera Girón

ened his grip on her hair. She tried to sneak a peek out the window.

"But they might . . . get hurt, or come in . . . or . . ."

"Fine . . . I'm not arguing with you." John turned her so that she was facing the window again. He pressed her face up toward the glass, which had her leaning over the sink.

"There, take a good look. You can watch them while I fuck you."

Before she could protest, he unbuttoned her jeans, rubbing himself against her back. His bathrobe was open and he wore nothing underneath. He pulled her pants down. She let him do it, knowing that if she fought him, it would just end in a beating. If she cooperated, it would be over before she knew it. She looked out the window as he pushed into her.

His breath was hot on her neck as she saw the children playing. Up in the nearby trees, a flock of crows screamed, wings fluttering, feathers drifting lazily to the ground. She wondered why they were making so much commotion today. It was always something. Several of them would flap away from the tree, circling, screaming, and then rejoin the others among the leaves.

John pushed her forward more so that her face rested on the windowsill, the wood digging into her cheek as he held her hips steady for his thrusting. She stared across the counter, past

The Birds and the Bees

the dishes, and over to the refrigerator.

John was taking a long time today. She hoped the kids wouldn't come in, although it certainly wouldn't be the first time they would see Mommy and Daddy in a compromising position.

The fridge clicked on and she listened to the humming. It was a nice soothing sound that distracted her from the panting string of obscenities John liked to whisper to her when he really got going.

She stared at the fridge, at the dirty white door with kiddie smudges on it. There were bills and a couple of paintings held in place by little fruit magnets. An apple. An orange. A bunch of grapes. As she watched the fridge, she could swear she saw the grapes moving, slowly edging along the fridge door. But it must be her, bouncing and sliding around, just giving the illusion that it was the magnet moving.

John pushed one of her legs up higher so that she was almost straddling the counter. She felt the window ledge digging further into her cheek, but she didn't dare move her head even an inch.

The grapes were definitely in a different spot than they had been a moment ago.

"You're my bitch, my whore, my slut..." John growled.

The refrigerator hummed and the grapes slid back again.

Sèphera Girón

John pushed into her one last time with a cry, and she felt as if her body would break in two.

As he shuddered and moaned, she watched as the grape magnet fell off the fridge and landed on the floor.

Chapter Four

Abraham walked down the city street with a spring in his step.

All around him, everything was so bright.

So new. So shiny!

The tall glass towers, bricks, stone, mortar. It all stunned him into silence with strength and magnificence every morning when he walked out of his little apartment. Tears sprang to his eyes. How lucky he had been. How fantastically lucky he had been that his number had finally come up!

It was only, what? Three weeks ago. Not even three weeks ago that he had never seen a sidewalk before in his entire life. Not a sidewalk that wasn't in a picture, at any rate. He had never seen a building that wasn't made out of mud and sticks. He had never seen people walk freely and quickly, clutching things called briefcases, suitcases, knapsacks. Men and women together. Sexes and colors intermingled. Rushing, always rushing to somewhere.

Rushing, yes. The cars. He was even more amazed at the cars. At the sheer numbers of cars. At the color and speed and beauty of cars. Where he was from, he had been witness to a few mud-soaked jeeps and buses, usually not able to go very fast and stalling constantly. Here, cars, buses, trucks, all went amazingly fast. Maybe not right now, in what was called rush hour, but on the way from the airport he had seen them.

That was another thing. Rush hour. Sure, everyone was rushing, but no one was getting anywhere at all. It was a silly expression. And one of many that he would learn.

It all was a strange wonderment to him, to experience all that he had in his lifetime, and yet there was constantly more. Always more.

He felt that God must really be calling to him. Speaking to him. He was blessed. Incredibly and fantastically blessed. Why else would he be shown such amazing wonderments?

Ah, but he had paid. Paid dearly with love and blood. Paid with nightmares of hunger and torment. He had been but a small child when it all happened, but glimpses of the nightmare haunted him now and again.

The Birds and the Bees

He owed his life to his brother, Dominion. It was he who had carried him from the burning village where his parents had been slaughtered like animals. It was his big strong brother who covered his eyes from the fire and soot, who strapped him to his back and carried him, for miles, endless miles, in a pilgrimage that no child should ever have to make.

Yet he made it.

His brother made it. And his dear friend Jeremy, who also had carried him and helped him when he felt he could continue no longer.

Hundreds of others too had survived to tell the tale.

They walked from Sudan to Ethiopia, where they had heard there was freedom. If they could make it to the promised land, their lives would be for the better. In the end they walked from Sudan to Ethiopia, back to Sudan, and then on to Kenya. A journey of a thousand miles and four years.

Wading through crocodile-infested rivers, creeping through bushes trying to keep the very youngest from making noise lest the wild cats hunt them down, their dreams of happiness and freedom dangled before them like a carrot. In the toughest times, they prayed to God. Joining hands, they cried and sang. Silently they prayed and begged. Redemption was surely just around the corner. If they could just hang on,

Sèphera Girón

could fight the brave fight, they would meet their reward.

They lost many children. Too many to count. Some were eaten by animals. Others were dragged away by the currents. Still more had been left dying in the heat of the sun.

Each child who survived was plagued by nightmares. Seeing brothers and friends torn apart by a lion, or succumbing to the fever or a snake. Hearing the screams of weak swimmers gulping down water, too far from the others as the currents made fast work of their bodies. The nightmares were more real in waking life than in death. Death was painful, but a daily ritual. Another day of walking and thirst would have been worse had they not thought there was a higher plan. A larger meaning for their journey.

So the weak fell, the strong walked. The children, the rest of the children, continued on, feverishly, across hundreds of miles, toward the promised land. Towards the place where there was hope and food.

There had to be hope, or the journey was for naught.

They walked, hope burning through them, carrying each other when they grew tired, hoarding what little food they could find on their travels.

A few had managed to grab books and Bibles before the villages burned, and they eagerly read to the other boys during times of rest. They

The Birds and the Bees

taught each other how to read from books, how to tell stories from both the page and the mind. They created their own story of their journey, each brother regaling the others with a tale, when they weren't quite so tired or quite so sad.

No matter what hardships they endured, they believed in two things.

God and education.

If they believed in God, if they believed there was greater purpose for their suffering, then it would be worthwhile. They were the chosen ones. They were surviving for a reason. Survival of the fittest. The lesson passed from oldest child to youngest child. The children taught each other to read, to draw letters in the sand, to add and subtract sticks and rocks. They learned about basic manners, they learned about forgiveness. They knew they could not forget, as wild as they were becoming. They were not much more than beasts after months, after years, yet they would not allow themselves to fall into savagery. They had to remain educated. They had to remain boys growing into men.

Survival of the fittest.

Many did grow into men.

After years of walking and braving the elements, of self-education and burying their brothers, they were offered safe refuge at a camp in Kenya. At long last, they were recognized by others, their self-sufficiency a surpris-

Sèphera Girón

ing lesson in human endurance. Their hopes and dreams only half realized as they still hungered for more in tents and mud huts. They still lived in hunger and poverty. There still was no real food, no real water. They had minimal shelter from the elements, but there were no cities save their own refugee camp. There was no way to better their lives. They lived day to day.

Then came the missionaries. And talk of the New Promised Land.

There was a place, far, far away, beyond the desert and the jungle and the water. A place of unlimited opportunity, if a person wanted it badly enough. If a person wasn't afraid to work hard and could live by rules and laws, they might be admitted to this place.

United States of America.

If they could keep learning English from the missionary teachers, and show a desire to integrate into a new culture, then they might be admitted to this land of opportunity.

Each boy worked hard, bettering his English, learning about cultural differences from flash cards and old magazines. There wasn't enough money for all the boys to experience the new opportunity. There was only so much funding. Only so many kindhearted people were willing to donate to charity to help out these struggling boys.

So to keep things fair, a lottery was created.

Every month, a few lucky names were drawn.

The Birds and the Bees

Tears were shed as friends parted for the first time since their horrendous adventure, off to someplace in that United States. In their guts, they knew they would never see each other again. They had seen the maps. This United States was a vast land, and they would not be able to meet at the water hole. They heard there were things called telephones. Things called computers and e-mail, but until they saw them for themselves, until they could understand how they worked, they could not begin to comprehend how on earth they would be able to use them. Or to see each other again.

Abraham was starting to understand it now. He could understand why good-bye didn't have to be forever. There was TV and e-mail. There were cars, planes, and trains.

Who could possibly wrap their heads around the miracle of this new land unless they saw it for themselves?

Sometimes at night, he would lie in the softness of his bed, his head sinking into the pillow, his body swathed in the freshness of clean, crisp sheets and he would cry. He would cry over how it could be that he'd spent years wandering through mud and dirt and weeds, sleeping with a rock for a pillow, one eye open for a snake, when across the world, people lived in tall stone boxes, safe as safe can be.

It wasn't fair, and he yearned to go back and get all of the Lost Boys. He wanted his friends,

Sèphera Girón

his brothers. He wanted all of them to live right here, in this very room. How could he possibly have three rooms all for himself when for so long, and still over there, people had no rooms at all? All they had were cloth and mud walls. No air-conditioning to cool them. No heat to warm them up. No way to get anywhere except to walk, and if you could not walk, you did not go. If you could not walk, you were prey for whatever and whoever came upon you, and they would do as they would.

He made a vow to get as much education as he could, to make as much money as he could, to go back and build a palace for the brothers left behind.

Abraham was on his way to his job. He had found a little bakery that wasn't far from his home that was interested in him and his stories. They had heard about him and his brothers on TV, the Lost Boys, as they had been dubbed on one of the news shows. The kind bakery owner, Mr. B, had called the embassy and requested that a Lost Boy be sent to him as soon as one came over.

So Abraham was blessed.

Mr. B also liked to talk about God, and even brought him to his church on Sundays. Abraham was pleased that there were so many opportunities to talk about God and Bible stories and to ask questions about things that he had been confused about.

The Birds and the Bees

After all, even though the boys had Bibles and they had prayed to God, there had been so many questions that none of them knew the answers to. It was one thing to believe that God would provide, but how did he pick and choose who was the recipient? Why was it that people Abraham loved and adored, from his parents to his friends, were perishing, yet Abraham remained? Sometimes being a survivor felt like a bigger punishment than not being a survivor.

Then there were other things that he was beginning to question. Mr. B didn't seem to know the answers to those questions either.

Funny how the longer he stayed in this new land, the less he understood some of the things he had been taught from a very early age. He even remembered his mother teaching him some of those ideas.

Love your brother.

It hadn't taken long to figure out how so many people judged and were judged by the color of skin. He hadn't been in the city a day before he was called a word that people described in whispered tones as "the N word." He didn't know it was a "bad" word till he asked Mr. B what it meant.

Abraham's English wasn't very good yet, but it was better than he gave himself credit for having. It was amazing how fast he picked up things, and he suspected it was partly because he could read people without words.

Sèphera Girón

He understood people's thoughts, and they didn't even have to open their mouths.

This wasn't unusual back in his world. His world was smaller and more instinctive.

The more time he spent in this New World, the more it was apparent that people spoke and judged before they thought things through. Abraham was getting good at spotting people who babbled on without regard for anyone's feelings.

Survival of the fittest meant something totally different in this New Land.

He realized that back home they had all known each other so intimately, that they'd had to rely more on their instincts than on each other to survive. So they had created ways of communicating without speaking, of reading each other's body language and smells. They knew when to love each other, and when to stay away.

He was realizing, here in the new land, in the land mostly of the White Man, that people mostly stayed to themselves. One of the first things he had learned in his classes at the missionary before coming over was not to make eye contact on the street. Especially Black Man to White Man. The teachers had been gentle in their descriptions of how White Man regarded Black Man. Maybe too gentle. Abraham wasn't prepared for most of the negativity that came his way. He even heard comments that he was

The Birds and the Bees

Blacker than most Black Men. After hearing those comments a few times, he'd asked Mr. B about it. Abraham had noticed too that he was Blacker than a lot of Black Men. Mr. B explained to him that a lot of black people in the United States had been in interracial families, so it was growing more unusual to see a man as black as Abraham. Since Abraham was right from Africa, from a purely black heritage, his skin was darker.

Abraham found the concept of skin blending very fascinating.

Genetics.

He wondered if maybe he should study genetics when he took some courses. Genetics was truly fascinating. Why were some people blacker? Why did some people have blue eyes, red hair? Why were some people more prone to colds than others?

Why did some people have a will to survive and others just gave up?

However, as long as Abraham could sense the White Man's thoughts, he wouldn't let him get the better of him. He'd just avoid eye contact. Avoid trouble. And pray to God for more tolerance.

In this land of plenty, there was a decided lack of tolerance.

Abraham breathed in the last of the city air. Fresh air, smog, trees, garbage. A jumble of smells fueling him with the desire to be at one with this city. To integrate into this city.

He entered the bakery, where rich lovely smells enveloped him. He loved the smell of the bakery. It smelled like comfort. It smelled like a new life. It smelled like freedom.

"Good morning, Mr. B," Abraham said as he walked into the bakery. Mr. B smiled at him from behind the counter, where he was arranging lemon tarts. Mr. B was a large man with a wide smile and rosy cheeks. He had told Abraham that he and his family were from Poland. That they had been brought to America, as he called this place, as children in a Big War. He had already told Abraham that even though they were white, they still had been ridiculed because of their roots. He told Abraham about how some people are incredibly judgmental and don't understand what a miracle it is to just be alive.

"Ah, Abraham! Good morning to you too!" Mr. B said.

"It's another beautiful day out there," Abraham said, and took off his jacket. He hung it up on the coat rack by the door and went into the back. It was hot back here. Huge ovens, huge trays and tables and knives and racks. Everything was so huge, and this was considered a little bakery. His mind couldn't even begin to comprehend how huge a factory bakery must be! He went over to the trays of breads and buns and started to examine them, picking out which

The Birds and the Bees

"Taking down some of the clutter around here. It's really out of hand."

"I thought you liked all those creepy pictures."

"It was more like I was just too superstitious to take them down."

"Superstitious?"

"They are relatives and so on. I've never been too sure why we started hanging pictures in the barn, instead of in the house like norm—well, I just never understood it."

"Who's that?" Deedee pointed at one of the pictures that was still stapled to the wall.

"That's your grandmother. She's dead." Mary Anne stood back, narrowing her eyes. "Funny, most of the people in these pictures are dead."

"You're not!" Jimmy said, pointing at a photograph of Mary Anne in a school group. There were about fifty kids standing all shiny-haired with big wide gap-toothed grins.

"I was in grade eight then," Mary Anne said, pulling the picture gently from the wall. As she tugged, a puff of dust hung in the air and a few dead insects fell to the floor.

"Euwww," Jimmy yelled, staring at the crumpled-up flies and hornets. Deedee stomped on them.

"Die, you mean old bees!" Deedee yelled. She kicked and scraped them until they were mere specks of dust.

Mary Anne still sat staring at the photograph.

Sèphera Girón

"Who's that mean-looking lady?" Jimmy pointed to the only frowning face in the sea of shining faces.

Mary Anne squinted, turning the picture around. The person in question had squinty eyes and ratty orange hair. At first glance, it was hard to determine whether the person was a boy or a girl. But careful surveillance indicated that it was indeed the dour face of a very unhappy girl.

"That lady is actually a fourteen-year-old girl, my dear. I don't remember her name, but I do remember how I often felt sorry for her. She was so . . . not nice-looking." Mary Anne ran her finger over the picture. Just looking at that sunken face reminded her of that year.

That was the year where all sorts of weird freak accidents had happened. It was as if every illness, every natural disaster from a flood to a few fires, to a vicious plague of tent caterpillars that threatened to cripple the farmers, all happened within a few short months.

That was the same year that girl had come to town.

That girl nobody really ever knew very well. She came and went within a few months, as if she had dragged the string of disasters with her and then whirled away again.

Mary Anne remembered all too well, for it was the year that her very best friend since grade one, Betty, had died.

The Birds and the Bees

That had been one of the more bizarre things that had occurred that summer.

The local kids had all gathered together at one of the more popular swimming holes. There must have been close to a hundred kids splashing and jumping and generally having a good time. It was like a graduation party for the eighth graders, lots of junk food and pop.

Tuna sandwiches on white bread were predominant, as were chips and dip and cans of pop.

Mary Anne remembered how delicious those sandwiches, straight from the cooler, had been. She and Betty had sat on one of the plaid blankets, giggling as they watched boys.

Betty had bright blue eyes and a ready smile. She was one of those people that made you feel good just being in her presence. Mary Anne adored her and was jealous of her at the same time. Betty could make you feel like you were the only one in the room when she talked to you, and she always had men flocking around her. She was Scarlett O'Hara, but with a heart of gold. And like Miss Scarlett, Betty liked to have a little bottle of gin or vodka in her purse wherever she went. She always shared a little something with Mary Anne.

Mary Anne and Betty were eyeing the tallest, most mature boy in the class.

Doug.

Doug was tall and blond, and well on his way

to becoming captain of the football team or maybe class president as the years went on. He hung out with several other boys, all of them cute and playful. They pushed each other, joking around, daring each other to take foolish risks. Like diving off the rope swing.

The rope swing was tied to a tree, and if you swung out far enough, you landed in deep water. However, if you jumped anywhere but in the farthest arc, you would land in shallow water and could get badly hurt. The kids all knew this, had been playing with the rope swing for their whole lives.

Already, people were diving off it, or just swinging out and back before handing over the rope swing to someone else.

Mary Anne had always liked the rope swing. She was great at swinging it out to the furthest part of the ellipse and then diving out even further, flying through the air gracefully like a professional diver.

Betty wasn't so skilled. She would clamber up the rope swing and cling to it like a little wide-eyed monkey, as if she were deathly fearful of it. Her usual easy smile was strained, and though she joked around while she was swinging, relief visibly coursed through her when her turn was over.

On this picnic celebration day, Mary Anne had already dove into the water a few times, and now was sitting with her wet hair and T-shirt

The Birds and the Bees

clinging to her bra-less breasts next to Betty. Doug stood nearby, laughing with a bunch of friends. So many girls had their eyes locked on Doug. He was so charismatic, so handsome.

Mary Anne saw that the new girl, Amy, was sitting apart from the others, munching on a sandwich and staring unabashedly at Doug. Amy's eyes were wide, her mouth automatically chewing and swallowing as the space under her neck flushed with lust.

Doug broke away from his buddies and walked past the place where Amy sat. Mary Anne saw the whole exchange.

"Hi, Doug," Amy said shyly, her face more flushed.

"Hi, Angie," Doug said. Amy coughed.

"It's Amy."

"Huh?"

"Me, I'm Amy."

"Oh, sorry." Doug nodded, and was about to walk on.

"Doug . . ." Amy said.

"Yeah?"

"Would you like a sandwich?" She tentatively held up a sandwich. Doug looked at it.

"Egg salad?" he asked.

"Yes."

Doug reached for the sandwich. Amy held it just beyond his grasp so that he had to bend over to take it.

"Would you like to sit with me?" she asked.

Sèphera Girón

Doug looked at her. At her round sagging face. At her immense breasts and floppy tummy. He looked over at his friends, who were snickering.

"I—uh . . . not right now thanks. I have to go talk to someone." He snatched the sandwich and took a bite out of it.

"Delicious," he said as he wandered over toward Betty and Mary Anne.

"And how are you ladies doing today?" Doug asked as he sat on their blankets. Mary Anne's heart pitter-pattered while Betty calmly batted her eyelashes at him.

"Much better now," Betty sighed. She reached toward Doug's sandwich and slowly took a bite. "Mmmm . . . egg salad."

Mary Anne's legs prickled. She scratched at her shin, knocking away some ant. Looking down, she saw that the blanket was being invaded by ants. She patted Betty's arm.

"I think we're on an anthill," Mary Anne pointed out. Betty looked down, still chewing, and nodded, watching as an increasing number of ants marched along the blanket, picking at food.

Doug continued to eat his sandwich. He made a face and stopped chewing. He spit out his mouthful in disgust.

"Jesus! What the hell was that?" he said, opening his sandwich. "Oh, for God's sake."

The rest of the sandwich was coated with egg

The Birds and the Bees

salad and a mixture of black beetle-looking things. Tiny yellow and black bodies were smothered in mayonnaise. Doug looked over to where Amy had been sitting, but she was gone.

"Good thing that bitch took off," he said.

"What a mean thing to do," Betty said, standing up, brushing ants from her legs that already were leaving tiny red welts.

"These things are nasty," Mary Anne said, hitting her legs with a towel. "I'm going in."

Mary Anne ran for the water, and kept going in until the resistance slowed her to a stop and she couldn't run any further. She dove under the water, feeling it swish past the itchy bites peppering her legs and hips. Mary Anne loved to swim, and she cruised along the bottom, eyes wide open, watching minnows dart among undulating plants.

When she broke the surface of the water again, she saw that Doug was helping Betty onto the rope swing. A couple of colorful dragonflies danced along the water right in front of Mary Anne, touching heads and tails, wings buzzing, long thin bodies twitching before flying off a little ways as a single being.

Mary Anne noticed Amy standing by the shore, a few feet away from the tree where Doug climbed onto the rope swing with Betty. There was something about the way Amy was standing that unnerved Mary Anne.

The rope swung back and forth, the tree

branch bending under the weight of two people. As Doug shouted, "Jump," Amy fixed Mary Anne with a cold stare, and a chill like a razor blade sliced up Mary Anne's back.

Mary Anne swam back toward the shore, watching with horror as Doug jumped from the swing, clutching Betty's hand. It was like slow motion as Betty hesitated, then lost Doug's grip, tumbled into the more shallow portion of the water, and hit the sand with a thud. Blood frothed up to the surface, and panicked children scrambled either toward Betty in an attempt to help her, or away in fear.

Doug reached Betty first, and dragged her lifeless body to the shore. He held her, tried to force air into her water-filled lungs, but there was too much blood pouring from her mouth and ears. Her head drooped lifelessly.

Mary Anne remembered feeling helplessness and anger as she used long, swift strokes to get back to the shore. One of her last memories upon reaching Betty was seeing Amy's fat ass crashing through the bushes.

"Mommy?" Deedee tugged at Mary Anne's arm. Mary Anne wiped her arm across her face, pressing the heel of her palm against her dripping nose.

"Yes, sweetie?" Mary Anne asked, pulling her daughter closer to her.

"I think we found the bees' house," Deedee said, and pointed up to the rafters of the barn.

The Birds and the Bees

Mary Anne swallowed as she beheld a rather large hive and a swarm of bees circling it.

"Wow . . ." Mary Anne said. She took each child by the hand. "I think I'll finish taking down the photos another time."

Mary Anne led them out of the barn and back toward the house. She meant to tell John, when he came home, about the bee hive and how maybe they should destroy it. She didn't think it was the same swarm as the vindictive bees from the day before, or she and the kids would have been attacked while still in the barn. The bees hadn't attacked, they had just flown along on their business, spindly legs hanging suspended while their swollen pollen-laden bodies emptied their loads into the hive. Mary Anne returned to the barn after the kids were in bed, and studied the hive a little longer. All that would have to be done was to get a big ladder and take the thing down. John could do that, or at least the old John who used to give a shit about her would have done that immediately.

However, by the time John walked in the door, Mary Anne was fast asleep, trapped in the nightmarish image of Betty hanging by her neck on the rope swing while a swarm of bees burrowed into her eyes.

On another branch, there was callous laughter from a giant crow. Mary Anne was trying to swim toward Betty, but her own body was rife with pregnancy and movement was slow.

Sèphera Girón

At last, Mary Anne reached Betty and tried to pull her down by her foot. Mary Anne felt her stomach roiling and rumbling. Looking down, she saw it rippling, a little dance up and down from her crotch to her neck. She touched it, and more ripples danced. Her nipples ached, and she saw they were leaking black. She touched her finger to a nipple and stroked it. The black thing felt hard, and it squirmed between her fingers. She saw the long throbbing body and long stick legs of a wasp. She tried to let go of the wasp, and watched as more of them made their way through her nipples. They poured forth, a cascade of wasps emerging from her by the hundreds. Once they hit the air, they buzzed their wings and went over to feast on Betty. Mary Anne thought she was going to puke, as her swollen stomach softened like an airless balloon while the hoards of wasps left their hibernation to go have lunch.

When Mary Anne woke up, John was beside her, smelling of pussy and beer. She turned over and pulled the covers over her head, hoping to block out the nightmare.

Chapter Five

Gabrielle pushed the tiny shopping cart through the narrow aisles of the produce department of the little European grocery store. A vast array of shiny fresh vegetables gleamed at her. She wondered how much time the workers spent polishing up the fruit and veggies every day. It must be a helluva job. There was so much, and each piece was artistically placed. Overhead, a few sparrows flew through the rafters.

It was odd, how this store always had little birds chirping and flying around overhead. She wondered if the manager ever tried to chase them out.

As she picked out a few things for the fridge, she picked up a bunch of bananas.

Sèphera Girón

A funny thing, bananas.

They always reminded her of a situation that had happened way back when she was in high school.

She must have been fourteen or fifteen at the time. She had been a bit of a bookworm, and would often hide in the library during school. Most of the time, she was just reading, but now and again, she would nibble on some cookies and write poetry or create little sketches about some guy she might have her eye on.

At this time, she had a big crush on Robert Towers.

She actually didn't know him, would just pass by him in the hallways now and again. Every time she saw him walking down the hall in her direction, her heart would slam against her chest and her palms would grow sweaty. Sometimes she would shake so hard that she would drop her books or pencils as he passed her by.

Robert ate a lot of bananas. No one knew why. Maybe he had just been hooked on them the way some people were into chips or candy bars.

As time went on, she gave herself the challenge of saying hello to him. He was in a higher grade, so she didn't expect him to actually acknowledge her existence. But he did.

He said hi back.

She thought she was going to die.

Robert Towers said hi to her.

The Birds and the Bees

She started to dress up in anticipation of running into him. Maybe she could somehow get him to ask her out. Or at least drop enough hints to see if she could figure out how to ask him out without rejection.

She knew he liked rock and roll; after all, he wore AC-DC T-shirts, had long shaggy hair and an earring. He sometimes wore a black leather bracelet. She didn't know why, but she found the idea of that black leather bracelet really hot.

The thing she liked the most about him was his green eyes. You could see their brilliance from a mile away. Emerald-green and as hypnotic as a snake.

She wanted to know what lay behind those eyes. Who was this guy? Why did she feel so attracted to him when she barely knew anything about him?

It was around that time that she started to read about soul connections. Soul mates. Lost souls. Souls that had traveled endless lifetimes together, searching for each other.

Through more of her reading, she learned new ideas about how there is no such thing as coincidence, that fate always has a pattern, that things happen for a reason, even if we are not sure how to interpret the message.

Gabrielle was convinced that Robert was her soul mate. Why else were their paths always crossing? Why else did she want to know him so badly? Why else did she want to crawl into those vivid green eyes and die?

One day, Gabrielle was walking down the hallway, squinting her eyes against the white glare of the fluorescent lights above her, cruising the area where Robert's locker would be. She hated how those lights buzzed and flickered, and she could swear that one of the things that annoyed her most from high school was the memory of those lights that peppered the hallways and hung garishly in the classrooms.

She noticed a girl with orange hair, sitting by Robert's locker. Gabrielle recognized her as Amy, the loner. Amy didn't notice Gabrielle as she continued to write something on a piece of paper. After rereading it several times, Amy folded the paper carefully and then slipped the note into the crack of Robert's locker.

Gabrielle stepped back as Amy hurried down the hallway. As she watched the girl walking away, she wondered how on earth Amy could ever think in a million years that a hunk like Robert would think twice about a large, sweaty girl who even if she were thin, wasn't likely to win any prizes for her looks.

Gabrielle was no beauty queen herself, but at least she wasn't fifty pounds overweight.

Gabrielle was burning with curiosity about what Amy might have written to Robert. She'd never know in a million years, though. Not unless fate had something to do with it.

The Birds and the Bees

As she was about to walk away from the locker, Robert turned the corner. He spotted Gabrielle and grinned.

"Hi, Gabrielle. What's shaking?"

"Just walking and thinking," Gabrielle said. She felt her face flushing, and hated it.

"I've been meaning to talk to you," Robert said, opening his locker. Amy's note fell out onto the floor. He picked it up.

"Did you leave this?" he asked, holding the note out to Gabrielle.

"Me? Why do you say that?"

"Well, you're standing right there and here's a note with no name on it."

Gabrielle peered at the note.

"You are the greatest guy in the world. I want to get to know you better. Meet me at 3:30 at the coffee shop."

Gabrielle shrugged.

"Well, isn't that a funny coincidence. I was going to ask you out anyway. Like today, after school. Wanna go for a coffee?" he asked.

Gabrielle flushed even harder than she had before, and found herself speechless.

"Sure," she said.

Above them, the fluorescent lights flickered annoyingly with a sporadic buzz.

They met after school at the local coffee shop. Gabrielle felt like the Queen of the World, walking in that door with Robert. That is, until she saw Amy sitting in the corner, watching her with mortified horror. A wave of guilt swept through Gabrielle, but then she brushed it aside. Robert was going to ask her out before he got the note anyway, so what did it matter?

Gabrielle felt Amy's eyes boring a hole into her, but what could she say or do? She barely knew the girl. She knew that if Robert had come into this coffee shop and seen only Amy sitting alone, waiting for him, he never would have believed in a million years that Amy was the one who had written the note.

"Hey, my mom's not home for a while yet. Wanna come over and watch TV?" Robert asked after about an hour. Gabrielle nodded speechlessly.

As Gabrielle sat on the couch, she thought for sure the whole world could feel her shaking. Her fingers couldn't stop the jitters. She was so nervous she thought she might pass out or throw up.

They were watching *Gilligan's Island*. Gabrielle hadn't watched it very often before, so she laughed a lot. She was having a great time with Robert, who had his arm around her. She wondered if he could feel her heart thumping right through her chest and into him.

When he turned her face toward his and gazed into her eyes, she thought she was truly going to die. His lips were soft on hers, hungry and persistent. She kissed back tentatively tasting him, thinking that she had never been

The Birds and the Bees

kissed like this before. Her mind started racing as his hands slid along her chest. He must really like her. Maybe they would be boyfriend and girlfriend. Maybe they would one day get married.

His fingers slowly touched her breasts, tapping them to find the nipple. She had only had her breasts touched a couple of times before, and couldn't believe how thrilling it was for her.

After they had kissed for a while, Robert took her hand and put it into his lap. She felt him hard through his pants, and pulled her hand back for a second, but Robert put it back on him again.

"Rub it," he whispered, his voice trembling. Gabrielle realized that he was as excited as she was, and rubbed his crotch through his jeans as best she could.

"Take it out," he said, pausing from fondling her breasts to unlocking his zipper.

Gabrielle looked at his cock. It was huge. She had never seen anything quite as big before. Of course, she hadn't had much opportunity to see many cocks at all at this point in her life.

He stared at her with his eyes shining feverishly.

"Suck it."

Gabrielle looked at him with stunned amazement.

"What?"

"Suck my cock. Gobble it good."

Sèphera Girón

"Gross," Gabrielle said, staring at his cock.

Suck it? God, she wasn't putting that thing in her mouth. That was the most disgusting thing she had ever heard of.

"Please . . ." Robert looked intensely at her, waves of desperation pouring from him.

"I can't . . . I don't know how," Gabrielle said.

"You just have to put it in your mouth. . . ."

"I can't do that. I'm sorry, I just can't."

Robert put her hand back onto his cock. She felt him quivering and pulsing as she danced her fingers along him. Robert reached over to the side table, where there was a bowl of fruit. He pulled out a banana.

"Eat this then," he said as he slowly unpeeled it. He handed the white phallus to her. She looked at it and started to giggle. She bit it.

"*No!*" Robert said. "Suck it. Lick it. Make it slow, like in a movie."

"I've never seen a movie where they do that sort of thing," Gabrielle said, tentatively kissing the banana, knowing in the back of her mind that she had to be as sexy as possible though she didn't know how to pull it off.

"That's better . . ." Robert sighed, rubbing at his own crotch as Gabrielle continued to eat the banana. Gabrielle started to feel silly and giggled.

"Maybe . . . maybe we can do something else," said Gabrielle.

The Birds and the Bees

"You mean, you wanna . . . make love?" Robert asked.

"No. I'm a virgin and plan to be that way for a long time."

Robert stroked his fingers along her legs and around her crotch. She felt herself getting excited at him touching her, but she wasn't going to fuck him.

"Are you kinky?" Robert asked.

"In what way?" Gabrielle wasn't even sure what kinky meant. She figured it had something to do with fishnet stockings, but she wasn't sure.

"Well . . ." Robert squeezed her crotch, rubbing his fingers along it until an involuntary moan slipped from Gabrielle's lips.

"What?" she gasped.

"Most teenagers . . . well, they are kinky . . . 'cause like, they don't want to get pregnant."

"In what way?"

Robert flushed.

"Instead of doing it the real way, you do it with, like, the other hole and that way no one gets pregnant or anything."

Gabrielle was about to protest again, but then stopped. If she kept denying him these things that he seemed to enjoy, then he was going to tell her to take a hike. She just knew it. At least that idea seemed a tiny bit less disgusting to her than putting that thing in her *mouth*.

77

Sèphera Girón

"What do I do?" she asked.

"Lie down on the couch there. On your stomach."

Gabrielle lay on her stomach, her legs trembling.

Robert kneeled above her and peeled her pants down so that her bottom was showing. He shoved a couple of pillows under her hips so that her butt was high in the air.

A cool breeze trailed in the room as the lights flickered. Gabrielle's butt was peppered with goose bumps. She felt him fumbling above her, heard the jingle of his belt buckle and the movement of him hitching his pants down. Soon his breath was hot on her neck as she felt him fleshy against her butt cheeks. He rubbed himself against her, his movements growing jerkier, his breath hot in her ear, his moans foreign and frightening. His pace quickened, and she felt her crotch starting to throb with a distantly budding pleasure.

He held her hair. Her face was smashing into the scratchy couch cushions and she had trouble gulping in air. His movement was more frantic, and suddenly she felt a stabbing like a hot fire had been shot up her butt hole. She realized that he was inside her now, and she flailed about, trying to push him out of her.

"Stop . . . it hurts," she cried out, tears welling in her eyes. She couldn't cry, though. She just couldn't. Cool girls don't cry. He obviously

The Birds and the Bees

knew what he was doing, and she would let him continue to do it, if only he would stop for a moment. But he wouldn't. It seemed as though he was just getting bigger and harder, growing inside her like an out-of-control plant.

No, tree.

A big hard branch sawing in and out of her. She knew she was ripping. She prayed he would be finished soon. The lamp flickered and buzzed above her head, while the back of the couch slammed into the wall repeatedly.

At last, he rammed into her with a shout, filling her with a hot warmth. He fell backward off the couch and tumbled onto the floor. She looked over at him.

Her prince with his pants crumpled around his legs. He didn't seem so glamorous anymore. The spell had been broken and he was just an everyday person.

Robert stared around the living room in a daze and grabbed a box of tissues while smoothing out his hair.

"You'd better get out of here," he said, his voice small and panicked.

"What?"

"My mom will be home soon and I'm not supposed to have company."

Gabrielle stood shakily, feeling liquid spilling from her butt.

"Oh, man, watch it. You're gonna wreck the sofa," he shouted, grabbing more tissues. He rubbed frantically at the milky, sludgy substance as the tissues disintegrated beneath his fingers.

"Goddammit," he swore.

Gabrielle stumbled into the bathroom, willing herself not to cry. She sat on the toilet and emptied her bowels. She pushed and pushed, trying to make sure all of him was out of her. When she wiped, she took great care not to trail any of the come where it might accidentally get her pregnant. She didn't know if she could get pregnant or not from that, but she wouldn't take any chances.

After she washed her face and bottom, she returned to the living room, where Robert had finished cleaning off the sofa and was settled eating another banana.

"So you're off then?" he asked.

Gabrielle nodded, grabbing her purse in a daze.

She stood by the front door, hoping he'd give her a hug or kiss or maybe plan their next encounter. Maybe he'd take her to a movie or something.

"Do you want to do something on Friday?" Gabrielle finally asked, realizing that he was just staring at the TV as if she didn't even exist at all.

"No, thanks. I have shit to do," Robert said.
Gabrielle nodded and unlocked the door.

The Birds and the Bees

"So, uh, bye . . ." she said. He nodded toward her and she let herself out.

She ran all the way, gulping in great lungs of air and sobbing at the utter humiliation she felt. When she arrived home, she wanted nothing more but to hide in her room forever.

However, the news came within minutes that her grandmother suddenly died, and now there was a funeral to deal with. Her favorite grandmother, Carmina, was no more.

All those long summer days, sitting at her grandmother's knee, watching the birds and the bees and the flowers while Grandmother told her fascinating stories. All those times Gabrielle had written her letters, and Grandmother had always replied. Grandmother knew secrets about Gabrielle that no one else ever did or would.

And now it was over.

Gone.

Grandmother was gone.

Gabrielle had stared at her mother, all words gone from her mind. Humiliation and grief consumed her for days, yet as time passed, she felt a sort of relief.

She had dreams for about a year of her grandmother coming to comfort her. That her grandmother would always be there for her, even when boys did wrong by her.

As the years had passed, the dream grandmother had become nothing more then a vague shadowy figure, haunting the various stories and adventures a young woman would have.

Gabrielle now stood in the grocery, realizing that she hadn't dreamed of her grandmother in a long time. She stared at the bananas, and was startled at how vividly she had suddenly remembered one of her earliest sexual encounters.

It was funny how, so many times, sex just did not end up the way it was hyped. That the reality sometimes was nothing short of horrific. She could feel the sense of violation and humiliation as if it had just happened. Yet the sex act itself, she couldn't remember. She had been sexually active for longer than she hadn't at this point in her life. There wasn't much she hadn't at least tried, yet nothing had been as humiliating as what happened with Robert.

Even one-night stands who never called back didn't give her that same sense of despair and horror as standing by the door that day, her ass sore and bleeding, hoping for an acknowledgment or a kind word and getting nothing.

She never really ran into Robert after that. She changed her route and kept her eyes down. Now and again, she'd see Amy around the school, leering from the shadows at her, eyes dancing with a malicious grin. Gabrielle often wondered if she had taken the shame that Amy might have experienced had Robert realized who had really written the note.

The Birds and the Bees

* * *

Gabrielle looked around the party. There was quite a turnout here tonight.

No surprise, of course, since it was the usual cast of characters.

From musicians to journalists to hangerson who had scored a freebie pass through a local radio contest or friends. This was a wide assortment of creative humanity.

Gabrielle took a strawberry tart from the buffet table and popped it into her mouth. She reveled in the delicate texture of the pastry and the tangy yet sweet taste of the fruit and custard. As she dabbed at her mouth, she turned to Marie.

"Nice spread," said Marie.

"Sure is. You can always count on these recording companies to put on a big party for their flavor of the week."

"I'll say. Look at the wine! No cheap stuff for us tonight!" Marie raised her glass and toasted Gabrielle. The women clicked glasses, then turned to survey the room.

Handsome men and pretty plastic women graced the room. Music at some point along the way had become the cult of beauty. Gabrielle missed the ruggedness of the rock bands of the sixties. The Joplins and Jaggers, the mike-throwing of Daltrey and the flailing of Townshend. The people who looked real, screaming into the microphone about war and society, in ripped jeans, tossing manes of loose wild hair.

Now it was about bellies pierced with rhinestones, about heaving cleavage, and glistening sweaty flesh. If you didn't have a pretty face, you were plasticized till you did. If you were curvy like early Madonna, it was off to the personal trainer until you emerged with Britney Spears abs, Courtney Love makeup, and Janet Jackson gyrations.

The same went for the men. The emergence of boy bands certainly took care of that. A hard-edged rocker was rare now. Even *they* were looking pretty.

Gabrielle longed for real music with real gut feeling. Music like she had heard the other night when Tommy played. He played from the heart, his fingers dancing along the frets like the old guard, not the new boom-box fakes of modern times.

Tonight's promotional princess was a tanned and toned nineteen-year-old with big hair and big breasts to match. She wore more makeup on her face than Gabrielle used in an entire year.

Blue, as her name suggested, had blue pieces woven into her multicolored hair, and wore a slinky blue spandex jumpsuit and blue platform shoes, and was sparkled with a sheen of blue that coated her flesh like a second skin.

Gabrielle stared with a combination of fascination and sheer wonderment. When she was

The Birds and the Bees

that age, there was no way she had a body that voluptuous yet childlike. Blue's cleavage was exposed teasingly as was the blue jewel in her belly through the magic of criss-crossing peek-aboo straps.

"Oh, to be so young again," Marie sighed.

"Young? Heck, I'd settle for an hour in that body," Gabrielle said.

They watched Blue move catlike across the party, nodding and smiling at various people, haughtily peering down at those she didn't recognize.

What was act?

What was real?

It was impossible to unravel the mystery from the woman, unless you had known who she was before. Blue mesmerized anyone in her path as she skulked along towards the bar.

Spotting Gabrielle, Blue stopped.

"Why, hello," Blue purred to Gabrielle.

"Hello, Miss Blue," Gabrielle said politely.

"It's Gabrielle, isn't it?"

"Yes."

Blue's lips twitched into a smirk. She batted blue sparkled eyelashes and took Gabrielle's hand.

"You know, I really have to thank you. You first wrote about me when I was no one. When I was still singing to my acoustic on talent night. You really gave me the confidence to be who I am today."

Gabrielle smiled. "You have a lovely voice. Don't forget it. Don't lose it in all the electronic garbage that passes for music these days."

Blue's smile faltered. She raised one of her taloned claws and patted Gabrielle's cheek.

"I'll remember that when I'm signing my million-dollar deal." She smirked and turned on her tottering heels.

Gabrielle watched Blue's tightly clad ass move away from her. She sighed. How much Blue had changed since she was the long-haired, gawky singer with the throaty voice. Hers was an exquisitely throaty voice, sort of like a cross between Marianne Faithful and Pat Benatar.

Gabrielle had been at the little cafe quite by accident that day. She had been making notes for her latest novel, and felt the need to go to a lounge to work. That unfinished novel still lay in pieces in a box. Cocktail napkins, notebooks, and floppy disks. All various stages of mutations, trying to morph, unsuccessfully, into something huge and important. But it wasn't to be.

Meanwhile, while she had been making notes about one of her characters, nearly two years ago it must have been, this young skinny waif had taken the stage. Jean McKay. She had long stringy blond hair, wore a baggy T-shirt and low-slung jeans. She didn't have much makeup. There was a sense of innocence and beauty that

The Birds and the Bees

echoed a forlorn sentiment. Gabrielle had wanted to run up to the stage, to tell the frightened child that it would be okay, that singing in this little club was only one step along the way. It hadn't been Jean's first time on the stage, and obviously it wasn't the last.

Gabrielle remembered being ready to dismiss the singer until she actually started to sing. Her voice was full and haunting, surprisingly strong and melodic. Instead of bringing her forgotten character to life, Gabrielle was filled with a need to tell the world about this undiscovered songbird. And so she had. The next day, her review was in the paper, and at Jean's next gig, the place was packed. After all, if Gabrielle said a singer was good, then her readers knew the singer *was* good.

Jean became Blue, and now here she was, perched on the brink of stardom, ready to fly across a chasm of a wondrous unknown world, where only the most beautiful and tenacious of birds could fly.

Jean had become Blue, yet Gabrielle still had not managed to mesh her characters into a passable novel.

"I think I've had just about enough," Gabrielle said, draining her glass.

Marie nodded. "Like I couldn't tell."

"Like you couldn't."

"I guess it's hard for you, watching the people you write about rise up and get rich and famous, while you still plug away day after day in the same old shit."

"Oh, it shows?"

"Only sometimes, my dear . . ."

They watched the scene a while longer, Gabrielle feeling her fingers clutching her glass so tightly that she wondered if it would explode.

"I'm out of here," Gabrielle said. Marie nodded.

"See you tomorrow," Marie said.

Gabrielle had started to walk away when a young woman approached her.

"Excuse me . . ." the girl said nervously, a slow flush creeping up her neck and across her cheeks.

"I'm in rather a hurry."

"Are you Gabrielle?"

Gabrielle stared at the young girl before her. She wanted to lie. She wanted to say no and get the hell out, but something about the young girl made her stop.

"Yes."

The girl's face flushed even redder as she held out a CD case.

"I read your column all the time. I think you really understand what is going on. Do you think you could listen to my CD sometime and tell me what you think?"

Gabrielle sighed. "You know . . . it's really . . ." Gabrielle looked into the girl's eyes. They were wide and full of hope, as if any word

The Birds and the Bees

that Gabrielle said would make or break her spirit.

"I'll try to give it a spin," Gabrielle said, and snatched the CD out of the girl's fingers. Gabrielle walked away before the girl had a chance to utter a word of thanks.

Once out of the hot sweaty crowd of the party, Gabrielle let out a big sigh.

"Thank God," she sighed, reaching into to her coat pocket for her cigarettes. She lit one up and walked down the street, staring into store windows. She had already forgotten about Blue and the young girl.

She felt annoyed.

No, annoyed wasn't the word for it.

She has a sense of disturbance, one that she hadn't had in a long time. It was an agitation, an impatience with people. It was at times like this that she felt like handing in her resignation to the human race. She was on a hamster wheel and no matter what she did, the wheel turned and turned and she got nowhere fast.

How was she going to change this? How could she get off of this wheel and onto a track that went somewhere? Anywhere?

She didn't know, but she knew she had to do something. She was getting into that stuck-in-a-rut head space again, and that was never good. She knew logically that she had plenty to live for. A couple of cool kids, a freelance career that many would kill for. She got invited to a lot of great parties, and had met some pretty impressive people in her time. They weren't all plastic pretension.

Tonight, she was soured.

Soured on the machine that spit out stars instead of music. Hair and clothes instead of sound. It made her crazy.

Her thoughts drifted to Tommy.

She knew he was playing again tonight, and thought that maybe she'd try to catch his last set.

There she was.

Almost as if he had called her through the notes slipping from his fingers. Tommy watched from under a lock of tousled hair as the small woman stepped into the half-filled room. She stood for a moment, and he sighed as her pale beauty was magnified by the slash of yellow light falling through the doorway. Shadows haunted her eyes and cheekbones, her long hair casually tangled into the straps of her purse. He noticed she wore glittery clothes, as if she were on her way to a party. She slid into an empty table and fidgeted around in her purse. He continued to sing and play as she pulled out a notebook and pen. She lit a cigarette, and drew on it. His eyes were drawn to the red glow of the tip. He watched her lips purse around the cigarette, and wondered what

The Birds and the Bees

they would feel like pursed around him. He blinked and turned his head away.

He was married. He had a child. His womanizing days were over. He had promised, long ago, that they were over. He hadn't cheated on his wife in years and years.

He thought of the last, well, the only real time he had ever strayed from his teen bride.

He had been barely out of his teens himself. He was playing a gig at a local outdoor rock festival and drinking far too much Jack that night. The band had been one of his first. A rock and roll band that covered tunes from Nirvana to the Ramones. He had been the lead guitarist and singer. He loved to sing rock and roll. He had a gravely voice that sounded great through a mike, and he was able to tear out riffs on his guitar in a manner that would put Pete Townshend to shame.

He was wailing away to some mournful grunge tune, when he noticed a woman swaying in front of him. He had noticed her all night long, really, if he was honest with himself, but the way the setting summer sun glistened off her streaked blond hair, the way her scoop-necked T-shirt clung to her sweaty cleavage, she was the vision of some sort of goddess.

All night long, she swayed and moaned in front of him, rubbing her body and shaking her shapely hips in time to the music. Tommy had forgotten he was married. And a new dad. He had forgotten everything in the world except for the music he was playing and beauty that enticed him.

After the band was finished the set, he left the stage, drenched in sweat. The guys high-fived each other. It had been a moment of triumph for all of them. Tommy was the youngest by five years, but he had pulled it off and the guys were pleased. Franky started babbling on about more gigs, about tours and record deals. The other guys joined in, and Marky sparked up a joint. As Tommy took a hit, the blond girl was in front of him once more. How she had made it past security was anyone's guess, but here she was. All curves and glistening sweat, ready to please.

She touched Tommy's arm and he stopped, the other guys walking on, not noticing that Tommy was now standing mesmerized by a pretty girl.

The girl rubbed her fingers along Tommy's arm.

"I really liked the show," she cooed. Tommy was certain his face was as red as the last lingering streaks the setting sun left in the clouds.

"Thanks."

She reached up and took Tommy's face in her hands. Her lips pressed against his, her tongue searching his mouth.

"I've been watching you. Watching you play for months," she whispered as she pressed her body against his. "I've been wanting you."

The Birds and the Bees

Tommy tried to unlock her arms from his neck, tried to step back from her writhing body.

"I'm sorry. I'm married."

"I know you are." She buried her face into his neck and licked him.

"I-I really have to go."

"Not just yet." The girl took his hand and placed it across her breast. He tried to resist, but the feel of her large erect nipple caused him to linger. She took his hesitation as acceptance, and placed his other hand between her legs.

"Touch me . . ." She sighed, throwing her head back. Tommy gently pushed her back and tried to walk away.

"No!" The girl leaped at him and clutched his hand. "You owe me!" she howled.

"I owe you?" he asked incredulously, amazed at the transformation from gentle seductress to predator.

"Yes. After all I've done. I've been to all your shows. I put up flyers for your shows. I get people clapping and dancing . . . you owe me."

Tommy looked at her. Really took a long look at her. Checked out her pretty blue eyes and her long full hair. He looked at her deliciously pouty lips and the button nipples pushing through her shirt. He could go with her. No one would ever know. Not his wife, who was home with the baby. No, she would never know. Just once, once he could taste what most rock stars got on a regular basis. When he became a big rock star, maybe he would again, but right now, who was he? Just a kid playing an outdoor festival.

No one would know, would they? He tasted beer being poured down his throat. Then he was led along the makeshift hallway, through and under tent flaps, until they were outside the festival, in a nearby cornfield. The floodlights tickled parts of the field, and flashing strobe lights from the next performing group sporadically lit their faces.

The girl. What was her name? She had never said her name. She lifted her top over her head as if it were the most natural thing in the world. Tommy stared in awe at the offering before him. Beautiful, blond, and wanting him. Actually wanting *him*. The sun was gone and more beer was in his hand. He drank down the bottle and threw it into the field while the girl lazily peeled down her pants. By now, his head sang with a wondrous song, the siren song of booze and sex, the heady thrill of a strange woman dancing in front of him. Wife and child were forgotten, as were the band mates and even the throngs of concert goers mere feet away.

She swayed, serpentlike, her hands winding their way over to him, flicking buttons open, spreading cloth away from flesh, pushing him down to the dirt. She was older and more experienced than anyone he had been with, and her ministrations teased and tormented him in

The Birds and the Bees

ones were stale and which ones were just not quite right to sell. There weren't that many, and he put them into a huge plastic bag. This was one of his favorite parts of the day. Gathering up the unusable goods and taking them out. It used to bother him to gather up the stuff and just throw it away. It used to make him cry when he thought of how many times he had gone to bed hungry, how just one small little stale moldy bun would have made all the difference in the world.

He used to try to hide the stale bread and take it home, but Mr. B would have none of that. If Abraham was good enough to work in the bakery, he was good enough to take home a few fresh goods at the end of his shift. The food bank didn't want the bread, Mr. B had explained, because they couldn't get it out to people in time and believe it or not, a lot of poor people were insulted to be given stale bread.

So they had worked out a compromise. Abraham could take the stale bread out back every morning. And whoever came along could have it.

He took the bag with the bread, and saw they were waiting there for him already, eyes gleaming.

He called hello to them. They called hello back in greeting.

"How are you today, my friends?" he asked as he took the bread out. A flurry of wings, and a large black crow perched on his shoulder. Another sat on his head. The birds cawed and swooped as he happily fed them. How he loved this new land!

"You're it!" Deedee giggled at Jimmy as they ran into the barn, bare feet slapping the old creaking boards. Jimmy dodged various rusted tools, zipped underneath the old tractor, and scrambled through the hay.

"You can't catch me!" Jimmy called out. Deedee was right behind him, stumbling and laughing. The children ran across the section of the barn where a bright light beamed, bathing the air with a sudden slash of sparkling warmth.

"Sun fairies!" cried Deedee, stopping to admire the floating shimmering of dust caught in the light. "Make a wish."

The children jumped into the air, clawing at the floating bits of fluff. When they grew bored of catching fairies, they resumed their game.

They ran past the old trunk, past the old section of the barn where there were photographs covering the wall. The children often ran past them, not seeing the brown curling papers for anything other than ancient faces that they didn't recognize.

Today as they ran, they saw Mary Anne hacking at the wall with a metal scraper. Bits of brittle and curling paper fluttered around her feet.

"What you doing, Mommy?" Deedee asked.

The Birds and the Bees

such a way that he was finished before he had even started. A sense of exhalation and then a deep sadness spread through him as he pulled away from her. She sat up, reaching for him.

"Wait . . . let's go around again!" she purred.

The spell was broken.

Tommy jumped up, pulling his jeans up with him.

"What was I thinking?" he muttered, fumbling with his zipper.

The girl wrapped herself around his feet.

"You were thinking about how much a fan wants to show you gratitude. Come here. Come back to me . . ." She reached for his hand, trying to draw it back between her legs. He jerked it away. As he turned, he realized that they had not been as alone as he thought. Standing there, watching with complete disbelief, was his wife. His wife holding their baby daughter.

Why was she not at home, safe where she belonged? What on earth was she doing here? Here where there could be nothing good?

His heart ached as he watched his wife turn on her heel without a word. He kicked away the siren, who was as shocked as he was. He zipped and snapped and tucked and tried to think about how on earth he could explain this, and even more, how he could explain that this had been the first and only time.

Tommy never forgot that day.

The disappointment burned into Sheila's eyes

took months to bury. Whenever he left the house, she would watch with that weird puppy-dog look, as if he would kick her, or worse, betray her again. And he never had. Not yet.

But now, watching Gabrielle smoking her cigarette in the darkness, Tommy wondered if he would betray his wife again.

The sun was streaming into the tiny hotel room where Gabrielle and Tommy sat on the bed, drinking from Tommy's nearly empty bottle of Jack.

"Morning . . ." Gabrielle marveled. "We talked the night away."

"We did."

They looked at each other, eyes bright with unspoken expectation. Gabrielle broke the gaze first.

"I guess I should be going."

"I wish you could stay."

"I have to get home. Get some sleep. I have work to do."

"You could sleep here."

Gabrielle looked at the pillows and imagined their heads on them, eyes shut, content in each other's arms.

"No. It's not right. You're married." She stood up and found her purse. She opened it and took out a business card.

"Here. In case you ever want to talk. I really did enjoy our talk."

The Birds and the Bees

"So did I."

His fingers brushed against hers as he took the card. Their eyes locked again, and Gabrielle turned for the door.

"Good-bye, Tommy."

"Good-bye, Gabrielle."

Gabrielle walked down a hallway that seemed so long, so foreign. She felt like she was in a strange land, like her mind was not her own. It was odd, the effect he had on her. Tears welled up into her eyes. How they had talked. How the subjects had ranged. She played them over in her mind. Hopes and dreams. Her dream of a best-selling novel. His dream of a breakthrough CD. Her divorce, her children. His wife and daughter, how young he had been when he had her. Just a teenager. How hard that must have been. He talked fondly of his wife, yet the way he looked at Gabrielle . . . She melted under his gaze. She imagined his lips touching hers a thousand times while they prattled on about the trials and tribulations of child-rearing and the latest music.

At one point, the talk had turned to religion. To God. He didn't believe in a God. Not in the way she did. Her belief was in a force, a spirit that connected all beings so that whatever affected one person would ripple along to another. His denial of that sort of thinking was vehement. If there was a God, he was not merciful, he was cruel. But there was no God, so it didn't matter.

She felt that the connection they shared was spiritual. That they had met before, and though she was walking down the street with the morning sun burning down on her and consciously lamenting that maybe she had lost an opportunity to share intimacy, they would be meeting again. If he felt the pull between them that she had felt, there was no way to deny that this was far from over.

There was small comfort in that thought. There was small comfort in anything anymore. Like clockwork, a big black bird glided down to a mailbox just ahead of her, and like clockwork, it screamed at her as she walked by.

The walk was waking her up, though she felt herself pulled further into an unreality. Just overtired. Just needed some sleep. It was as if she was in a time slip, that weird space between sleep and wakefulness, but usually she felt like this as she drifted off, in the dark, lying down.

It was foolish, she knew. Staying up all night, talking, as if she were still in high school. As if she had nowhere to go, nothing to do, for the rest of the day. Yet her day was going to be quite busy. Lunch with the kids, an amusement of some sort, and in between playing with the kids, she had to work on a column.

The Birds and the Bees

Why was it that when she finally met someone she had something good in common with, he was married?

Life wasn't fair.

Chapter Six

Amy was only about five when she wandered out of the door and into a field. Her mommy was in another room. She wasn't sure where, but she figured she was probably with that big scary man. Amy didn't like that man. She didn't like most men. They were big and loud and always angry about something.

Amy didn't want to stay in the house. It was hot and sticky and worse, smelled sour and rotten like that man. She wanted to go outside where the grass was green and there might even be a breeze. She opened the front door, waiting to hear if her mother noticed. But she did not. Mommy was otherwise busy doing something. Amy stepped out onto the front porch and felt the door slam shut behind her.

Sèphera Girón

Again she waited for Mommy to scream out after her. Again there was silence.

Amy ran down the stairs and down the sidewalk until she made it to the nearby park. It was a hot sticky afternoon, that was for sure. She pushed the tangle of her hair away from her eyes. Flowers were everywhere. Flowers as far as she could see. Pretty little flowers. Yellow and white and purple. All neatly tucked into the grass like the most beautiful pattern on a blanket.

Amy ran into the flowers, her bare feet slapping the soft grass. There was no one around but her, and nothing but the grass and the flowers and the hot sun.

She kneeled down to pick the flowers, tucking them in her hair. She made little chains out of them, peeling open the stalk of one end to push a flower head through another. It was painstaking work for tiny chubby fingers, but at last she had a crown that the pickiest of fairy queens would proudly wear.

Amy made bracelets and anklets, the hot sun pounding down on her, the thick summer air filling her lungs. She sang snatches of songs, "round and round the circle."

At long last, she was finished her weaving, and she lay her head down for a bit of a rest. She breathed in deeply of the fragrant perfume, and listened to the gentle hum of nature around her.

The Birds and the Bees

When she woke, it was to a louder hum. She was reluctant to open her eyes, the noise was so loud. It frightened her, this vibration. She felt the fluttering of wings against her bare arms, felt tickling against her cheeks. She opened her eyes and started to sit up. She froze as she saw she was covered in bees. Plump yellow and black bees, with spidery legs and buzzing wings. She was too afraid to cry, too afraid to move as she watched them crawl up and down her arms and legs, along her body. The humming was so loud.

She felt something tickling inside her ear, could imagine tiny little bee legs picking their way around, deciding whether to burrow deeper into that hole. The idea of it was enough to get her moving. She screamed and bolted. Once the scream was let loose, she couldn't stop. She wailed like a siren, and the humming of the bees turned to an angry buzz. Then the stinging began. They pierced her time and again and she howled, thinking she was going to die.

Where was her mommy?

Her frantic attempts at brushing them off made them angrier. They followed her as she ran, her little feet smashing all the pretty flowers she had so admired earlier. She watched bees hovering and diving, as if they were fighter planes. She felt the stings tingling through her. That sharp pinprick burst and then a liquid pain. She stood at the foot of the porch, exhausted. Tears ran from her face and she could taste salt on her lips. The bees were relentless. She noticed, however, that despite what seemed like an endless attack, bees were falling to the ground. She watched them kick their legs in the air and then, amazingly enough, lie still.

The pain was everything now. It had always been there. It would always be there. She knew that. When she thought about it, it was no worse of a pain than when one of Mommy's men smacked her across the face or butt. It was no worse than getting burned with a cigarette on her arm or back. She pulled the dying flowers from her wrist and tossed them to the ground. A few bees followed the clump. She ran her fingers through her tangled dirty hair, pulling at bees and flowers and stems, trying to pull them out as she cried. She wiped her snotty nose along her puffy red arm. Stings were swelling in her scalp, her cheeks, her legs. Every part of her body had been attacked.

Now some of the stings were itching. Burning, itching, throbbing. She cried harder, and more bees fell to the ground.

Amy sat down heavily on the stairs, her head on her knees. The bees would come or they would stop. There was nothing she could do. Her fingers felt little sticks in the welts. She looked, staring at the little black stick things.

The stingers.

She picked at one, digging at it, and finally

The Birds and the Bees

pulled it out. She held it up, staring at it.

That tiny little thing, ripped out of a bee. She looked at the growing pile of dead bees beside her. Rip off their stingers and they die. She smiled as she pieced it together. The bees were dying because they'd stung her. In hurting her, they'd sacrificed their lives. She laughed. She only had pain, but she was still alive. The bees, they had wounded her and now they lay dying.

Her giggles verged on the edge of hysteria as she picked at her wounds. She swatted away the remaining bees.

"Amy!" She heard the shrill sound of her mother's voice.

Amy was jolted out of her hypnotic state and back into reality. She started to cry.

Amy's mother stormed down the stairs.

"Where have you been?"

"I . . ."

"Look at you! Where the hell have you been? I've been worried sick about you!"

"I went to pick some flowers and then. . . . and then . . ." Amy cried harder, snot dripping from her nose.

"Look at you! You are disgusting!" Amy's mother shook her. "My God . . . what the hell is going on?"

The full scale of the pain she had been subjected to pounded through her blood.

"It hurts, Mommy. It hurts." She pointed at the welts. There were still a few bees buzzing around, seemingly not terribly interested in landing.

"Jesus . . . what do you expect by running off like that. . . ." Amy's mother dragged the girl through the house, up the stairs, and into the tiny bathroom. She fumbled with the tub taps with one hand, and stripped down the crying child with the other. The full force of the itching, throbbing welts swelled to the surface, and Amy's cries turned to shrieks.

"Shut up," her mother said, and put the child in the tub. Amy shrieked louder, lifting up her feet.

"Too hot! Too hot!" she cried.

"Nonsense. We have to get the poison out."

She left the room with Amy sitting in the tub. Amy reached over to the faucet and turned the knob so that more cold water poured forth.

Amy's mother returned with a box of baking soda.

"The only one I could find was in the fridge. Hope it's not gone bad or anything," she said as she poured the contents of the smelly box into the water. Amy watched the white powder clump and swirl and dissolve. Her little legs were covered with splotches. The baking soda stung the wounds, but at the same time, it felt good. She could see in some places where the stingers were still attached to her body.

Her mother ranted above her, the water swirled, a vacant stench of stale fridge smells

The Birds and the Bees

filled her nostrils, yet all she could think about were the bees. How resilient they had been. So strong. So brave, to attack a giant like herself, knowing it was suicide.

She wanted to know everything she could about bees, and made it her mission from that day forth.

Katey lay in bed, clicking the TV stations idly. Where was she going? What was going to become of her? She was so confused.

On the one hand, she was madly in love with John. Or so she had herself convinced. She liked his rough manner. She liked the idea of him coming to her instead of going home to his wife. She adored the feeling of him inside her. No one had ever felt as he had inside her, and she knew already, in her young life, that such matches of physicality were indeed rare. No one could make her body sing and tremble the way he could. Or at least, no one she had ever met till now.

The Sound of Music was on a movie channel. It was the scene where Liesl is singing away in the rain, violet eyes brilliantly shining.

Katey remembered seeing *The Sound of Music* as a child and staring up at the screen at those beautiful eyes. There had been something about Liesl's eyes that had sent shivers through her, something about her eyes that made Katey want to touch her. Touch Liesl's lips with her own. Touch Liesl's breasts and dance around the gazebo with her in those Austrian pinafores.

But she knew too that it was a movie, and movie stars were supposed to be glamorous. She didn't think much more of it than that, for everyone admires a magnificent-looking person, man or woman, don't they?

She clicked around, found amazing psychics baffling their phone-in callers. For a while she watched, trying to understand how people could figure out events from a bunch of cards, or stones, or just by closing their eyes. She figured that most of the readings were just setups. Prescripted, prefabricated, prerehearsed.

She clicked again, and watched a red-faced preacher shout about corruption in the world today. He screeched about the gays and the unholy unions of the unmarried ones. He pointed the finger at the lure of alcohol and drugs, railed about children's minds shot to hell by the repetition of video games. Katey noticed that he didn't say much about cults that begged for money to spread the word of God.

The preacher prattled on about the plagues and how they had been materializing as predicted. Sure, the actual New Year's Eve events had never transpired as predicted, but there was more to come. How about the crazy weather patterns? Terrifying floods and hurricanes, earthquakes and fires. All the fault of those gays and pagans.

The Birds and the Bees

She continued to click, past comedy, past Baby Blue movies that never showed "the good parts," and returned again to *The Sound of Music*. As the story of the nun who married a rich man continued on, Katey grabbed a beer and a smoke and wondered whether one day she would find her life mate.

Or was John it?

It was funny how one day she could find herself all weepy over some schmaltzy love story, and the next she could be cynical as hell. *The Sound of Music* was one of those movies that did it to her. She found the idea of a little dormouse like Julie Andrews winning the heart of a handsome rich man on the verge of preposterous. Of course there was the thought that maybe he was just a dirty old man who wanted to be the first one to pop the virginal cherry.

To each his own.

With *The Sound of Music* blaring in the background, Katey went into the very back of her tiny closet. She didn't know why she kept anything hidden. After all, she was the only one who lived here. But she had felt it was important to keep this part of her self hidden. From John. From everyone. She didn't know what John would think. Part of her felt that he would find it exciting, but part of her was worried that anything that stretched the slightest bit outside his own realm of experience threatened him. She was pretty certain that his experience

Sèphera Girón

pretty much consisted of work, home, booze, and small-town girls. She doubted he'd even been in a regular dance club. She figured the furthest he would explore would be a rock-and-roll dance tavern, as long as it had draft and a pool table.

Where she was going was far more interesting than any dance club or rock-and-roll hall. She was pretty sure he'd never even heard of such a place, or if he had, would never have believed that it existed in his very own town. She would love to see his face if he ever stumbled into one by accident. But there was no way that would ever happen. The dress code and security were pretty tight.

She pushed through the closet of stuff. There, way back, was a box underneath a box of books. She dragged it out.

As she opened the box, a little thrill went through her. Her heart beat a bit faster and she realized, as she always did when she opened that box, that she missed this side of her life. And as she always did when she opened that box, she wondered why she bothered living any life at all but that one.

Well, she knew the answer to that.

The answer was the same as it was for most people.

Katey pulled out a pair of handcuffs, a whip, and several leather straps. Her fingers ran across the leather, so new it was pretty much

The Birds and the Bees

uncreased. So new it still smelled delicious. She put them gently on the ground and pulled out more items. A leather halter bra, several types of leather garters and waist cinchers. A chain-linked corset.

The corset was her favorite and, of course, the most expensive item in the box. Her fingers stroked the leather and PVC, jingling the chains. Another thrill ran through her as she stripped off her clothes. Her tiny body was molded even smaller as she cinched up the corset by pulling the strings at the back. The chains fell strategically between her breasts, down her middle, and along her hips. Her butt swelled out applelike where the corset ended, and she wondered whether she should wear fishnets or regular stockings.

The corset wasn't done all the way up, so she was able to crouch back down to the box and pull out several pairs of shoes. Long, shiny black stilettos, short leather-chained pumps, a pair of Doc Martens.

She was feeling nasty. Horny and nasty, so she pulled on the stilettos and walked over to the mirror. She felt tall and proud and in control. With a smile, she took up the whip and handcuffs and strutted over to the mirror. She waved the whip around with one hand, making sharp smacking noises in the air while dangling the handcuffs with the other.

"Come to me, baby," she cooed to the mirror.

Sèphera Girón

She stuck a foot out in front of her. "Lick my boot."

Tapping her foot impatiently, she kicked it out.

"Not like that. Like you mean it."

She cracked the whip again and laughed haughtily.

"You have been a bad, bad boy...."

The phone rang. Startled from her play, she blushed even as she went to answer it.

It was Miranda.

"Are you coming out tonight?" Miranda asked.

"You bet," Katey said, catching a glimpse of herself in the mirror. "You know how much I hate to miss my monthly fix."

"Well, I keep telling you, if you want to take off some weekend, we can go to that other one that's twice a month."

"It's so far, though. Then we'd have to get a hotel and everything. We don't make that kind of money just to play dress-up."

Miranda laughed. "Maybe one day I'll be rich!"

"Or marry rich!"

"Hell, you won't be marrying rich if you keep hanging out with loser trash like that married man you've been screwing. What the hell do you see in him anyway?"

"I like him. God help me, for some reason, I like the bastard."

The Birds and the Bees

"Drag him along sometime! Then we'd really have some fun!"

"Wouldn't that be hysterical? But it'll never happen."

The girls chattered on a while longer. After she hung up, Katey saw that *The Sound of Music* was now over. As the Von Trapps stood high on their mountain, trudging toward a new life, she wondered, again, what the hell was she doing with her own.

Each moment she spent with her children was a moment she wrapped up and put aside to cherish later. How quickly they were growing. Turning into humans that sometimes she barely recognized. She could look into her son's face and see the echoes of herself and his father in there. Watching him walk just like his father, she could envision a time when he would be pushing at the limits, testing everyone to become a man. Learning and growing, her children were branching away from her. Sometimes she wanted to take them home with her forever. She had visions of packing up the car and driving, driving for a long time, until they reached some faraway place where it would be just her and her children, like it had been a long time ago.

But how times changed. She was no longer a mother. Not a full-time mother. There was another mother for her children now. Even though it was for the best, it sank like a dagger into her heart whenever she thought about it. As much as Gabrielle wanted her children back, how would she care for them? How could she continue on with her pennies-for-pages lifestyle to feed and clothe two rapidly growing kids? Where would they even go to school?

She watched them, sitting on her couch, eating popcorn, watching TV. Two little children. People that had grown inside her, that she had suckled and bathed. Two little children that had stirred so many hopes and dreams and wishes for her own future.

Cameron was now twelve. He must have grown five inches in the past year. His voice was a tiny bit deeper every time he came over, yet inside the elongating face, she could still see the round apple cheeks of the baby.

Cinthia was eleven. Long blond hair, a bit of the currently trendy blue eye shadow, and budding breasts. Gabrielle and Cinthia had actually gone bra shopping a couple months back. Gabrielle was pleased that Cinthia had wanted her and not the stepmother to guide her into this new ritual. It was the little benchmarks that reminded her that even though she didn't live with them, she was still their mother.

There still were hopes and dreams and wishes. They were growing into fine people. They spoke excitedly of school, of friends, of the latest movies and TV shows. As much as it hurt

The Birds and the Bees

constantly, like a seeping wound, she had done the right thing by giving them up. Her children were a marvel and a miracle. Whether she had raised them day-to-day or not, she still had created them. They were still her, she was still them.

"Hey, Mom!" Cinthia said, pointing at the TV. "Look at that!"

There was a news flash about a swarm of bees that had taken up residence in the back alleys around City Hall. Apparently they were living in dumpsters, but were taking over more and more of the block daily. If anyone wandered into a back alley, they didn't last for long. Either they were able to escape the bees by some miracle, or they were consumed.

"They've been talking about those killer bees from Africa for years," Cinthia said. "Now they are here, just like it was predicted. Why is everyone so surprised?"

Gabrielle looked at her daughter with a renewed sense of pride. A simple observation, but so true. Even as far back as when Gabrielle was a teenager, there had been warnings and scares about killer bees. How they were making their way north, inch by inch. There had even been a rash of killer-bee horror movies, explaining how they had been bred by cross-genetics. How the mild-mannered honey bee had been crossed with a more aggressive African bee so that the hives would manufacture honey faster. Yet another example of a genetic experiment gone horribly wrong. The bees had been time bombs for at least twenty years, maybe longer. Her daughter was right. Everyone knew that.

"Do you think they will be able to destroy them?" Gabrielle asked Cinthia.

"I don't know. I guess if they find the queen for that hive, then they won't have any more orders and might just stop. At least that's what I've always understood."

"I think it's quite interesting that the bees are invading City Hall," Cameron said. "Don't you?"

Gabrielle patted his head, letting her fingers linger over his bangs.

"In what way?"

"It's like a political takeover or something. I bet this isn't just a random act of bees. I've always thought the killer bees were genetically engineered by terrorists. Just like AIDS, and even the epidemic of children with learning disabilities and rage issues. There is biological warfare afoot, and it's only going to get worse."

"How on earth did you come to that conclusion?" Gabrielle asked.

"Me and my friends talk about it a lot. There are even sites on the Internet. We've been infiltrated for years. Slowly. Carefully. The underpinnings of society are being chipped away by random fatal illnesses and biology."

"Good Lord!" Gabrielle said. "Sounds like you read a lot of science fiction."

The Birds and the Bees

"Science fact, Mom. It's 2001. Maybe in your day there weren't even home computers yet, or Game Boy, but now there are transplants, clones, chemical and electronic warfare. Insidious attacks we don't even know exist."

"I bet the Secret Service does!" Cinthia piped in.

"You two . . . How on earth did you get so embroiled in these conspiracy theories? So there are hives in dumpsters. It's not the first time. God knows, any summer day you can walk by a garbage can in any city and have wasps come after you."

"These aren't wasps, Mom. These are killer bees. There's a huge difference."

"Killers bees are like attack dogs, Mom. They are trained to kill."

"And who is training them?"

"Terrorists!"

Gabrielle rolled her eyes. "To what purpose. To sting us all to death?"

"It's insidious, Mom. Everyone at school knows that. It's the new millennium and doomsday is near."

"Oh, you two, stop that. I know you're just kidding!"

Gabrielle wedged herself between the kids on the sofa and hugged them both.

"How did you two grow up so fast and get so smart? Where did you even learn all those big words?"

Sèphera Girón

"From you, Mom!"

"You made us figure out all those big words."

"And those big ideas? Terrorists? Armageddon? It's not the truth, you know."

"It's a theory. And judging by the random attacks of nature lately, who knows what is really going on?"

"Well, just don't go wandering around downtown alone until things calm down," Gabrielle said. "There have been enough random attacks of animals and even children, high school shootings and such, that I want to keep you guys locked up and safe forever."

"You can't lock us up, and don't worry... we'll be as safe as safe can be," Cameron said.

"Good," Gabrielle said. "Now who wants to order pizza?"

"Yay!" Cinthia shouted. She crossed the room to find the pizza flyers. On her way, she passed the balcony door. She stopped and peered out.

"I like your view, Mom. I always feel like I'm in the heart of the city when I'm here. Like I belong."

Gabrielle stood beside her daughter, and slipped her arm around her.

"You do belong, my darling. You will always belong."

Gabrielle kissed the top of Cinthia's head. Sitting on the balcony rail was that big black bird, watching them.

* * *

The Birds and the Bees

The music was booming out into the street as Katey approached the club. She looked around and saw Miranda hurrying up the street, the sound of her stilettos clacking along the pavement. Katey smiled, her lips a reddish black, her eyes heavily ringed and shadowed with black and reddish colors. Miranda had red and black hair and heavy Goth makeup as well. They hugged each other and entered the club.

The evening was in full swing already. Katey lit up a cigarette and stared around the room while Miranda ordered drinks. All around her, people were dressed in various costumes. Leather and PVC dominated, yet there were feathers and silks and ruffles. Men and women alike wore makeup, hair pieces, a Halloween of sexual freedom and self-expression. People were dancing, bare breasts and chains bobbing in the strobe lights. Katey breathed in deeply of the tribal sweat beading on the bodies. Miranda handed her a rye and Coke, and together they walked past the dance floor and up a staircase to another room. Here, the music wasn't as loud and there was no dancing. Instead, there was a large cross and several bench-type pieces.

A woman was tied with her face toward the cross, arms strung high, legs akimbo. She wore a white Merry Widow, white stockings, white high heels. Her hair was bleached white, her face hidden. Katey watched as a large man with a muscular chest and tight leather pants slapped a whip against her ass. The sound was sharp, even over the music.

The whip left a red mark, and the man ran his hand over her cheek. Rubbing her gently, massaging the flesh, he kneaded and prodded the entire cheek until once more, he let loose with a well-placed smack.

Katey's breath hitched in her chest as she watched. Miranda wandered off to join a group of mutual friends.

Katey watched the flogging of the woman in white, ignoring the games being played on the other apparatus. She didn't care about the man squirming beneath the boot of a round heavy-breasted mistress. She didn't watch as a boy carefully placed clothespins on the thighs of a strapped-down person whose sex couldn't be determined by outfit nor face, even as the victim squirmed.

No, she was mesmerized by the round apple cheeks of the woman in white. Those soft round cheeks marred minute by minute by a fresh strip of red. She watched the man do his work. The way he touched her, kneading her like a piece of meat. She watched the way he waved the whip, how he drew it out and back, how he gauged how hard to swing it and where it would land.

It was like poetry, watching his ministrations. She could tell, by the way he worked, that they

The Birds and the Bees

were not a couple. They were no doubt strangers, here to play.

The man rubbed the woman's back, touched her shoulder-length hair. Katey sighed.

The spell was broken as he untied her from the cross. The woman turned around and laughed. Katey watched her shake his hand and self-consciously adjust her breasts back into her corset. The man kissed her hand. The woman laughed again and stroked his cheek with a lingering finger, then wandered off toward the bar. Katey followed her, watching her weave through the crowd until she reached the bar. The woman ordered a drink and waited, tucking a piece of her bleached hair behind her ear. Katey studied her face. It was hard to see in the dim light, but she liked what she saw.

The woman noticed Katey staring at her, and smiled.

"Hi," she said, reaching for her drink. The woman paid the bartender and turned to face Katey.

"Hi," Katey said. She looked down at the woman's breasts. One of her nipples still peeked over the top of the corset.

"I like your outfit," Katey stammered, and took a sip of her drink. The woman smiled widely.

"Thank you. I like yours too." This time it was the woman's turn to study Katey from stiletto heels to bust-popping corset.

"Black and white." The woman giggled. "Opposites."

Katey tossed her hair. "Maybe."

"I'm Donna," the woman said, holding out her hand.

"Katey."

"Nice to meet you, Katey. I need to use the ladies' room. You are welcome to join me."

Katey nodded, and followed Donna through the throng of flesh and shiny material until they reached the bathroom. Already it was flooded and crowded. Part of the reason the ladies' bathrooms were horribly crowded at these fetish parties was the extra traffic of transvestites preening in the mirrors. Donna and Katey stood in the line, primping in the mirror and glancing around at everyone else.

"I don't think I've seen you here before," said Katey.

"I've seen you, honey. I think you just don't recognize me."

"Oh, your hair and all?" Katey squinted at her, trying to envision her in other hair and costume colors. What she could see about Donna was that she was pretty, sculpted, powdered, painted, and underneath it all, unremarkable. Beautiful. Chiseled. But unremarkable.

"I like being a bleached blonde. It's true, you know, blondes do have more fun."

"I know, I've been having fun for years."

"You are looking for something, though . . .

The Birds and the Bees

someone," Donna said, holding Katey's chin in her hand and staring into her eyes.

"Are you psychic?" Katey asked, trying to look away from Donna's gaze. But Donna wouldn't let her.

"A little. But you don't have to be Miss Cleo to see your haunted eyes. Even under your makeup, it is clear you don't get much sleep or peace."

"Working, you know."

"Among other concerns . . . he's not very nice to you."

"Who?"

"Your man. And I don't mean that in a fun way either. Getting spanked in playtime is fun and sexy. Getting spanked in anger is abuse."

"I-I . . ."

Donna draped an arm around Katey. "Honey, I've been there. Really. That's how I know. And believe you me, the minute I dumped the abusive asshole and came out to play, life got a hell of a lot better."

"I-I . . ."

"Hey, you wanna go next?" Donna nodded at the stall that had just been vacated by a tall willowy redhead wearing a garter belt, stockings, a feather boa, and not much else.

"No, you go on."

Katey looked at herself in the mirror. Did it show that much? How could that be? Donna must be messing with her. Yeah, she just must be guessing what was going on. Or was she? Maybe Katey really was that transparent. Regardless, she was torn between running away from Donna or finding out more. As if in reply, Donna emerged from the stall.

"Wanna go play?" Donna asked as she washed her hands.

"Play?" Katey asked. She looked at Donna's red-streaked bottom.

"Sure. We'll put you on the cross and I'll spank you," Donna said.

Katey stared at her. "No, thank you." Katey heard the words fall from her lips, but she couldn't believe she was saying them.

No, thank you?

No, thank you?

What the hell was that?

Of course she wanted to be spanked. She had always dreamed about being tied up and spanked, and now this delicious woman in front of her was offering to spank her, and her mouth was saying *no*? What the hell was wrong with her?

"Oh . . . okay . . . I just thought . . ." Donna pouted. Katey grabbed Donna's mouth and pulled her face toward her own. She planted a juicy kiss on her lips.

"I did . . . well, I mean, I do want to . . . I have thought about it . . . it's just . . ."

"You aren't ready for a public display?" Donna nodded knowingly.

The Birds and the Bees

"That's the main thing."

Now it was Donna's turn to kiss Katey. "Don't worry, honey. We can just go dance. Would you like that?"

Katey nodded.

"Let's shoot a couple of orgasms and do it."

The women slammed back several shooters at the bar, and then made their way to the dance floor.

Hours later, Katey woke up in Donna's bed. She ached all over. She sat up, rubbing her head. Her clothes were on the floor. Donna slept quietly beside her. She remembered flashes of the night. Dancing, kissing, laughing, stumbling back to Donna's apartment. The smell of Donna was all over her. Perfume, musky, sweet. A slash of dawn splashed across Donna's back, and Katey lay her head against her, listening to her breath. Donna. A lovely sultry woman. And a lovely sultry lover.

Outside the window, a bird called. Screamed, actually. It seemed to shriek and scream in a very unbirdlike manner. Katey crept out of the bed, toward the window. The bird continued its shrill noise, and she had to crane her neck to see where it came from.

A large black bird was down on the fence post, flapping its wings and cawing. Katey watched in amazement at the way it puffed up really big and stuck out its neck. It shook its

Sèphera Girón

head, apparently telling off someone or something.

Katey saw a woman walk by. There was something odd about the woman. Maybe it wasn't a woman at all. It was a vision, a blur, a redheaded bundle, walking quickly by the bird. The bird shrieked loudly and lifted itself off the fence, hovering above the woman. The woman swatted at the bird, missing it. A couple of feathers fell from the tail as the bird swooped at the woman's face. Katey watched in disbelief as the bird swooped again, claws smoothly skating across the woman's cheek. Beads of blood bubbled scarlet in the dawn's early light, and the bird pecked, plucking black things from the air and snapping them with its beak. It swooped in again at the woman, circled once, and was gone.

The woman lifted a hand to her face, wiping the blood with a finger, staring at it, then licked it off. She ran her arm across her face and the blood was gone. Katey couldn't see her features; she was like a picture softly out of focus. Katey knew there was a head, a face, holes for eyes, but her image seemed like a moving blur, a swirl. And then, as the woman walked under her window, Katey saw why. The woman walked with a swarm of bees enveloping her like a halo. They hung around her, and Katey could hear the droning even through the glass of the window.

The Birds and the Bees

"What are you looking at?" Donna asked sleepily.

Katey turned around to where Donna lay among the rumpled bed sheets, one hand propping up her head.

"Nothing," Katey replied, and returned to the bed.

"Mmm, I can't believe it's morning already." Donna signed, running a finger lazily along Katey's arm. Katey looked at Donna, flashes of the previous night of lips and breasts and warm mouths sucking warmer places playing in her mind.

"Me neither. I have to get going soon."

"Oh, I hope not too soon," Donna said, softly kissing Katey's shoulder. Katey smiled and brushed Donna's tousled hair away from her forehead.

"Not this very minute, but soon," Katey said. She watched as a fly loudly buzzed around the bedroom, lighting on the ceiling fan, then flitting over to the window.

"Do you want to do something later on?" Donna asked.

Katey shook her head. "I can't. I'm seeing my boyfriend tonight."

"Oh . . ." Donna pouted. "I guess you were just out cruising then?"

"I . . . guess," Katey admitted sheepishly. "I mean, I really liked seeing you on that cross last night. I just had to talk to you."

Sèphera Girón

"And more."

"I didn't think there would be more. I am pleasantly surprised."

"I'm glad."

Donna stood up, staggered a step, and giggled.

"Whoah . . . the room is still spinning. I'll go put coffee on."

"Okay."

Donna left the room, and Katey returned to the window. The woman and the bird were both gone. She wondered if she had really seen what she had seen, and figured that it must have been part of a dream.

Chapter Seven

Mary Anne woke in the night to the sound of a baby crying. She was halfway down the hall when she remembered that there was no baby.

Yet still she heard the crying.

She peered into the tiny room where the children slept. They were still, unaware of her presence. Such beautiful innocents, lying unaware of their mother creeping in to stroke their hair and fuss with their bedclothes.

The baby cried a frantic mewling, but she knew there was no baby. She used to run around the house, searching for the crying. Panicking as the crying shifted from room to room and she couldn't see the baby, couldn't find the baby. She knew better now.

Sèphera Girón

She went into the living room and sat on the couch.

"Shhh . . . Nigel . . ." She whispered, cradling her arms. "It's okay."

The crying shifted as she started to sing a lullaby.

"Round and round the circle . . ."

A cooing and gurgling echoed around the room. Mary Anne leaned her head against the back of the couch and shut her eyes.

"Niiigel . . . Niiigel . . ." she sang. A cold breeze blew by her head. She laughed, reaching her hand up.

"I'm glad you're here tonight."

I'm glad to see you too, Mommy.

It was like a feeling more than a voice. A wave of goose bumps ran across her arms.

The room was much colder now. The air went from calm to agitated. A new sound was low in the background.

Mommy.

"I'm right here."

The sound grew louder, a low humming. The climate in the room had changed from a calm peacefulness to the brooding sense of a storm brewing.

"What is it?" she said aloud.

She couldn't sense Nigel anymore, and it frightened her. The sound grew louder, and she recognized it as the buzzing of bees. Shadows

The Birds and the Bees

darkened the corners of the room. Shadows moving, elongating and shrinking, creeping from corner to corner.

"Nigel."

The sound was overwhelming, and she put her head in her hands.

"Stop it."

When she lifted her head again the room was so dark, not even the moon was shining in. A blackness hung like a fog in the air before her, and she swatted at it. The sensation was thick, the noise overwhelming.

Mary Anne stood up.

"Nigel!"

It was useless to shout out at him. He wasn't there anymore.

Mary Anne hurried out of the room and returned to her bedroom. Reluctantly, she shut the door. The heavy snores of John and his rancid breath filled the room.

Which was worse?

Crawling into bed, she tried to still her thumping heart. Not for the first time, she wondered why Nigel had come to her. Not for the first time, she wondered if she really was going mad.

Mary Anne waved good-bye to the school bus as it pulled away in a haze of dust kicked up from the country road. John had already left for work, so she was safe to spend the next few hours however she wanted. She took Jimmy and Deedee by the hands and walked past the house and out into the field. Though it was still early, she could tell it was going to be a scorcher. One of those delicious, hot fall days. In the trees, the birds sang. Every now and again, a flock would lurch up from the branches, sending leaves falling and swirling like rain around them. The children would laugh and giggle, catching the leaves and chasing each other. Mary Anne would watch them, sadness in her eyes. She loved her children so much, she couldn't understand why their father was indifferent. Why he was such a prick most of the time?

However, there was not much she could do at this point. He was the boss, she was the mom. Until the kids were older, she might as well hang in there. Maybe once the kids were older, he'd grow to appreciate them more, and maybe things would change.

Maybe he'd actually treat her like he loved her again, instead of like a sperm receptacle.

In the dream, her grandmother was there.
Carmina.
Watching her from the shadows as Gabrielle clawed at the water, spitting out gallons that relentlessly rushed down her lungs. Gabrielle had managed to fight the turbulent current and flail over to the shore, where she lay gasping. She

The Birds and the Bees

could almost feel the touch of her grandmother on her shoulders. How she missed her grandmother. She was so confused. So lonely. Grandmother was the only one who had ever understood her.

No one is going to stick up for you but yourself.

Gabrielle squeezed her eyes shut, tears leaking out of them. Her heart ached at the idea that she would never truly hug Grandmother again. As she lay gasping on the riverbank, she watched a crow picking at things in the earth. It lowered its beak and then swung it up, as it wolfed down a tasty treat. Gabrielle saw little spindly legs briefly before they were swallowed down.

The bird had found a hornet's nest, and every time a bee came toward Gabrielle, it snatched it with its beak.

Gabrielle closed her eyes again as she coughed up more water.

I will always be here.

"Then why am I so lonely?" Gabrielle sobbed into the dirt.

Gabrielle checked her e-mail. There were a few hundred messages in the queue, most of them from various mailing lists. However, there was one, from *lonesong*, that she didn't recognize. Clicking it open, she realized who it was almost immediately. Her face flushed as she read the note.

Sèphera Girón

Dear Gabrielle,
Just wanted to drop you a line to let you know how much I miss you. It was great to meet you and I hope we can get together next time I come to town.
Tommy

Gabrielle nodded.
"Miss you too, Tommy, but so what? There's no point."
She pressed delete and stood up.
It was too quiet in here. Lonely and quiet. A week had passed since he had left. Many days had passed since she last saw the kids, and she wasn't due to see them this weekend. Maybe it was a good time to work on her novel.
She opened the file and reread some of what she had last written. Her mind drifted back to the club, back to where she had watched Tommy strum his guitar and sing. It was only a week ago, yet it felt like a lifetime since she had gazed into those warm green eyes. She wondered if she would ever see him again.
People like him had ambitions, could talk a good talk, but so many of them never made it. They failed before they even got started. It was typical. Maybe they ran out of steam or interest. Maybe they just couldn't get the money together, or they started to believe the naysayers more than they believed in themselves.
Whatever the reason, she knew musicians

The Birds and the Bees

were a dime a dozen, and she also knew that Tommy certainly had the talent to get to where he needed to go, but he had already fallen behind a few wasted years.

Not that she was any prize. At her age, she still hadn't published her first novel. That had been one of the things that had widened the marriage gap. Her yearning to be a writer. Yet what was she writing, really? Music reviews, a bit of news, that was it.

Her eyes glanced along the e-mails, and she opened her horoscope, which was always paired with news items. It wasn't the horoscope she looked at, however. It was a news item that caught her eye.

Unusually large flock of crows and other types of black birds have been spotted in parks around the city. There have been reports that the birds have been attacking small animals and even people. Scientists have been trying to study why the birds are landing and staying in the city, but so far, there seems to be no answer. If you see a large flock of birds in your neighborhood, keep your pets inside.

Birds.
Black birds.
Black birds that stared at her with black soulless eyes.

Birds that screamed for no reason when she walked by them.

Birds that swooped around her head, that flapped by her ears.

It made her skin crawl.

What was the deal with the birds?

She decided to punch in "news about birds" on her search engine. Interestingly enough, there were several articles about the unusually large number of large black birds roaming the city. Several theories were bandied about, but none of the experts could seem to agree. It was too early for migration, unless there was one hell of a winter coming. It was as if nature was restless.

The fact that birds had sporadically attacked people for no reason was unusual. Especially when they didn't seem to be nesting or protecting anything in particular.

Or were they?

Or were they messengers from the other side?

Lord knows there were enough stories written about birds from the other side. *The Crow*, *The Raven* . . . endless folklore and legends about birds as spirit, as messenger, as trickster, as shape-shifter. Almost every culture had something about birds, from the smallest sparrow to the mighty phoenix. Gods and goddess with heads of birds, flying creatures, beaks and wings and feathers.

The legends had to start somewhere. They

The Birds and the Bees

had to have been grounded in some sort of reality.

What was happening lately could not be explained away by any legends or folklore. New reasons why birds flock to cities were manifesting, and new legends and folklore were being born.

The Instant Messenger dinged, and he was there. She hadn't believed that he would have the courage, the balls really, to talk to her. Yet there he was, blinking a hello. She typed back a hello, then caustically asked, "Where is the wife?"

He said she and the girl were at her mother's house, and he was home alone.

How convenient.

"How are you?" she typed.

"Been better . . ."

"Oh?"

"Not getting anything done . . . she's always on my case about something."

Gabrielle nodded, her fingers hesitating over the keyboard.

"Maybe you need to get away. Come to a place where you *will* get something done."

Now the hesitation came on his end.

"Have a place in mind?"

"How about a beautiful desert island . . . hot sun, lapping beach . . ."

"Wouldn't get much done on an island. Too busy watching everything else."

"Like what?"

"Ocean, girls swimming in the ocean . . ."

"I sea what you mean." Gabrielle chuckled at her own pun. "Maybe you need to go somewhere else."

"Like where?"

"How about you come back here again?"

"I can't afford a hotel."

"Who said anything about a hotel?"

There were a few minutes of hesitation. Gabrielle began to wonder if he had wandered off, or maybe the wife had returned. At last, she saw a new screen of words appear.

"Is that a proposition?" he wrote.

"It's an offer, of sorts, I guess."

"What is the offer?"

Gabrielle's face went red. What *was* the offer? What *did* she mean by that? She figured in a perfect world she would ask him to come and stay with her for a while, where he could compose and record, and they could hang out and have more of those wonderful talks they had had, and have great wonderful sex.

It sure would be nice to have sex again one day. Or at least, sex with someone who wasn't just a one-night stand. She could just imagine Tommy. Touching those wonderful ringlets, feeling his mouth warm against hers, his hands . . .

The Birds and the Bees

"You there?" The Instant Messenger chimed.

Now *she* was the one drifting off into thoughts.

"I'm here," she wrote.

What was she offering?

A future, for starters.

Katey studied John's face. Splotchy with broken vessels, and he wasn't even middle-aged yet. She wondered just how much he really drank. She wondered how much longer she could live this way. Forcing him to choose between her and his wife was going to be a challenge that she needed all the strength in the world to deal with. John did not take ultimatums very well. He was a stubborn son of a bitch. Maybe that was part of what she liked about him. He passed her the joint and she drew deeply on it.

"Do you ever wonder?" she asked, her mind lazily drifting as the pot took hold.

"Wonder what?" he asked.

"Wonder . . ." Her mind hummed the "I Wonder" song from *Sleeping Beauty*. "Wonder where we are going."

"You know, Kataroo," John said, "I like to not wonder at all when I'm with you. That's part of the fun, ya know?"

"Well, I know that's how it's been in the past. But it's been a while now. Are we going to go on like this forever?"

"Can't I be in love with two women at the same time?"

"Now isn't that a switch? I thought you resented Mary Anne, and was only hanging in 'cause of the kids an' all."

"Hmmm." John took another drag from the joint. "Sometimes, when I look at Mary Anne, I see the teenager that I adored. That young, smiling, thin little child that I wanted to put into a little cage and keep forever and ever. Then sometimes, I look at her and wonder how I ever got trapped with such an old bitter hag. Funny thing, isn't it?"

Katey took a swig from her beer bottle and stood up. She stood in front of him, putting one leg up on the bed so he could look at her in all her naked glory.

"And what do you see when you look at me?" she asked, running her fingers along her thigh. Her legs were goose-bumpy, and there was an odd chill in the air. John took one last toke on the joint and crushed it into the ashtray. He leaned forward, burying his face between her legs. She felt his tongue flitting along her pussy. The sensation was nice, but not the same as when Donna had tasted her. There was something about a girl knowing just what to do to another girl. It made sense to her. After all, they had the same equipment, so of course they would know what the best way to tease and torment each other would be.

The Birds and the Bees

He breathed heavily on her, then blew on her. She didn't know why he did that. It was more annoying than erotic.

"I see a young girl, much like my Mary Anne used to be. Ready to face the world, yet not sure how." He sucked again on her pussy. Katey laughed. She knew John thought she was laughing in pleasure with him, but she was laughing at how she was so *not* like Mary Anne. Or at least, as far as she knew. Wouldn't John shit if he knew about her dark half?

He stopped and lay back down on the bed, drinking from his beer.

"What were we talking about again?" he asked.

"We were talking about how you're leaving Mary Anne and coming to live with me in a life of decadence and sin!" Katey said.

"Oh we were, were we?!?!" John said, pulling Katey down on top of him. They kissed, rolling along the bedsheets. Katey unzipped his pants and took out his dick.

"You *are* going to run away with me, aren't you?" she asked coyly, stroking his hardening member with strong fingers.

"Mmmm . . ." John sighed, lying back and closing his eyes. "I still have to decide. Who is worth more to me?"

"You *know* I am all you ever dreamed about and more," Katey said, looking harshly at him.

The look was wasted, however, since John still kept his eyes shut.

"Suck me, bitch," he said. Katey stayed still. John opened his eyes. They flashed now with a commanding look as opposed to the dreamy stoner gaze he'd had a minute ago. Katey's lip raised a bit in a sneer, as if egging him on. John's hand lashed out and grabbed her by the hair. He pulled her head back. The first tug sent her adrenaline racing and she nearly came on the spot, but now he was too harsh, shoving her face toward his cock. She licked it.

"Harder. Take it all in."

She opened her mouth and nearly gagged as he used two hands to pull her head onto his rock-hard member. Something about the way he pulled at her head turned her on. Whether it was the hair being pulled around her scalp, his strength, his force, or something else, she had no idea. All she knew was that she loved it when a person was dominant, if but for a moment.

Abraham loved Sundays. Not only was Sunday his day off, but it was God's day off too and he thought it was great that they coincided. Often he would take the bus to a suburb just outside of town and wander off to a park. His favorite park was just the tip of the iceberg toward miles of wild fields leading towards a woods. He knew people owned homes around and in the woods and fields, so he was careful when he walked

The Birds and the Bees

around not to disturb the land so that they couldn't be angry with him. If there was one thing he knew about, it was how to walk as quietly as a big cat, barely rustling the leaves, breathing as shallowly as he could. His instincts were still remarkable, his senses toned to the point where his boss often joked that he was psychic, anticipating customers' moods and needs.

Instinct? Psychic? He wasn't sure.

What he was sure about, though, was that there was change in the air. Not just in this delicious fragrant country air, but in the tide of humankind. He couldn't put his finger on it, but he sensed something coming almost like he sensed a storm brewing in the distance.

There was something coming, all right. It rippled at his flesh, it danced along his mind like staccato pinpricks. He wished he knew how to decipher feelings when he had them. When he was with the Lost Boys, it was easier to predict, for there was so little to gauge. Weather, war, friends. Not too much else. But here in North America, everything was so complicated. Things that he had never even heard of were big deals. Feelings, emotions. People spent a lot of time pampering their minds and bodies. Maybe people here in North America had too much time to think, not enough time to hunt and hide and fight for survival.

The sun beat down on his face. The same sun

that beat on his lost brothers. He wondered how many more of them would get the opportunity for this land. He wondered if he would even see any of them again. It would be so cool to get together, to compare notes on what had happened, on where they'd ended up. They had been through so much together, and maybe they were meant to be connected just a little bit longer.

He missed Jeremy most of all, next to Dominion. Jeremy had been like a brother, a father, a best friend to him. It was Jeremy who had pulled him along with the tribe of Lost Boys on the march of a thousand miles when all Abraham had wanted to do was curl up and die. Abraham had witnessed his parents dying, his sister raped and then chopped up into pieces like an animal.

How men could show such hatred for other men, for children no less, was still beyond his comprehension, though he had seen it over and over again.

The day Abraham had won the lottery to come here was bittersweet. He had been thrilled, ecstatic to be offered the opportunity of a new life, but as name after name was called, he realized that Jeremy would not follow him. Even if they hadn't ended up in the same city, they could have ended up in the same land. But it was not to be. God had not smiled on Jeremy that hot morning.

The Birds and the Bees

Abraham was torn the day he left. Part of him wanted to throw down his little duffel bag, which had been given to him by the Red Cross, and say no, he would not go unless Jeremy would go. But the other part of him knew that he had to go to the new land. War was constant in Africa. The camp was often without food and drink. There were endless days of hunger, and always the fear that he would have to walk again, for another thousand miles, dodging animals, searching for water, crawling in hunger, digging in the dirt for a bug, a leaf, anything that he could put on his tongue. He never wanted to be that hungry again. He never wanted to feel that ache again. In the new land, he had heard that if he worked hard, he would never be hungry. And right now, that was true. He didn't make as much money as he wanted to, and his dreams of school would be on hold for a few more years while he saved up, but he was so lucky that he worked with a generous baker who fed him. Fed him so much that on some days he felt his tummy swelling with the bread. It amazed him, to feel a bulge of food in his body, slow to digest, like a snake, when he came from a land where a bloated belly meant you were starving and very likely to die.

Today, he walked across the field, looking at the green everywhere. Green so far, farther than he could see. A gentle swell of hills was also green in the distance. And farther still, a mountain that was green and brown and usually covered with cloud. He loved green, he felt like green was his favorite color in the whole world. It was a color he hardly saw when he was back home. Green was the color of grass, of money, of hope.

He had even renamed himself Abraham Green, although his papers said Abraham Seventeen.

The wind touched his face and he smiled. A wonderfully cool wind cut the heat perfectly. Kneeling down for a moment, he slipped off his shoes and spread his toes in the grass. Soft. Just like the carpet in his new apartment. Dots of yellow and purple flowers peppered the grass. As he walked, dandelions caught between his toes and snapped off. He picked one of them up, held it up to the sun. Bright and happy, the flower reflected his mood.

Yes, his overall mood was bright and happy, yet there was still that undercurrent of unease. Fear of a shift that was going to affect him and this bright new world. Sandwiched into the hope and dreams of optimism was an unsettling dread that tickled his bones. But more than that, there was loneliness.

Some nights he ached with loneliness. Not only for his friends, his Lost Boys, but for something more. Now that he was in the free world, he had access to television and was bombarded with images of couples. Of women, dancing,

The Birds and the Bees

undulating, talking, and laughing. He saw beautiful glistening bodies of all races. Singers, dancers, actors. Even a simple commercial could bring tears to his eyes, for he realized that he needed, wanted, a mate. Yet he had no idea how he could make that happen.

Yes, women came into the bakery, but he knew they looked at him not as a potential partner, but as someone who baked and bagged their bread and pastries. He learned quickly how to flirt with them, for despite his hardships he had an easygoing temperament and a sense of humor, though the language differences sometimes played jokes on him. However, he found that as long as he kept a smile on his face, he was forgiven his mistakes.

There were a couple of women that came in who didn't seem to mind his very dark skin and broken English. But they were women of class and money. Another thing he had been quick to realize was that even in this land of the free, there were class differences, even among people of color.

One thing walking in the desert had taught him was patience. Like the lion stalking his prey, he had to be patient.

Watch and learn.

Take everything in as best he could.

Learn from the television, and from the people he met, what women like and want in a man. He would learn how to become a man that a

Sèphera Girón

woman would be proud to have. He would get a degree, he would work hard, buy a house, buy a car. He would have everything he had ever dreamed of and much more. Back in his former life, there was no such thing as having your own car and home. Yet here, it was normal. It was expected. So he had to watch and learn.

He reached a hill and walked up it. It was pretty high, and he often liked to sit on a part about halfway up, where there were several large flat rocks. From there, he could see people playing in the park, cars zipping down the distant highway, the mammoth buildings of the city. He could see smog on the hazy days. He imagined that he would see mountains of snow in the winter. He wondered what snow was like. Would he be able to come here in the snow, or would it be too deep to wade through to get here?

The rock waited, warmed in the sun. He sat on it, briefly thinking once more of African heat. Another wave of loneliness and unease swept through him. He tried to push it away by focusing on the pretty flowers that thrived nearby. Tall flowers unlike anything he was used to back home.

Home.

This was home now.

When he first left Africa, he thought he'd be able to go home one day. But as the days slipped into weeks and the reality of money and how

The Birds and the Bees

things worked became clear to him, he wasn't sure he would ever actually get back to Africa. He wasn't even sure if his friends would still be there. They were in a camp, with few resources. What if the workers got tired of them and went on to help others?

Now that he was on the other side, he realized it was a huge world out there and so very many places were in need of help. He saw places that treated people as badly as, and even worse than, anything he had seen in his flight to freedom. He knew now how incredibly expensive it was to help people, entire villages even, and that most people wanted to help, most people felt sorry for the plight of the "underprivileged," yet generosity of spirit only went so far, and generosity of money went even less.

In one way, it seemed strange to him that anyone helped anyone at all outside of America. Just in his short stay, he'd seen homeless people propped in the doorways, sleeping on the park benches. There were homeless and needy people right here. Why didn't they help their own first?

Surely there were reasons. He just didn't understand them yet. There was so much to absorb, so much to understand, and more paradoxes to unravel than anyone could ever believe.

The humidity was tiring him out after his

walk. He lay down on the rock, staring up at the sky.

What should he do about finding a lady?

It seemed like here in America, he didn't have to worry about being with the same lady forever. He could test-drive a few.

Test-drive.

He found that a funny expression. He had first learned it was about trying out cars, but in his observations of this new culture, he found that it could refer to the ritual known as dating. He liked saying test-drive; it tickled his fancy in an odd way. However, he was observant enough to know not to actually tell any future date that he was test-driving them. He expected that would earn him a slap or a cocktail in the face.

His eyes were heavy.

In his mind, images swirled. A red and black haze coalesced behind his eyelids, then danced into images. A tiger. A snake. Clicking beetles, raging elephants. He stood by a water hole and watched as the animals came to drink.

Hyenas laughed in the background, then darted in quickly, tails between their legs as they lapped at the muddy water. Elephants sprayed their backs and their young. A cacophony of snorting and braying filled the air.

Abraham watched from behind a tree. A young boy crept to the edge of the water. Big brown eyes searched the animals as he hurriedly scooped the dark dirty water to his

The Birds and the Bees

mouth. Flies buzzed around him, invading his ears, landing on his arms, and flitting off again. He scratched his leg where the skin was raised slightly. It itched like crazy, more so in the heat as the day stretched longer and the dirt crawled in. Lying on the ground, he scooped more of the filthy water into his mouth and looked around. Not only was he looking out for animals that could hurt him, he also was looking for something else.

He was missing something. He could sense it. He was missing something that was supposed to be there. But what was it? It should have been there. *They* should have been there, but as far as his eye could see, they were not.

Had he been left behind?

He scratched his leg again. The bump was higher and longer now. Tiny bugs bit him and flew off, leaving little welts that itched chronically. Those bites he was pretty much used to. He couldn't remember a day when he wasn't scratching his arms or face or swatting away the annoying insects.

His tongue was still dry. Again he knelt to the pond and drank of the stagnant water. A water snake rippled by, hissing at him in passing. The lion had drunk its fill and wandered off while the lioness and her young rushed in, long cat tongues scooping the fetid water, eyes searching, warily watching the elephants most of all.

A movement caught his eye.

There was something, not that far from him, in one of the few clumps of brush that sprang from the water. He stayed crouched, scratching his leg, scratching his arms from habit. The bushes rustled again, and he saw the lioness staring with great interest. She was already poised on her haunches.

The boy, Abraham, didn't want to approach the brush, but something told him that things were different now. His throat was parched, his legs ached, but something was different. The sun was different. It blazed in the sky in a different way. The animals were different, though he couldn't put his finger on how.

He was different.

He was thinking with logic.

He was thinking with the mind of a grown-up.

He was thinking in English.

A shudder passed through him.

How did he know?

Colors rippled once more, and now he stood above the moving creature in the brush.

It was a baby. A little white baby. It cooed when it saw Abraham's face. Abraham had never seen a white baby before.

Oh, yes, he had, but when? How could he have?

He was confused, and scratched his little-boy head. The lump in his leg was huge now, spreading from his knee to his ankle.

The Birds and the Bees

He wanted to touch the little white baby. He wanted to see if its skin was as soft as it looked. He reached out his fingers toward it, and felt the lump in his leg shift.

Abraham stared at the lump as it slid around his leg and up into his belly. Nausea filled him as he looked back toward the baby. He put his fingers on baby's head, touching the fine little curls, and saw in disbelief as the lump suddenly flew along his arm and shot out in a black shiny stream toward the baby. The baby was covered with hundreds of black shiny beetles.

Abraham screamed, and the sound of his own screaming woke him up.

As Abraham lay gasping in the heat of the sun, he slowly pulled himself up. That was enough of that. Meditation, message, warning, or just freaked-out nightmare, he didn't want to go back into that state.

It was time to go back home and rest up for another day.

Chapter Eight

Wendy brushed her long blond hair. Sometimes life just plain sucked. It was bad enough that Becky Wood was the prettiest girl in the class, but now, she was going out with Mac.

How could that be?

Wendy liked Mac way more than Becky ever would. Wendy understood Mac. She saw how Mac was a dangerous person. How he could be volatile if spoken to the wrong way, or at least, what *he* perceived to be the wrong way.

But it didn't scare her.

Wendy understood his pain and rage. After all, she had been watching her parents eke out an existence in hell for the past thirteen years. She had enough pain and rage boiling within her to fuel a rocket ship to Mars.

Sèphera Girón

Sure Sheila could drone on and on about how she had wanted Wendy so badly, even waxing poetic about it if fed enough beers, but the truth of the matter was that Sheila and Tommy were barely older than Wendy when they had had her.

How on earth could people in their teens think they made a wise decision by bringing a baby into the world when their own parents were still taking care of them?

Sometimes Wendy was totally disgusted with her parents. She was ashamed of living in a shack. Not even a nice trailer, but a shack with no real heat and crappy water pressure. She never had a decent bath in her life unless she went over to a friend's house.

She remembered her first really good bath. There were loads of bubbles and the water was deliciously hot. Steam rose up and made her face all sweaty. Her whole body had tingled and throbbed as if it had suddenly been awakened from a long, dirty sleep. She couldn't believe that most everyone had this sort of thing at their beck and call. Most people took a warm bubble bath for granted.

Well, at least she had a couple of friends she could go hang out with. She didn't think her parents had any friends at all. They mostly hung around the house, sitting at their computers, clicking away in chat rooms. Both parents slept all day, and would click away deep into the

The Birds and the Bees

night. She had been getting herself up for school for years.

It was a joke, actually, that her dad fancied himself a musician. Sure he'd plink away on his guitar now and again, but for the most part, most of her memories of him were sitting at the computer, talking to God knows who in chat rooms, or lying on the couch with a towel on his head, whining about a headache.

Funny thing, most of the fathers of the other kids actually left the house and went to work. Jobs seemed to be the norm everywhere but in her house. She had heard her parents fighting about it endlessly over the years. Sheila wanted to go out to work, but Tommy wouldn't let her. Sheila was tired of living in a shack, in poverty, but Tommy would scream that she should be grateful that she had anywhere to live at all. That she should be happy to be living on his grandparents' land, that they fed them and clothed them.

Wendy flung herself onto the little cot with sleeping bag that was her bed. She stared around the room. It was a disaster. She had tried to keep it neat for a while, but it wasn't happening. Boxes were piled everywhere, mostly belonging to Sheila, who would "clean" once in a while, which mostly consisted of flinging things into boxes that she would "get to later" and never would. Some of those boxes had been in Wendy's earliest memories.

Sèphera Girón

Now her dad was "on the road" again. Trying to make it as a guitarist and singer. A solo act. Wendy didn't have much faith in him. Sure his voice was pretty good, for an old guy, but that was it. He was too old and too damn lazy. He would lose interest, and then another pipe dream would be blown away in a puff of smoke. She had been old enough to watch the cycles of dreams come round and round. Every couple of years, he would get the itch to "go on the road" and "get material for an album," but then he'd fall back into his malaise, spending what little money he made on anything but a CD.

Wendy wished she had the same optimism her parents seemed to have. They must have it, or had they really just plain settled? There had to be more to life. She knew there *was* more to life. She had seen it. She had been to other people's houses, had parents make her real food on a real stove. Like it was commonplace. She had been into houses that had nice furniture, clean carpets, walls that had pictures and no handprints, cats walking around but you couldn't smell them.

Wendy sat up. Every house that she had been to, every friend she had ever met had a bed, not a cot. A bed with a bedspread, not a sleeping bag. A bed with matching pillows, in rooms that were bright, where you could see the floor. A floor pretty much clean. At least cleaner than this place, where she practically had to leap

The Birds and the Bees

from the doorway to the bed. Even when she cleared away the clutter, there was so much sticky stuff and years of goop and gunk that she sometimes would scrape it with a knife, but it never helped much. She was tired of pointing things out to her parents. Tired of hearing that, yeah, her dad was going to fix the sagging step, the crooked bookcase, paint the room, fix the oven that hadn't worked in her recent memory.

Often she thought about running away. Anything to get away. Anywhere had to be better. Why was it her grandmother cooked almost every meal? Her mother was capable if she ever dragged her ass out of bed or away from the computer. Wendy would cook herself, except there was never any food in the cupboard or fridge.

On a little bookcase, she had a few items of joy. There wasn't much she had, although her dad always had a smoke hanging out of his mouth, and her mom wasn't any better. But Wendy had a few items, and she treasured them greatly. She had a little china animal collection.

As a little kid, someone had given her a little porcelain dog, and she'd adored it. Over the years, people had figured out that she loved china animals, and she was given a few for special occasions.

In times of pain, like today, she reverted to playing with them.

She picked up the black dog and moved it

Sèphera Girón

around, and it barked a hello at the other animals. She dusted them, talking to them, organizing them. As often happened when she was deep in thought with her animals, they started talking to her. Or at least, she thought they did. She felt like they were saying things inside her head and she could understand them. They were telling her, again, to be patient.

Things are changing.

Times are changing.

"In what way?" she asked, skipping the little black dog, Blackie, along the imaginary street. "In what way will things change?"

Round and round the circle.

The white poodle, Frenchie, nodded solemnly.

It will be all clear soon enough. You are part of the plan.

"How am I part of the plan?"

You have the key.

"So you keep telling me," Wendy said. "Obviously, it's not a real key, but a way or path or something."

The kitten, Mr. Mittens, did a little back flip.

You are ready!

"I just want Mac."

You could have Mac! You could have anything you want, Mr. Mittens purred. Wendy stared at the animals, her hands moving them around, her mind filling with the buzzing of their voices.

The Birds and the Bees

Whenever they started talking, a low-grade buzzing hummed in the back of her head.

"How do I get Mac to stop liking Becky?"

We'll show you! Don't worry, we'll show you!

Wendy laughed, clicking the dogs together.

Outside Wendy's door, Sheila stood, trying to peer through the cracks, listening to her teenager play with the animals. She couldn't really get a sense about what Wendy was doing, except for the fact she was playing with toys. Sheila lit a cigarette and went into the bedroom to talk about it with Tommy. However, Tommy was still sleeping.

Sometimes it really annoyed her, how late he slept. He could sleep right up till six o'clock. She used to try to keep normal hours, especially when Wendy was small, but she would be so lonely, watching Tommy sleep. She found talking on the Internet was a good way to pass the time, since she had no friends around here.

Sheila placed her smoke in the overflowing ashtray by the bed, and crawled on top of Tommy.

"Tommy, wake up." She shook him. He was out cold. It was so frustrating when he was this far asleep. She tickled his toes, pulled his hair, even pinched his nose shut, but he was gone.

Sheila left the room, taking her cigarette with her. She passed by Wendy's room again, and tried to close her ears to the murmuring of her daughter. She pushed open the screen door, and carefully picked her way down the three broken steps and out in to the overgrown yard.

What was she doing with her life?

She smelled the woods, loving the smell of cedar and pine and warm earth. The woods calmed her senses and she walked further into them. There had to be more. Even with a high school education, there had to be more to life then sleeping and fucking and talking on the Internet. She yearned to travel, if only Tommy would take her with him when he went out. He had seen more than she had, and he hadn't seen that much more. Just bars, which were all no doubt the same.

But maybe they weren't. Maybe some of those bars were like the ones she saw in movies. Not that she had seen many movies either since they didn't have a TV and hardly ever got to the bargain matinee. However, she had seen enough movies to know that there was more then one type of bar. They weren't all tiny little scum buckets like the one in town.

Yes, she really should demand to go with him. That way she would at least know what was going on. Maybe one day he'd see someone else, and then what would she do? She would be trapped forever in this tiny town in a shack.

Grinding out the cigarette under her foot, she thought that maybe it was time to push her in-

The Birds and the Bees

dependence. Maybe she should get a job.

How could she get a job, though? She couldn't even drive.

She ran her hands along her breasts. Maybe she could start an Internet site like some of the people in the chat room kept telling her to do. She already had topless pictures on her Web page, and Tommy didn't mind that at all. As a matter of fact, she had caught him once or twice jerking off to the pictures on her Web page. And if her own husband thought she was hot, who knows what a world of men with credit cards might think, or pay!

That way, she would have her own money, and she could buy some new clothes, maybe even get to go to a full-price movie for a change. Wouldn't that just be great?

In the meantime, she was worried about Wendy. A teenager shouldn't still be playing with toys, should she? By Wendy's age, Sheila was already out partying and getting high and thinking about having a baby. Wendy should be thinking about starting a family too. Find a man so that Sheila and Tommy could stop supporting her.

Yet, on the other hand, Sheila thought about Tommy's grandparents. How they had raised Tommy, and still did, as a matter of fact. She didn't want to be the one raising Wendy's kids. That would just suck. Well, she couldn't anyway, not here. Maybe if she could get that porn idea off the ground. Waiting for Tommy and his so-called music career wasn't going to work. He was already back a few days, and all he'd done was sleep, smoke and drink, and talk about making the CD and talk about the ideas he had for new songs, while never writing them down. Never picking up the guitar, or even turning on the little tape recorder, let alone booking a studio and getting going.

Tommy was king of the pipe dreams, and she was pretty much all piped out. It was up to her to figure a way out, and she was pretty confident that she had.

She continued her walk through the woods, her thoughts racing. Above her, the tall pines stretched to the sky, blocking out all but brief blue patches of the sky. Insects hummed around her, the usual assortment of mosquitoes and black flies. Living in the woods had immunized her to the chronic slapping of bugs that her fingers knew by rote. The scent of bug spray was her perfume; red welts of bites on her arms were her jewels.

Yes, she would be a porn star. That was definitely the ticket. She wouldn't have to leave the house and she would rake in the dough.

Tommy squinted open his eyes. She was gone. He sat up, stretching. The last thing he wanted was to be woken up by Sheila bitching at him about something. He had heard the screen door

The Birds and the Bees

slamming shut and her footsteps on the porch, so she had probably gone walking in the woods. Creeping to the front room, he peered out the window and saw her in the forest. Great. While she was roaming around the forest, he could go check his e-mail.

Tommy pulled on his sweat pants and first went into the washroom. As he peed, he looked around the tiny cramped room. He wondered when was the last time Sheila had scrubbed out that bathtub, if ever. It was caked with a brown ring and gray smears and streaks. Looking at himself in the bathroom mirror, he could barely make out his reflection. Long blurry streaks of God knows what from years gone by blocked his view. Spiders had not only spun webs in the ceilings, but had caught and sucked dry several flies over the years. After the reasonable cleanliness of the hotel rooms on his tour, he noticed more what squalor he lived in. Of course, hotels were relative luxury, but still, it would be nice if the wife would actually clean once in a while.

He walked past Wendy's room and heard her singing to herself. He smiled. She was going to be like her father, no doubt. Maybe she could sing backup in his band one day. A pop-and-daughter team. He chuckled. Over his dead body. No daughter of his was going to shake her booty and put herself on display.

The computer hummed, and he saw he had a couple hundred new e-mails. He knew most of them were from the lists he was on. He had to go to a special site and type in a secret code to access the in box where Gabrielle might send him anything. A sly grin crossed his face. There were several messages from her. A couple of newsy articles and, of course, a couple of e-mails. He peered out the window, didn't see Sheila, so he opened them.

Their affair, if that's what it was, was growing steadily hotter and heavier. Gabrielle's words fairly steamed off the page at him. He read soft words of longing, words speaking of desire to see him, to touch him. His heart raced as he digested the fact that this woman seemed to be totally smitten with him. It had never really happened to him that a woman wrote him so much and so lovingly. Sure he had gotten a few scrawled fan letters over the years, mostly from girls who were obviously half-corked. But never was a woman, yes, a real woman, so enthralled by him. He knew his music was good, and he figured that was really what she was responding to. His composing and singing. That was the real magnet. It figured that it took an older woman to appreciate him, but he had always known he was ahead of his time.

He read over her words. Weird how brave they had both become in such a short time. They had only spent that one night talking. All night they had talked. And now they wrote to each other about the color of their eyes, the

Join the Leisure Horror Book Club and
GET 2 FREE BOOKS NOW—
An $11.98 value!

Yes! I want to subscribe to the Leisure Horror Book Club.

Please send me my **2 FREE BOOKS**. I have enclosed $2.00 for shipping/handling. Each month I'll receive the two newest Leisure Horror selections to preview for 10 days. If I decide to keep them, I will pay the Special Members Only discounted price of just $4.25 each, a total of $8.50, plus $2.00 shipping/handling. This is a **SAVINGS OF AT LEAST $3.48** off the bookstore price. There is no minimum number of books I must buy and I may cancel the program at any time. In any case, the **2 FREE BOOKS** are mine to keep.

Not available in Canada.

NAME: _____
ADDRESS: _____
CITY: _____ STATE: _____
COUNTRY: _____ ZIP: _____
TELEPHONE: _____
E-MAIL: _____
SIGNATURE: _____

If under 18, Parent or Guardian must sign. Terms, prices, and conditions subject to change. Subscription subject to acceptance. Dorchester Publishing reserves the right to reject any order or cancel any subscription.

The Best in Horror!
Get Two Books Totally FREE!

An $11.98 Value! FREE!

PLEASE RUSH MY TWO FREE BOOKS TO ME RIGHT AWAY!

Enclose this card with $2.00 in an envelope and send to:

Leisure Horror Book Club
20 Academy Street
Norwalk, CT 06850-4032

The Birds and the Bees

smell of their hair, how they would feel in each other's arms.

The Internet had changed everyday life so dramatically. Though computers had pretty much always been around all his life, and he had understood the thrill of the Internet at a very young age, he was aware that things had not been this way that long. That people of Gabrielle's age had used typewriters, listened to records, found it hard to grasp the idea of instant messaging and instant mail, although most used it. He thought back to the sixties. And to times earlier still. How odd life must have been, without answering machines, Nintendo, computers, and the Internet.

Looking out the window, he saw that Sheila was still gone. Did he dare?

He clicked on an icon and his messenger popped up. He saw that Gabrielle was on-line right this very minute. Would he have time to say a brief hello? Oh, but of course he would. Lord knows when he would be alone again once Sheila came back in. Their computers were side by side, and they seldom left each other's side. Often he wondered if he could live without Sheila, though other times he worried that he would have to. Sheila had always been there.

He had first noticed her when he was in grade eight, and he had set his sights on her from that moment on.

Sheila would always be there, though Lord

Sèphera Girón

knows what she would do if she knew he was talking so much to Gabrielle. He clicked on the messenger and said, "Hello, sweetheart."

Gabrielle clicked back immediately.

Several moments passed as they flirted unashamedly. While the chimes of the messenger sang, Tommy quickly typed replies to the letters she had sent. He didn't know when next he'd make it back to the secret mailbox.

A telltale screech from the front porch signaled that Sheila was walking up the stairs. Tommy quickly clicked that he had to go. He closed the messenger window and hid the unsent mail. He opened his screen to a horoscope page.

"I see you're finally awake," Sheila said.

"I missed you next to me," Tommy said, grabbing her hand as she walked by. He pulled her down to him and kissed her fully on the lips. She kissed back.

"Mmm, I see someone woke up frisky," Sheila said, her hand roaming to his crotch. There was a hard bulge beneath his sweat pants. Her fingers massaged him as he moaned.

"Your horoscope says you must keep your husband happy." Tommy whispered into her hair. Sheila pulled on him a little harder.

"Don't I always make you happy?"

"Make me happier," he said as he stood. He led her back to the bedroom. They passed

The Birds and the Bees

Wendy's room, where she was still singing to herself and playing with her toys.

Sheila shut the door and turned lustily toward Tommy. She was already unbuttoning her shirt, swaying her hips seductively.

"I was thinking..." she said, sliding onto the bed and rubbing against him.

"Mmm," Tommy said, reaching over to her naked breast and rubbing the nipple in his finger.

"I was trying to think of ways to make money," she said, kissing him several times along his face.

"Money is good..."

Her fingers clamped his half-hard penis and rubbed it into an erection.

"You know how much I love it when you take my picture, especially when I'm naked."

"You are beautiful naked." Tommy took a nipple into his mouth and flicked it with his tongue.

"I love to be naked." Sheila writhed under his touch. They fell into their pattern of licking and sucking, and soon the only words exchanged were those of lust and desire.

Wendy heard the sounds of her parents fucking, and it disgusted her. They never had time to talk to her, yet they could fuck forever. It pissed her off.

Wendy slipped Blackie into her pocket and

went outside. She stared up at the sky and wished that she lived closer to where her friends did.

Overhead, a huge flock of black birds fluttered by, screeching and screaming at each other, as if they were in a hurry. Several of them swooped down toward her, and she ducked, covering her head. Birds often swooped around her, though she didn't know why. She didn't much care for it either. It freaked her out, feeling the whoosh of air around her head and hearing the ear-splitting piercing calls.

Behind the main living shack, there was a smaller shack, where rusted-out gardening things were kept as well as her bike. She pulled the rickety door open, and stared with dismay at how her dad had once again slung his shovel and the hand lawn mower over the bike.

She had saved up for that bike. It was nice and shiny. About the only nice and shiny thing in this whole house was this bike, which she had hoarded money for from birthdays and baby-sitting.

No one had any respect for anything around here. It pissed her off even more than her parents fucking like rabbits all the time. As if fucking could block out living and life. As if fucking would stop the world from turning, people from growing, children from needing shoes and clothes.

The birds circled around her again, flying

The Birds and the Bees

closer, and more swooped and cawed. She stopped pulling at the bike for a moment, and went out to look at them.

Things are changing.

Times are changing.

Wendy watched as the birds settled down, perching on the roof of the shed, along the grass, all coming to a standstill, staring at her with shiny beady eyes. There must have been fifty, a hundred? She had no idea. All these birds, just staring at her.

Tell them what to do, Blackie said from her pocket.

Wendy furrowed her brow and blinked. The birds waited.

Tell them about Mac and Becky.

Wendy snickered.

Yeah, right, like she was going to tell a bunch of birds about her problems.

Wendy turned away from the birds and continued to carefully lift debris from her bike. At last, she pulled it out. She brushed away the dirt and grime, and checked the air pressure in the wheels.

Everything was fine with her bike. She pushed it a little and jumped on it. The birds watched her as she traveled down the gravel driveway. The air felt good on her face.

"Follow me!" she said in fun to the birds. To her great amazement, the flock rose up with a mighty flutter of wings and followed her. It freaked her out, but it also made her laugh. She felt like the Wicked Witch of the West, peddling her bicycle with a swarm of flying monkeys at her back.

She peddled faster, the birds keeping pace, swooping and cawing as they followed her.

It wasn't that far to the variety store, where she knew Mac was working tonight. She bet a million bucks that Becky was conveniently hanging out. Sure enough, they sat on the front stoop of the old wooden store, sharing a cigarette.

Wendy's skin crawled as she saw them. Wasn't that special, oh, so, cozy, blond bimbo Becky sucking on the smoke while Mac held it, his eyes fixated on her tits. Wendy hopped off her bike.

"Hi!" she said, trying to sound casual. Becky blew smoke out her nose, which went directly into Wendy's face.

"Oh, look who came by. Lost Girl Wendy. Still looking for Peter Pan? Or just a peter?" Becky smirked. Wendy clenched her fingers. Her whole life people had made stupid comments about her name. It was either Wendy from Peter Pan or some Wendy Witch from old comic books. Whatever it was, they were never meant as compliments.

Wendy could never think of good comebacks till she was out of a situation, so she didn't even try to verbally spar with the bitch.

The Birds and the Bees

"I just came to get some smokes," Wendy said, stepping past them on the steps and going into the store. Mac stood up and followed her in. He went behind the counter and tossed her a pack.

"Put it on my old man's credit," Wendy said.

"Sam'll kill me. Your old man owes a shitload of money. Still, I'll add it on for you." Mac winked at Wendy. Wendy blushed. She felt her legs tremble. She loved it when Mac winked at her. His eyes were so blue, and he had really black hair, so that they looked even more blue.

They were as blue as the sky, she thought.

As blue as the lake and, boy, did she ever want to dive in.

"Thanks Mac," Wendy said.

"Hey, want a slushy? On the house," he said, nodding toward the machine.

"Sure." Wendy went over to the machine and poured out a slushy. Mac watched her with that grin that made her melt.

"When do you get off work?" she asked shyly.

"Oh, not for a long time," Mac said noncommittally.

"He's going out with me after work anyway," Becky said as she slouched in the doorway. "We already have plans and they don't include you."

"Whatever," Wendy shrugged.

Tell them what to do, Blackie whispered from her pocket.

Wendy looked at Becky. She was so typical

she could have been torn from a teen magazine. Britney Spears hair, low-slung jeans, too much glossy glittery makeup, especially for this nowhere town. When Becky was around boys, she used an annoying baby voice, as if she could gurgle orders and men would obey. And so far, they usually had.

It made Wendy sick.

Wendy walked back onto the porch and saw the birds in the nearby trees, the weight of them causing the branches to sag.

Don't be afraid, tell them what to do.

Wendy went to her bike.

"Still riding a bike like a baby girl, aren't you?" Becky catcalled.

Mac walked out to watch Wendy mount.

"She's only a kid," Mac said.

"I'm only a year older and I'm already driving my dad's pickup."

"Underage."

"Big shit. He lets me. Oh, that's right . . . your daddy doesn't have *any* trucks, does he, little lost girl? He's too busy sleeping all day and pretending to be a big rock star."

"Don't you talk about my daddy that way. He was just on tour."

"Touring the local dives, my old man said. Probably drank more than he made."

"Shut up, bitch. You don't know anything. He's making a CD."

"Yup . . . whatever." Becky put her hand up in

The Birds and the Bees

that annoying "talk to the hand" way that made Wendy seethe.

I wish you were dead, you stupid ugly cunt.

Wendy had no sooner thrown a leg over her bike when there was a scream as the sound of a hundred pairs of wings swooped down from the trees. Wendy leaped from her bike and lay on the ground as the entire flock of birds descended on Becky. They screeched and cawed, drowning out the screams of the hysterical girl. Mac tried to beat them off with his hands, and then he grabbed a nearby broom and swung at them. The birds were not to be deterred from their goal. They wanted one thing and one thing only. Claws peeled and scraped away at the screaming girl's flesh. Beaks pecked at her eyes, until the sockets were bloody and sightless. Wings flapped in her hair, in her face, around her legs so she couldn't run. Every time Mac took a swing at the birds, several of them would flap in his face, beating him back with their wings, yet not touching him. He couldn't get close to the girl, who was now collapsed on the ground, nothing more then a wriggling, twitching pile of meat.

Wendy watched the scene, horrified. As much as she wanted Becky out of her face, she didn't really mean . . . did she?

Her emotions raged from elation to terror. She wondered if the birds would turn on her next, yet knew, somehow, they wouldn't. Seeing

Mac screaming, and now tears of fear flowing down his face, made her heart ache. She knew he was freaking out, yet she hoped, on some weird subterranean level in the pit of her soul, that once he got over the horror of this day, it would be she he turned to for comfort. For after all, weren't they sharing the same ugly moment?

A smile twitched on her lips but for a second, and she quickly capped it with her hands. She hoped to God Mac hadn't seen it. Judging by the pale sweaty sheen of his face, she knew that he was in too much shock to register much of anything right now. And that was just fine.

As quickly as the birds had swarmed in, they swarmed off, leaving behind a corpse that could only have been picked cleaner by vultures themselves.

Things are changing, Blackie said.
Times are changing.

Mac ran over to Wendy.

"Are you all right?" he asked her, holding her face, staring at her up and down.

"Yes, I'm quite all right," she said, breathing in his fear-scented sweat. He smelled delicious, panic and terror all rolled into one trembling sixteen-year-old boy who needed comfort.

"They didn't touch me. I tried to kill them and they didn't so much as peck at me," he said in shock, pulling at his own clothes.

Wendy took his hand and tried to lead him

The Birds and the Bees

away from the blood-soaked corpse.

"We need to call someone . . ." He trembled. "We'll call the cops, I guess." He tried to look over at the corpse, and a wave of nausea overtook him. He spilled his guts over the railing and onto the grass.

"Who's going to believe that a bunch of birds came and did this?" Wendy asked. "What if they blame us?"

"Don't be stupid. They aren't going to think that we stood here, peeling away her flesh from her bones and poking her eyes out. For what? She's my . . . she was my . . . she was my . . ."

Mac sank to his knees as new waves of realization overtook him. He sobbed. Wendy tried to stroke his back for a while, but he wouldn't stop crying. Every now and again, she'd glance over to the corpse and tried to get it through her head that this was real. That it wasn't a movie prop lying there in blood and bone. That only minutes ago, that corpse had been the biggest bitch in town.

And Wendy had killed her.

No, she hadn't killed her. The birds had killed her. No one could prove it was any other way. It was the birds. Plain and simple. They just went nuts. Just 'cause *she* hated Becky didn't mean that she had killed her, or told the birds to.

Though she *had* told the birds to.

No, she hadn't. She had wished the bitch dead, that's all.

And that was no crime. Everyone wishes someone dead once in a while, don't they?

Of course they do, Wendy. Of course everyone has wishful thinking now and again. Just not everyone has a flock of birds ready to do their bidding.

Wendy looked up at the tree where the birds sat and watched, waiting. Waiting for what? Waiting for their next order?

There were no more orders.

The damage had been done.

Wendy looked one more time at Mac crying on the porch, and felt a wave of disgust wash through her. He was just a boy. A crying baby boy, heartbroken over the biggest slut in town. What on earth did she want *that* for? She was bigger than that. She was stronger than that. Hadn't she just proved it? Hadn't she just committed the perfect murder?

Wendy opened the new pack of cigarettes and took one out and lit it. She took a couple more drags, staring at crying Mac and the corpse with narrowed eyes.

God, this town sucked big-time.

She hopped back on her bike and headed for home, and prayed her parents had stopped fucking by now.

Chapter Nine

Gabrielle browsed back over the messenger conversation that she had just finished with Tommy. Her face was flushed and her fingers trembled. She didn't know why she felt the way she did, but she did. It was not like her to be swept away in the moment. Years of loneliness, years of listening to lies and more lies, had jaded her. But now, she reveled in being swept away. It felt right somehow. His music had touched her in a way she hadn't been touched in ages. They were able to talk about things she had seldom been able to discuss with others.

She clicked on an audio clip he had sent her of a piece he was working on, and sat back in her chair, her eyes closed. The music washed over her, his voice tickling her ears. What she was doing was dangerous and wrong, yet she couldn't help how she felt. And he must feel it too, or why was he constantly writing to her and messaging her? Ending his messages with love and kisses?

Somehow, she had to get him back here so that she could finally show him what he meant to her.

In just the short time since their paths had crossed, she felt the weight that had been hanging around her start to lift.

The doorbell rang.

Gabrielle opened the door, and was pleasantly surprised to see Lisa standing in her hallway.

"Gabrielle!"

"Hey! How are you?"

"What's up, girlfriend? I haven't heard from you in a while. What's going on?"

"I guess it has been a while. I didn't realize it."

"Can I come in?"

"Sure."

Lisa looked around the small room as she came in, and threw her purse and coat on the nearest chair. Gabrielle wandered into the kitchen and rummaged through the cupboards.

"Should I put on coffee or do you want something stronger?"

"Hell, it's after four, let's have a cocktail."

The Birds and the Bees

Gabrielle found a bottle of red wine in the cupboard and popped the cork.

"So what have you been up to? Writing that novel?" Lisa asked.

Gabrielle's face was flushed. "Picking away at it . . . not as much as I wish I was."

"So what are you up to? New guy?"

"Well, yeah . . . there is, in fact."

She studied Gabrielle's face. "You're not still hung up on Tommy?"

Gabrielle shrugged. "Well, it would appear he's also hung up on me."

"You know better."

"I do, do I?"

"He's married, for God's sake. You know that it's always the woman that gets screwed."

"I can only hope."

"It's not funny. Don't fall for it." Lisa held her wine up to the light, pretending to study the hue.

"He hasn't made me any promises."

"I know you, you are vulnerable. Forget him."

The messenger chimed. Gabrielle's face brightened.

"It's him." Gabrielle and Lisa went over to the computer.

"I'm back, sweet thing," the message read.

"I'm glad," Gabrielle typed.

Lisa pulled a face. "How do you know that isn't the wife clicking at you?"

"Why would she?"

"To mess with your mind . . . who knows? There are a lot of crazies out there."

"He's not crazy."

Gabrielle's fingers flew quickly along the keyboard as she conversed with Tommy.

"How do you know?"

"I can tell. We think alike. He writes beautiful music."

"Uh-huh. Well, I'll always be here for you, but you know, you *know* that this is a bad idea."

"I'm only talking to him."

"Yes, I can see that. Look at how you're talking to a married man. A man who belongs to another."

"How happy can he really be there with her, if he's talking like this to me?"

"Just be careful. I've seen this game too many times."

"So have I. But this is different."

"Why? Why is it different? Because it's you? Because married men fuck up everyone else's lives but not yours? Not Gabrielle Light?"

"It doesn't feel like that."

"I'm sure it doesn't. It never does. I know, I've been there."

Gabrielle sighed. "I'm just talking to him. Hell, you know yourself we've never even kissed."

"Sex is all in the mind anyway. Don't you remember? The brain is the biggest sex organ going on?"

The Birds and the Bees

"So we're having sex now?"

Lisa looked at the screen. "Only you know that." She winked.

"Okay, so you don't approve. I hear you."

"It's not for me to approve. I could give a flying fuck about morals. I'm just worried about my friend getting hurt, that's all. I've seen this shit far too often, and so have you."

"I'll be careful," Gabrielle said.

"I'd like to believe that," Lisa said as she wandered over to the TV. The volume was off, but on the screen there was a frightening picture. An incredible number of black birds were pecking around what appeared to be a pile of rags.

"Holy shit," Lisa said as she turned up the volume. "Check this out."

"—died from over one hundred forty-seven stings on her body," the announcer said. "The woman, believed to be in her fifties, was known as the Bird Lady of Baker Street. Her morning ritual was known to many in the area. She would go into the neighborhood bakery to collect stale bread to feed the birds. Some residents complained, but for the most part, the birds and the woman were harmless enough. Until about a week ago, when instead of just a few city pigeons, more and more large black birds started showing up at her feedings. Then today, the startling discovery of her body, covered in bee stings. As you can see, the birds are still here, as if to share in the mourning." The

Sèphera Girón

reporter waved his hands behind him, and the camera pulled back to reveal hundreds of huge black birds smack dab in the center of the city.

"Birds . . . Bees . . . After last week's random bee attack, and now this. A warning has to be issued to watch for swarms of killers bees."

Gabrielle turned to watch in amazement as the reporter continued to talk.

"Be careful, if you are walking in the country, not to do or wear anything that will attract bees. Killer bees are tenacious and will follow you anywhere once they start an attack, so don't try to dive into a pond and hold your breath. If you are stung, scrape off the stinger with a credit card, don't squeeze or pick at the site. Watch the eleven o'clock news for more detailed killer-bees tips."

"Holy shit," Lisa sighed again. "The Bird Lady killed by bees? How freaky is that?"

Gabrielle shuddered and went over to the window. It was still dusk, and she could see what she had seen for days now.

"Then check this out."

Lisa went over to the window and her hand flew up to her mouth. On Gabrielle's balcony rail sat at least a dozen huge black birds, sitting silently, staring at her.

"What the hell? Are you feeding them?"

"God, no. I hate birds, I would never feed them."

The Birds and the Bees

"What are they doing there? Are they on everyone's rails?"

"How high is this building? Twenty stories? And yet, they choose *my* balcony to sit on. *Mine*."

"But why?"

"I don't know, and it freaks me out. They are there when I get up and they are there when I go to bed."

"Have you tried to go out and scream at them?"

"God, no! I hate the things."

Lisa went into the kitchen and found a steel pot and a large metal spoon. She returned to the balcony and opened the door.

"Don't go out there!" Gabrielle begged.

Lisa ignored her and stepped out of the sliding door, clanging the spoon against the pot. The racket was annoyingly loud, but the birds sat and stared, unblinking.

Gabrielle shook. "Don't . . ."

"What is wrong with them? Are they dead?"

"I don't know . . . I don't know. . . ." Gabrielle quivered, tears running down her face. "They freak me out so much, I can't bear to look out my window anymore."

"And that poor Bird Lady, what's up with that?"

"I don't know . . . I just don't know."

The messenger chimed a few times in a row, and when Gabrielle returned to it, she saw that it had been Tommy saying good-bye. He was off to eat dinner at his grandmother's once more.

"Lose the dude before you get too deep," Lisa suggested, pouring more wine.

"I'll think about it," Gabrielle said halfheartedly, pulling the curtains shut on the birds.

A week had gone by. Another week of aching loneliness and chiming on the messenger. Another week when she got up, made a pot of coffee, diddled around on her computer, went to the office, came home, and talked to him. Yet times were changing too. It wasn't rare to hear about random attacks of nature against humans. It was as if nature was shifting the balance and man was evolving or devolving. Now, when people left the house, they carried umbrellas, knives, sprays, all sorts of stuff. There was debate on the news about bringing in the Army, but for what? How could the Army prevent random bird swarms, or killer bee attacks?

In the case of the bees, scientists followed them, destroying nests in the alleys, in the parks. They wore special clothes to prevent stings, and always made certain to destroy the queen. Yet the bees continued to swarm, continued to multiply.

The birds were harder. No one could gauge who they were attacking or why. No one could figure out if they were all mad with rabies, or some other odd illness that made them sud-

The Birds and the Bees

denly kill and eat humans. Even more strange, the birds seemed to appear out of nowhere. No matter how many were shot down, there were always more. It was as if the heavens would spontaneously open up and drop a hundred birds on an area, only to have them disappear again.

Gabrielle made notes about it all in her journals, but it made no sense to her. The new millennium had arrived and instead of plagues of locusts and world war, there were other issues to contend with.

How quickly she too adapted to her new lifestyle. The shock of turning on the news was gone. She even found herself flipping channels to comedy shows to block out the now-repetitious reports of random attacks on the weak and the homeless.

Instead, her mind was turned to other things.

She had to see Tommy. The desire was so strong in her that she thought she would explode from the ache of it all.

He told her he was playing a two-night gig in a small town not far from hers. She knew she could get permission to cover it, and even if she couldn't, to hell with it. She would go to see him. She had to see if what was there was real or was just an aching illusion.

So now, here she was, eating up the miles in her car, watching the endless white line stretch before her, leading her to Tommy.

She cranked the car stereo. One of her favorite albums was spinning and she sang along. Her kids always laughed at her old-fashioned taste in music. Classic rock. Back when rock was cutting-edge.

It wouldn't be long now before she could see him again. This town was small and not too hard to navigate. She found the tavern where he was performing, and drove past it to the coffee shop where they had planned their rendezvous.

Nervous, she looked at herself in the rearview mirror. She checked her makeup, quickly adjusting her eyeliner, and ran the brush through her windblown hair.

"Just take a deep breath," she whispered to herself. "God, I feel like a teenager all over again."

She parked the car and went inside. He wasn't there. She ordered a coffee and sat by the window, watching and waiting.

At last, she saw him. Walking. He walked with a bounce in his step and as he saw her in the window, he grinned sheepishly.

She could hardly contain herself as he came into the shop.

"Hi," she said shyly.

"Hi," he said, blushing.

It seemed so sweet and innocent. A grown man blushing. Over her. Her heart skipped a beat.

The Birds and the Bees

He slid into the seat across from her.

"So how are you?" he asked, pulling out a cigarette.

"I'm all right. You?"

She realized she was twisting a napkin into a thousand pieces, and put it down.

"I'm doing well, thanks. Better now actually." He smiled.

"Me too."

There was a silence, and Gabrielle sipped her coffee.

"You want a coffee?" she asked. He shrugged.

"I'll go get you a coffee," she offered, anxious to be moving around. Her knees were trembling. Trembling. How crazy was that? Almost forty, and her heart was beating and her knees were trembling. Maybe she was having a heart attack or something.

She ordered his coffee and brought it back to him. As she placed it before him, she lingered long enough to feel his closeness. How she longed to just grab him and kiss him. But she couldn't do that. She was a woman. He was a married man.

What was she doing here?

His hand caught her wrist and he pulled her back toward him.

"Aren't you going to kiss me hello?" he asked.

"I wasn't sure . . ."

Tommy pulled her toward him and kissed her long and hard on the mouth. She found herself gasping when he pulled back. Flustered, she returned to her seat.

"I missed you," he said.

"Missed me? You don't even know me," she said.

"I missing not knowing you. I want to know you."

"I want to know you too."

They stared at each other.

"You are married."

"Yes, I am. I thought I was happily married too . . . now, I'm not so sure."

"You aren't?"

"No. I think sometimes of how life might have been if I hadn't married, or at least hadn't married so young. But I know I would have married. I like having a companion."

"Humans are made to desire companionship."

"Why did you never remarry?"

"I haven't found the right man yet."

"Surely you have found men you like."

"Not enough to take a chance on."

"And why are you here? With me? A married man?"

"I honestly don't know that."

"You came all this way because you don't know?"

Gabrielle sighed. Her mind was racing. There was so much she wanted to say, she yearned to say. She wanted to tell him how he had brought

The Birds and the Bees

light into her darkness, how she felt an energy between them that she had never felt before, how she yearned to reach into his mind and know everything about him. What he liked to eat. What he liked to read. How he slept.

But nothing came out. Nothing at all. She stared stupidly at him, at his beautiful eyes, and swallowed.

"You do this with all the guitarists you write about? Go rushing off to another town to sit in silence?" he teased.

"No, actually. I hardly ever have gotten involved with someone I write about or work with. It's not smart business, you know?"

Tommy nodded. "So, why are you here? To interview me?" He winked.

"I am here 'cause I wanted to see you. I want to know you. Everything about you."

"I want to know you too."

"I don't want you to hurt me either. You are married. And I should just forget it."

"Maybe I won't always be married."

"Maybe you always will be. How do I know? Are you leaving her today?"

Tommy stared at her for a few minutes, then dropped his gaze to his coffee cup. He tilted his cup, watching coffee slosh against the side.

"She's been getting on my nerves. Money's been tight. We've been squabbling a lot, and that I could do without. Yet I don't know if I would leave her. I'm all she has."

Sèphera Girón

"She has a life, doesn't she? She has your daughter. She must have a job or a hobby or something."

"She takes care of my daughter, that's about it."

"Maybe she needs to get a life. Maybe you both need to get a life. Then you wouldn't be bored with each other."

"Maybe. Or maybe I'm falling out of love with her. Maybe I'm . . ." He stopped and took a sip of coffee.

"Why are you here really?" he asked.

"You said we could meet. I wanted to see what there could be between us. We're adults. We both know that is what this is about."

"Is there something between us?" Tommy asked, searching her face.

Gabrielle smiled and reached over for his hand. She patted it.

"I would say there is definitely something between us. What it is, I can't say. I don't know. All I know is that I feel a connection. Like I've always known you."

"I feel that about you too. It's the strangest feeling in the world."

"It is, isn't it?"

"So what are we going to do about it?"

"I don't know."

"Are you going to leave your wife?"

"I don't know . . . I don't know what to do. I'm really confused."

The Birds and the Bees

"I can see that."

The words hung in the air. Around them, the coffee shop bustled with people coming and going. Snatches of stray conversation flitted here and there.

Suddenly, a woman screamed and stood up, knocking her coffee over.

"A bee!" she cried, running from her table. The chair skidded out from behind her and she tripped into another table. Cups were knocked off the table and smashed to the floor. More people stood up in a panic. Chaos ensued as people ran from the shop. Gabrielle and Tommy stood up and watched as the bee flew in wide circles around the shop, soaring over the heads of people running, and then retreated to a high spot on the window.

"Where there's one there's more," a woman cried out.

A rather large man wearing a baseball hat ran behind the counter and emerged with a broomstick. He dashed to the window, swinging at the bee.

"Don't! You'll anger it. More will come," a woman cried.

"Kill it!" a woman with teased blond hair shrieked.

The man couldn't quite reach it. The bee flew off again, sending another stream of panic through the place.

Sèphera Girón

"Let's go," Tommy said, taking Gabrielle's hand.

They left the coffee shop and walked out into the street, where people pushed them aside, frantically staring up into the air. There wasn't a bee in sight, yet the ripple of panic was spreading as news of the bee in the coffee shop was frantically shared by the worried patrons with passersby.

"The world's gone mad," Gabrielle said. "Haven't you noticed it?"

"I think we've all lost our minds in one way or another."

"The weather. The animals. The insects. I don't understand it."

"Nature trying to find a new balance, maybe. Or maybe God is just plain pissed off with us all."

They walked on. The afternoon was already turning into evening. A light wind blew, and Tommy took Gabrielle's hand.

"I have to go back and get ready for tonight."

"Okay."

"Are you going to watch the show?"

"I want to . . . but it's a long drive back. And the kids are coming tommorrow."

"Yeah. I know. You mentioned that. It's too bad. I'd love to play for you."

"I'd like to have you play for me too. Maybe next time."

"Yeah. Next time." Tommy grinned.

The Birds and the Bees

They walked around the block in silence until they returned to the coffee shop. People had gone back inside. It seemed the panic had been momentary and now life went on.

Life always went on.

No matter how strange things got, people adapted and life went on.

Gabrielle opened her car door and stood to face Tommy.

"What do you think is going to happen?" she asked.

"With us?"

"Yes, with us."

"I know what I want to happen. I just don't know if it's a reality, is all." Tommy said. "I'm so torn, you know. On one hand, I want to run away with you. Yet on the other, I don't want to lose what I already have, even if it isn't really working right now."

"Yeah . . ." Gabrielle sighed.

Tommy took her face in his hands.

"Don't be sad. I just need a bit of time to think."

"This is sudden, I know. We just met . . ."

"You know what I want to do right now?" Tommy said.

"What?"

"I'd like nothing more than to sweep you up into my arms and make mad passionate love to you."

Gabrielle shivered. "I would like that too. But

I can wait. I can wait for you to figure out what you really want. I'm no man's mistress."

"I know that too."

Tommy hugged her, rubbing her back. She nestled her head into his chest. His heart beat against her. He was so strong, so solid. She yearned to be with him like this, freeze-framed in time always.

How could it be that she had finally found someone so right for her and yet so wrong?

She closed her eyes and wished that things would work out in her favor. Yet she didn't want to ruin another family. It would have to be his decision. Made without pressure. She fought hard to keep from crying. Fought hard to keep from saying a thousand things she yearned to say. She held him, breathing him in as if it would be the last time she ever got to touch him.

And for all she knew, it *would* be the last time. Or maybe not.

They broke the embrace and Tommy kissed her.

Warmly.

Passionately.

Her head spun as she slipped into the driver's seat. As she drove away, waving at him, watching him in the rearview mirror, the tears she had been holding at bay leaked into her eyes and dribbled down her face.

What a mess.

The Birds and the Bees

Why did falling in love have to be such a mess?

She knew she was doomed for that was exactly what was happening. She was falling in love with a married man and she had no one to blame but herself.

Chapter Ten

Little Jimmy ran ahead, up to the mouth of the cave.

"Don't go too far," Mary Anne said, pulling out a can of wasp spray. "There could be anything at all in there."

"Nothing's here, Mommy," he called out. She saw his form against the wall, a slat of sunshine illuminating him. He looked like a cherub, her little angel.

A flutter of wind fanned across her and she wondered if it was Nigel. Goose bumps rippled along her arms. Her Nigel was near. She hurried into the mouth of the cave with Jimmy and Deedee. A bee zipped over their heads and traveled with a buzz into the darkness.

"Be very quiet," Mary Anne whispered, and

Sèphera Girón

held the children close to her. The mouth of the cave was already a great deal colder than the air outside. This seemed like a plain old cave. Nothing remarkable. She wasn't even sure if any animals made their home here. Every move she made, she wiped strands of spiderwebs from her face. If animals or people made their home here, these webs wouldn't be so thick. She didn't even want to think about the spiders that made them or where they were right now. She imagined she already had several creepy-crawlies inching along her hair, but she didn't want to think about it. All she cared about was finding that hive and seeing if it was possible to destroy it. The bee was a very good sign.

More bees flew into the cave and buzzed down the tunnel. They came one by one. Weary travelers heavy with honey. Mary Anne smiled. Her gut instincts had been right. The damnable bees were in this cave. Were they the same attacking bees as before? She figured they must be. She didn't know much about bees. She didn't know why they had attacked that day. She didn't know if they knew she and the children were here and if this was a good idea. There were enough cans of spray and wasp bombs to smoke out a nest.

She opened the bag very carefully and pulled out three wide-brimmed netted hats.

"Here, put these on," she said to the kids. She helped them pull the nets over their faces.

The Birds and the Bees

"This feels gross, Mom."

"I know sweetie, but it will keep the bees out of your face, in case it comes to that."

Mary Anne pulled out the little can filled with frankincense. The smell of the incense wafted out. She loved that sweet smell. It reminded her of being in Sunday school when she was a little kid. How she used to love to put on her best dress and shine up her black patent-leather shoes. Her hair was always perfectly in place. Walking into that church on a bright Sunday morning was one of her favorite things in the world. And the smell of frankincense brought it all back.

Her mother always wore a little blue hat and her dad always wore a suit, as if it were sometime in the fifties, even though it was the eighties. During the week, they were T-shirt-and-jeans types, her mom slinging beer in the bars, her dad all greased up from wrenching cars. But come Sunday morning, no matter how many they might have tied on the night before, they all woke up and dressed like some bizarre *Leave It to Beaver* family and trundled off to church. Mary Anne would head down into the basement with the other kids for an hour or so and lose herself in the Bible stories. She liked the stories, the magic and miracles. The world flooding and the few who survived, the woman turned to salt, strange and wondrous creatures floating down from the sky in rays of heavenly light bringing news that brought fear or rejoicing. Her favorite stories were of the slaves running from the Pharaoh and the Red Sea parting by the command of just one man. A man who had talked to a burning bush, who preached the one true word of God above false gods.

When she got older, she questioned how Moses knew it was indeed the true God, and how anyone could say who is a false god, among other things. Her questioning was always met with resistance and hushed, hurried answers. She grew disinterested in the fantastical stories. She considered them nothing more than stories as she grew older.

But as a child, she found the stories amazing and exciting.

After they heard their Bible story of the morning, and talked about it and sang a song or two about Jesus loving them, the kids were collected by their parents and taken up to the main part of the church. Mary Anne would stare in awe at the huge vaulted ceilings, the glistening gold columns of the organ spiraling to the roof, the stained-glass windows depicting gory and depressing images. The ethereal music of the choir echoed around the church, and then the man in the robe would start ranting about something.

She never really listened to the man. She didn't understand what his point was most of the time, and would sit and smell the frankin-

The Birds and the Bees

cense and listen to the music and stare at the many depictions of Jesus scattered throughout the church.

Sometimes she would rub her wrists and wonder what it must have been like to have been crucified. To be strapped to a cross in the heat of the desert, left to scream and rot, while carrion birds circled, and people screeched tormenting words.

It must have been horrific. Sometimes she would stare at the pictures and cry, wondering about man's cruelty to man. How could it be possible that someone would speak his mind and be killed for it?

Yet, as she grew up, she could very well see how that would happen. She just had to look at her husband wrong, or use the wrong tone of voice, and she would get a wallop across the jaw. It was very easy to see how mass hysteria could crucify a man for nothing more than trying to help people.

She peered down the cave, at the darkness within, and sniffed the frankincense some more. Would her children get further in life than she had? She certainly hoped so. She hadn't brought them to church or anything of that nature. Over John's dead body, that's for sure.

What would be in store for her kids when they grew up? As long as they got the hell out this

Sèphera Girón

town, it would be a step better than anything she had managed to do so far.

A few more bees soared overhead. She watched in amazement as the smoke billowed and rolled from the little can. As the bees flew through the clouds, she could see them slowing down.

She could even hear them slowing down; their buzzing wasn't as frantic. She watched them bounce around, confused after the smoke hit, then slowly continue down along the cavern.

Other bees came into the cave, and some of them immediately dropped to the ground once they hit the smoke. Others twirled for a little while, and then continued on about their business. No matter what happened, none of the bees paid any attention at all to her and her children.

They were on a mission.

"Kids, I'm going to go in a little further. I need you to stay here and wait. If the hive is large, you might get hurt again, so I want you to just wait."

"Okay, Mommy. I will."

"If you hear anything bad, just run home, all right?"

"Sure, Mommy."

"If you stay near this smoking can, you will be all right."

"Yes, Mommy."

The Birds and the Bees

Mary Anne hugged the children and kissed them each on the forehead. She put a can of wasp spray in each of their heavy coat pockets.

Nigel's presence was very strong around her, and it gave her incentive to continue down the dark corridor. She held a flashlight in one hand and a can of spray in the other. Her mind raced. If the hive was huge, she would have to come back with more stuff.

Bees continued to pass her, flying low, drugged by heavy sacks of pollen and thick smoke. She knew she was on the right track. It was part of her job, to make her children safe.

Her heart pounded, and as she walked a few steps more, she realized that there was no way she was going to be able to handle this hive by herself. What was she thinking to even come here alone, or worse, with the children, after all the weird attacks?

No one else was going to stop this, though, were they?

Once she found it, she would bring John back to see what to do about it. He would know how to destroy it. Of course, he was so unpredictable, it might be weeks before she could get him out here. If she caught him on a good day, then it wouldn't be long, and maybe their home and all the surrounding areas would be free once and for all from the random swarming.

There was a dull light glowing way up ahead. Perhaps it was the reflection of rocks or condensation, or maybe there really was a shaft of light, flickering through a crack somewhere in the cavern. Mary Anne turned off her flashlight, and the glow remained.

There must be something just up around the corner.

The humming of bees was very loud, more loud with the hollow acoustics of the cave, and she dreaded turning that corner and seeing just how big this hive was. Whatever lay around the corner was definitely no match for her. But she might as well take a quick peek so she could tell John, or maybe even animal control, about the nest and that it needed to be destroyed.

Even from here, she could see bees crawling along the walls, could see the ripples of their bodies in the bouncing light. Maybe they were stopping to rest before making their way into the hive.

Her arms were goose-bumpy. Nigel was certainly here. She scratched at her goose bumps and felt the hard bodies of bees landing. Her touch angered them, and needle pricks peppered her at an alarming rate. She reached for the can of spray, but it was as if her movement had set off some sort of alarm. The mellow hum turned to violent buzzing as bees swarmed her. While swatting at them, she fumbled with the can, trying to find the button. It fell from her trembling fingers and bounced to the floor. As her mouth opened to scream, bees were already

The Birds and the Bees

burrowing under the hat netting and crawling along her face. She scrambled along the floor, grappling with the cans of spray, and she managed to press down a stream of chemical at a few of them.

The sound, the smell, something, infuriated the bees even more, and another wave flew toward her. She couldn't see; the netting was totally infested with the crawling insects. Pain soared through her as they violently stung her. She cried out for the children to run, despairing that they would even hear her at all.

Wendy put some jeans and a T-shirt into her knapsack. She would have packed a sweater too, if her mom had washed any. But all that she had were still dirty, too dirty to bring with her. It was still hot out these days anyway.

Wendy . . .

Wendy smiled and turned to her china animals.

"I'm going to miss you," she said to them. "I would bring you, but I know you'll get broken. Blackie will take care of me."

Wendy wrapped the little china dog carefully in a handkerchief.

You know I will . . . we have much to do. . . .

Wendy nodded.

"I'm ready for anything. I really am."

Wendy double-checked that she had everything. Well, she didn't own much and there

Sèphera Girón

wasn't much to have really. All she needed were some clothes, and whatever money she could scrounge up. She peered into her parents' room. What a disaster. It was piled high with dirty clothes and boxes, plates with half-eaten food, tin cans piled high with butts. Not only did it look disgusting, it smelled disgusting. Like rotten food, body odor, stale air. She had poked around a tiny bit over the past week while her parents were on the Internet, trying to find any money at all. All she had found was a crumpled-up ten-dollar bill and some nickels. If her parents ever went anywhere, she could have done a more thorough search, though she doubted she would find anything anyway.

To have money, you needed a job, and her parents didn't work. Even if Tommy had made any cash on his trips, it was probably in a bank or tied up in debts.

Wendy quietly searched both their jeans pockets one last time, and came up with nothing. She crept out and went into the living room. She moved around overflowing ashtrays and a few magazines. Over by her dad's computer, there were several books. He liked to read detective and horror stories. There was more than one movie she had seen in which money was hidden in a book. Very quietly and carefully, she flipped the pages of the books, and then, there she found it. In an old paperback of Clive Barker's *The Books of Blood*.

The Birds and the Bees

Five twenty-dollar bills.

Good work! Blackie barked.

Wendy nearly laughed, she was rocking now. She took the money and put the book back.

As she was about to turn on her heel, her eye caught the beat-up paperback of Stephen King's *The Shining*.

Trembling, her fingers pulled out the book. Inside, another five twenty-dollar bills.

Tears filled her eyes as she couldn't believe her good fortune.

Carefully she put the book back onto the shelf. She wondered how many more books held secret treasures, but she didn't care. She had two hundred dollars, and that would do. She had never stolen from her parents before, but this time, it was necessary.

She had to get the hell out of this house before she went insane.

Looking at the clock, she saw it was eight A.M. The school bus would be by soon, and she needed to catch it to get into town, at least so she could get to the bus station.

Hurry, Blackie urged.

"I'm hurrying, I'm hurrying," Wendy sang. She slung her knapsack over her arm and took her mother's light windbreaker, just in case.

As she pushed open the screen door, she thought about leaving a note, but she figured what the hell. It might be days before they noticed she was gone anyway. Once she had stayed at her friend's house all weekend, and her parents had never even noticed she was gone.

When she finally came home, they had looked at her stunned when she pointed out they didn't even know she was away. They had said they had figured she was at school, and she had told them there was no school on weekends. They were so self-absorbed in their small backward worlds of Internet and sex that they never knew what she was up to.

Well, now she was on her adventure. Blackie was leading the way, and she would follow.

The school bus lurched around the corner and came to a grinding halt. Wendy climbed up the stairs, and looked around at the kids in the seats. It was like they were all strangers. In fact, they might as well be, since hardly anyone ever talked to her.

A strange sensation tickled her gut. It hummed, as though one of those weird massage-chair things that she had seen at the local mall was trapped inside her body. The sensation spread down to her fingertips, dancing along her blood and into her toes. It made her feel warm and happy inside, and she knew she was doing the right thing.

Of course you are, Blackie reassured her. *Why wouldn't you be doing the right thing?*

Thoughts of her parents rose to the surface, then fell away again. One less mouth to feed

The Birds and the Bees

would be all right with them and with her grandparents. It would be nice not to hear the vague mutterings of her grandparents expressing exasperation at Tommy. They didn't understand his music "thing," and most of the time, neither did Wendy.

Wendy knew about rock groups and music. She knew that her dad was good, but she knew that her dad was lazy, unfocused, washed-up already.

You will be the special one, Blackie promised. *You have a special place in the world. Everyone will adore you.*

The school bus stopped at the school and the kids piled out. Wendy looked for the on-duty teacher and darted away. She crept along bushes until she was safely off the school property. Now that she was gone, what could they do?

Nothing.

Wendy felt the sun on her face. It was a great day for a new adventure. There was a spring in her step that she hadn't felt in a long time, and the buzzing in her belly grew like a caressing lullaby.

The walk from the school into the downtown district wasn't far. Of course, in this tiny town, there was no real downtown to speak of. It was more that there were a few more stores and bars than on the other streets. And most important, a bus station.

Sèphera Girón

Wendy entered the bus station. Once inside the door, she stopped. Maybe this wasn't such a good idea. Where was she going again?

You are the special one. Go to the city. You will find the answer there.

Wendy bought a bus ticket, and even as she boarded the bus, she wasn't sure at all what she was doing. But she was convinced that anything was better than the life she was leaving behind.

Anyone would leave *that* life behind.

Hell, half the time she felt like she lived on the Springer show.

Trailer trash. Rednecks. That was all her relatives.

She'd be trailer trash too, if she were lucky enough to have a trailer. She was shack trash. But now, with the help of Blackie, she could go to the city and see what real life was all about. Blackie would tell her what to do, where to go.

There was a plan to all of this.

She had dreamed it a thousand times. She had dreamed that she was someone very important in a plan. She was being trained for something spectacular. Blackie told her so.

She could see it now.

Wendy, the teenager, would do what several generations before her could never do. Have the balls to grow up and move on.

Chapter Eleven

Gabrielle waited in the bus station parking lot. Her heart pounded, her fingers slick with sweat on the steering wheel, watching the people leaving the station.

Lost people, people looking for relatives, people looking for a new life, people running away from whatever it was that they could stand no longer.

She longed for a fresh new start herself. Maybe this was it. Maybe this was what she was waiting for. Even if she wanted to go into the station, she was loath to leave the car.

On the lips of the roof, clutching eaves, troughs, and railings, a sea of black birds watched. More and more of them flew and landed on the roof. She knew what would happen if she left the car. It was her they were after. She felt it in her bones. They followed her. They watched her.

In front of the station, several homeless people wandered. One woman sat on the steps. At first Gabrielle had mistaken her for a pile of rags, but then she saw the dark wizened apple face beneath. A face that was ancient and ageless at the same time. Who knows how old the woman was or what the woman was. She could have been twenty, she could have been a hundred. Her face and hands were burned and leathery, covered with years of dirt and dust and decay. Hands that pawed through the trash, searching for that last drop of coffee or a piece of forgotten bread. Amazing how many people threw out half a sandwich or a nearly full can of pop. Those fingers had searched and trembled and touched in a thousand garbage cans.

The woman didn't aggressively panhandle as the others did. She just sat, still as a rock, still as a pile of rags could be. Gabrielle wondered if perhaps she had done drugs or gone into a coma, or was just reminiscing about better times. Or were there better times? Perhaps this was as good as it got, a pleasant day sitting in the sun on the steps.

A lone bird swooped down from the roof and circled the woman. It flew back up to the others, screaming with a series of caws. There was murmuring among the birds, as if they were

The Birds and the Bees

discussing something among themselves. A ripple spread along the flock, as they hopped from one foot to the other, ruffling their feathers, fanning their wings. Now two birds soared down from the roof, as if performing some sort of duet. They squawked at each other, and circled the homeless lady. She stared obliviously ahead, as if the birds didn't exist at all.

The two birds settled slightly ahead of her, hopping around on their little claw feet, beaks snapping open and shut. Two more birds swooped down, and then more and more were joining the original two, hopping around in front of the woman, who still never moved a muscle.

As more birds went down to the woman, others flew from somewhere else to join the throngs on the roof.

Gabrielle turned up the car radio slightly to drown out the din of the birds chattering. She fiddled with the stations and when next she looked up, she saw the woman was covered in birds.

Still, the woman did not move. A nearby panhandler stopped his begging to turn and look at the woman. It was a bizarre tableau, and Gabrielle forgot what she was even doing here to be witness to such a spectacle. The woman on the stairs, covered in black birds, slick with shit and downy feathers, not even blinking an eye.

And the man in multilayered clothes watching her.

His face was tanned and leathery as well, his jeans ratty, his hair wild, his scraggly beard wilder. His age could have been twenty or twenty hundred. Poverty made people ageless. Poverty made people accept situations that regular people would find bizarre and unacceptable.

Suddenly, the woman screamed and stood up, lumbering to her feet like an angry bear. Birds fluttered up and down like a wave, squawking in protest. The woman's scream was just one long shout as she raised her arms. It was as if she had finally broken out of the reverie, or perhaps the drug trance, to realize the flock enveloping her. She jumped around in a panic, flapping her arms as if she were trying to fly herself. Her movements seemed to upset the birds, and their protesting grew louder. Beaks snapped open and shut, faster and faster, some so fast they were a blur as they pecked away at the woman's arms and face. She screamed, louder now that she was being attacked. Her cries, or maybe the blood that was seeping along her arms, caused more birds to soar down and join their friends.

Gabrielle watched in disbelief as shards of meat flipped through the air. Spurts of blood fountained up and before long, the sidewalks were stained crimson with puddles of blood.

People, seeing what was happening, either

The Birds and the Bees

stopped to stare with horrified fascination, or ran screaming. The birds, having picked clean the beggar woman, now turned their attention to others. They swooped and screamed, dive-bombing the running people. More birds flew down and landed on Gabrielle's car. She honked her horn, but they continued to descend. She could hear them clattering on the roof, tiny claws scraping the hood, beaks flapping in squawking chatter.

A wind blew up and the birds were caught in it, swirling and twirling, a black vortex, spinning higher and higher. The wind was strong and whistled along the tall buildings, pushing the birds further away. The birds lifted like a giant cloud and swarmed out of sight over the buildings.

Gabrielle put her head down on the steering wheel, realizing her face was wet from dripping tears. A tapping on the window startled her, and she turned, fully expecting to see more birds. Instead, it was Tommy, standing there, looking in at her. Beyond him, she could see emergency crews and TV camera cars. Reporters scurried around like rats on a sinking ship, shoving their microphones into everyone's faces.

Gabrielle shook her head, wondering if she had fallen into another dream. The stains on the ground were too real, though. Tommy standing there, sunlight falling on his hair like he was a golden angel, was no dream. This was the moment she had been waiting for.

She pushed open the car door and stood up to greet him. They stood, staring at each other, savoring the moment as if it were suspended in time. They reached for each other, wrapped their arms around each other.

"I missed you," Gabrielle whispered into his curls.

"I missed you too," Tommy sighed. They held the moment for a little while longer, wanting it to never end. But they couldn't stay like this.

"We'd better get going."

The voice came from a faraway place as she lay on a stone slab. She stared up into darkness.

"Here is how it feels to die ... for five minutes," a deep voice said calmly.

Before Gabrielle had a chance to respond, she felt her body freeze, as if it too had turned to stone. Her heart slammed once and was still; her eyes stared ahead, seeing a flash of light, then nothingness.

The nothingness shifted and stirred into a long tunnel, then burst into a whiteness. She tried to hide her eyes, but her body was as heavy as the stone. She was melting into the stone.

A rush soared through her and she felt as if she had dropped on the first hill of a roller coaster, a free fall, except she hadn't moved. She struggled to say something, but no words

The Birds and the Bees

would form, no sound would come out of her mouth or throat.

"Enjoy the ride," the voice said.

Gabrielle's thoughts raced. She would enjoy the ride if she knew it would end safe and sound. But right now, it felt as if her heart was frozen. Not just emotionally, but as if an ice-cold metal pick had been shoved right through it and skewed her clear through to the other side.

There was another flash of light, and the free fall again, and suddenly, she burst awake, panting.

She moved her arms and legs and instinctively put her hand to her heart. It thumped the same as it always had, as if it had never stopped at all. Steady. Rhythmical. Just like the deep breathing beside her. She turned to look at Tommy. He slept, oblivious to all that she had just experienced.

Just another bad dream.

And here, here was Tommy, right beside her to protect her.

She watched his face as he slept. His hair was all tangled, his mouth slightly open as his breath pulsed in and out.

The night had been odd and not at all how she'd imagined.

Her mind had played their meeting so many times over, yet the reality had been so different. So disappointing.

Sèphera Girón

Of course, bearing witness to the horrific death of the beggar woman hadn't helped at all, but even so, she had thought the excitement of their anticipation would overshadow things at least for an hour or so.

But it wasn't to be.

When Tommy first entered the apartment, it was as if he were suddenly registering for the first time the reality of what he was actually doing. He had put down his guitar and knapsack inside the front door and stared around, looking like a lost little boy. Gabrielle had put her arms around him, pursing her lips against his in the hungry way she had been yearning to kiss him. He kissed her quickly back, almost pushing her away as he walked into the room.

She showed him around the apartment, suddenly shy. He looked out the balcony window and she peered out with him, relieved to see the birds weren't there for a moment. However, she did see a bee lilting along the flowerpots.

As she opened the sliding door, she happened to look up, and saw a honeycomb in the process of being formed in the rails of the door. Several bees flew in and out of it, bodies heavy with pollen. The sight of the nest unnerved her, but she didn't say anything to Tommy at the time.

"Nice view," Tommy said, scanning the scenery. She saw a tear glistening in the corner of his eye, and she looked away.

The Birds and the Bees

"Yes, it is," Gabrielle admitted. "I love this town."

She took his hand and led him back into the living room and to the couch.

"Are you thirsty?" she asked. "Or maybe you are gritty and need a shower?"

"A drink would be fine," he said, nervously perching on the couch.

Gabrielle went into the kitchen and pulled a couple of beers from the fridge. There wasn't a sound from Tommy as she popped them open. He was staring out the window.

"You're finally here, yet you're still far away," she said softly, putting a beer into his hand.

"Oh, I'm here," Tommy said, the faraway gaze shifting into a penetrating stare. He clicked his bottle against hers. "Cheers."

"Cheers." Gabrielle smiled, sitting close to him.

She took another sip of beer and started to rub his back.

"That feels good," Tommy sighed. "I don't know the last time I had my back rubbed."

"Me too." She smiled, kneading her fingers along his shoulders, playing with the tense muscles.

"I'll give you one later," Tommy promised.

"I'll look forward to that!" Gabrielle smiled.

Gabrielle's fingers danced along his back, pressing into the knots and tight muscles, pushing and pinching the flesh. Tommy took a long sip on his beer and stared at the computer.

"So that's where we talk, huh?"

Gabrielle nodded. She touched his hair tentatively, lifting the curls from his neck so she could rub it better.

"How were things when you left?" she asked.

Tommy sighed. "Wendy was at school, so I didn't have to worry about confronting her. And Sheila, well, she was sleeping. I . . . uh . . . left a note," Tommy drank more of his beer.

"A note? Saying what?" Gabrielle furrowed her forehead.

A note.

"Just that I was tired of living the way we were and I wanted more."

"In a note?"

Tommy shrugged. "She knows. It's hardly a surprise."

"But still . . ."

Tommy shifted restlessly. "You know . . . maybe I should drop her an e-mail, ya know?"

"An e-mail?"

"Sure. Do you mind?"

Goose bumps danced along Gabrielle's arms as a great sense of uneasiness surged through her.

"Uh, I guess . . . if it helps make things go better," she said. The words fell out of her mouth with gentle ease, but in her mind bells were going off. This was not how it should be, yet what could she do? If she didn't let him send the

The Birds and the Bees

e-mail, he might chew it over all night. He'd just gotten here, and she didn't want to fight so soon. Yet why was he sending the soon-to-be-ex-wife e-mail when he had barely kissed his new lover?

Then again, Tommy was different than other men, as near as she could tell. That was part of the attraction. That he was a bit odd. If he cared about the ex, then he would surely care about her. She was a big believer in getting along as best as possible, especially when children were involved. It was best if she stayed mellow and not fuss about a simple e-mail.

"Okay, go to it," she said, waving to the computer. She walked over to the balcony and looked outside.

There were no birds, and a couple of bees wove among the plants. In the distance, there were sirens. Closer, she heard the wailing of a cat, over and over. The wailing rose and fell, as if it were tossing on a ship in a storm. She clutched her beer bottle, picking at the paper label with her short nails. What was that saying? If you could pick and peel the label right off without a single tear, you were a virgin. Who thought that up?

Her eyes were welling up and she fought back tears.

Okay, so things were going pretty crappy so far.

Random bird attack at the bus station.

Sèphera Girón

Tommy so distant that he had barely touched her in greeting. Now he was sitting on the computer, e-mailing his wife.

Yes, his wife. Not his ex-wife, but his wife.

She narrowed her eyes at the thought of it. Warnings from a hundred advice columns floated through her head.

No, she wasn't going to crash and burn, though. This was different. This was meant to be. She was so sure of it, right through her bones and into her heart.

She glanced over at Tommy, who was hunched over the computer screen.

Her heart fluttered.

They had so much in common. She had never met someone who shared such similar ideas with her. Someone she could really talk to, about so many things, it seemed. In just the short time they had been communicating, it was as if they had explored so much. Everything except the flesh.

The cat wailed louder, the traffic roared and honked.

She drained her beer bottle and went back inside. She saw on the screen that Tommy wasn't writing e-mail.

"Are you finished?" she asked.

"Just about," Tommy said. "I saw that she was on-line, so I thought I'd just talk directly to her."

"Oh." Gabrielle felt her stomach tighten.

The Birds and the Bees

What was wrong with this picture?

"What did you say to her then?"

"I just told her I was here with you, much like I did in the letter," Tommy said, clicking the screen closed. "She's pissing me off."

"Well, of course she's going to piss you off. You just left her for another woman, so she's bound to be mad."

"It's not even that," Tommy said. "She just keeps going on, like she always does, about how I'm a loser, and now I'm going to have you to look after me."

Gabrielle reached her hand under his curls.

"Of course I'm going to look after you. That's what I promised, isn't it?"

"I guess. Though I don't know why."

"You are going places, that's why. We'll go to that party that I told you about and I'll introduce you to everyone."

"Party?" Tommy raised an eyebrow.

"You remember. The party where all the bigwigs will be?"

Tommy nodded, his eyes distant again.

"Right . . . party. Man, I hate the schmooze thing."

"I don't think anyone truly enjoys it, but it's all part of the deal."

"But why? Why can't I just make music and everyone hears it and loves it?"

Gabrielle patted his chin and said with a wry grin, "Poor deluded boy."

She stood very close to him and touched her lips to his.

He was startled at first, and then pressed his to hers.

She wrapped her arms around him, resting her head on his shoulder.

"I don't even know you, yet I've missed you so much," she said.

"It's like I've known you forever."

"You feel it too?" she asked, looking up into his face to see if he was teasing her. He looked down at her and touched her nose.

"How could I not? Why do you think I'm here?"

"It's a pull . . . a tug . . ."

"An instinct . . . like you are the half I was missing for so long."

"I think that I am. Why else would I have been so suddenly inclined to just up and leave. . . ."

Gabrielle kissed him again, this time undulating against him, as if trying to pour all her feelings into one kiss.

He kissed her back, sucking on her lips hesitantly. They pulled their arms around each other tighter. Gabrielle felt his heart beating against her chest.

Thump-thump.

Thump-thump.

Her nipples hardened as she pressed and swayed against him. He cupped her ass full in his hands.

The Birds and the Bees

"The first thing I noticed about you was your delicious ass," he sighed as he licked her neck.

They kissed a little longer, and then broke the embrace. They stared at each other. Tommy broke the stare by pacing toward his knapsack and patting his pockets.

"I need a cigarette," he said.

"Oh." Gabrielle bit her lip as he went over to the couch and lit up a cigarette. He stared at the smoke as it curled upward from the end, blowing rings through it.

"What do you think it was?" he finally asked after a few minutes of staring and smoking.

"What?"

"That bird attack?"

"Yeah . . . that bird attack . . ."

"There was one around my parts too, you know. Just a couple days ago," Tommy said.

"A bird attack?"

"Yep. Hoards of black birds pecked a teenager to death. Went to Wendy's school."

"No shit."

"Something's in the air, man. I can feel it."

"Well, certainly that's for sure. I mean, I've never heard of bird attacks, killer bird attacks, ever . . . not outside of the movies."

"Me neither."

"And now here they are."

"What with the weird weather . . . the crazy bird stuff . . . sort of like the apocalypse is coming or something."

"Scary stuff . . ."

"Like nature going crazy."

"What does it mean, I wonder."

"I don't think we'll ever know."

"Armageddon? Doomsday? Judgment Day?"

"Sure as shit hope it isn't Judgment Day or I'm in for a hell of a penance," Tommy said.

"We all are, Tommy. You aren't the first person in a marriage breakdown. Hell, look at me. I've been through it and I'm still alive. Nearly killed me, but I'm still alive."

"You are strong, Gabrielle. I'm not so sure that I'm as strong."

"You said yourself your marriage was stale, that it was time to move on."

Tommy lit another cigarette. "In theory, sure . . . but, man, it's an emotional killer. . . ."

"At least you have someone to help you through it," Gabrielle said, kissing him softly on the cheek. "I didn't have anyone. My heart was sealed shut for years."

"I still love her, you know."

"Well, she is the mother of your child. I hope you do."

"She isn't that bad. . . ."

"Tommy . . . no one said anyone was bad. You just grew apart, is all. That's not a crime. It's actually quite normal. We all grow up, and sometimes, we just grow apart. Who we were as kids is not who we are as adults."

"I don't know. It still seems . . . I don't know."

The Birds and the Bees

"You are just tired . . . maybe if we just go lie down for a while."

Gabrielle went to the fridge and got a couple of more beers.

"Follow me," she said as she led him into her bedroom. She sat on the bed and watched him pace around the room, and finally sit down on the edge of the bed.

"Can I smoke in here?" he asked, patting his pockets.

"I guess," she said.

She watched him check his pockets and then remember his smokes were out in the living room. While he retrieved them, she turned the TV on and flipped it to a music station. She lowered the volume as he reentered the room, a lit butt hanging from his mouth.

"You just need to relax," Gabrielle said.

"Yeah . . ."

Gabrielle edged over to where Tommy sat and looped her arms around him, pressing her breasts into his back. She played with his hair, twisting his curls around her fingers.

"You will be happy here, you'll see."

Tommy stared around the room. Gabrielle watched him look, trying to see things as he saw them. She didn't have much, but she treasured what she did have. She also knew that she was a clutter-bug. A few clothes tossed over the chair there, a couple of books cluttering up the dresser, a couple of the kids' dolls and toys left in mid-play, a spare roll of toilet paper that she had meant to take to the bathroom before getting distracted rummaging through the sock/underwear drawer from hell. Guiltily, she realized a few cobwebs hung from the ceiling. She had been so busy vacuuming, she'd forgotten to look up.

"I'm not the cleanest person in the world, but I try."

Tommy laughed. "I'll let you get away with it this time!"

"Well, I'm sort of always this way, so get used to it. I'm not changing my ways now. Hell, I'm pushing forty."

"No, you aren't," Tommy said, slipping an arm around her. "You have a long way before forty."

"Mmm, maybe now I do, but somehow I think time is just going to get away from me and one day I'll wake up, and not only will I be forty, but I'll be forty-one!"

"Then all hell will break loose." Tommy kissed her forehead. "Don't worry."

"I wonder if hell already hasn't broken loose."

Gabrielle kissed Tommy along his back as he finished his cigarette. Once he butted it out, he turned to her and slowly pushed her back. He kissed her repeatedly. Their hands roamed along each other, touching first clothes, and then sliding under to stroke bare flesh. Before long, they lay naked. Kissing. Legs and arms en-

The Birds and the Bees

twined. Gabrielle ran her hands along his back, scraping her nails gently down his spine and squeezing his bottom. Tommy stroked her torso, and she arched up at his touch, murmuring into his hair. She reached between his legs and held his penis in her hands. He was soft, but she stroked him, pulling on him, first slowly and then faster. He grew firmer under her touch, and she grew wetter as she felt him responding to her.

She took his hand and placed it between her legs, and he touched her for a moment, then drew his hand back. She undulated her hips against him, rubbing her aching groin against him, pulling on his cock faster.

At last she felt he was hard enough, and moved herself under him. He slid into her and she sighed, relishing the sensation. He started to pump into her, the first few strokes filling her with pleasure. She arched against him, pulling him into her deeper. She heard him grumble under his breath, and she felt him grow soft again. Her fingers sought him out, danced along his shaft, coaxing him to firmness once more, yet again, the minute he entered her, he lost his erection again.

"Dammit," he said, rolling off her.

"It's okay," she said, trying to touch him. "We can just play."

"No, no. It's just not going to work. I can tell."

"We can try . . . we're just nervous, that's all."

Gabrielle scooted down so that she could take him into her mouth. He moaned a little and put his hands in her hair. She sucked and licked him, stroking him several different ways with her hand. He grew hard for a moment, then lost it again.

"I don't understand," Tommy sighed. "It's never happened before."

Gabrielle kissed her way back up his chest until she reached his lips.

"It's all right. We can try again another time."

She nuzzled her head into his chest, and lay, staring into the darkness. She heard him breathing deeply, and then lightly snore. He was asleep already, while she lay frustrated.

This was not at all how she'd pictured their first night.

Not at all.

She had fallen asleep for a while and had that horrible dream. Now she was more awake than ever. Confused and frustrated, she looked at Tommy for a little while. He slept soundly, so soundly that as she slipped away from the bed, he didn't even move or shift.

She wondered if he ever had nightmares. She wondered if he was even dreaming of her. Did he think he was home? Did he ever lose it for his wife? Was it guilt that had interfered, or was he always this way?

She thought of all the steamy letters and messages. Maybe there had been too much buildup

The Birds and the Bees

and he'd had stage fright. She wasn't sure that was possible. But men were weird. Maybe the buildup had been too much. Maybe he had hoped too hard for a perfect first night too and freaked himself out. Or maybe he really was impotent.

She wandered into the living room and lit a cigarette. She sat naked on the couch, staring into the darkness. Christ, but she was horny. She had waited so impatiently for this night, and now here she was, alone on the couch.

He had felt so good that brief moment inside her. How she wished it had lasted just a little longer. It wouldn't have taken much for her to come. Her hand strayed to her swollen pussy, still wet from earlier anticipation. She played with herself, imagining how he had felt for that brief few minutes. Within seconds, she was filled with a warm shiver, and her mind flashed on how crazy sex was. How animal and instinctual. How you could go without it for so long, yet the minute you thought you might get it, it could make you half crazy. How half crazy she was, out here masturbating in the dark, with a married man that she thought would be her sexual dynamo snoring away in the other room, oblivious to her confusion and frustration.

She would be patient. Everyone had problems now and again. It just had never happened to her before. She lay on the couch, her eyes closed, her fingers tapping at her groin, and as

Sèphera Girón

she dozed off, she heard a bird cawing just outside her window.

Damn birds. They probably saw it all.

She wondered what it felt like to have a bird tapping at her pussy. Her fingers slid inside herself once more. Images of birds, beaks, and feathers flitted through her brain as she moaned into the couch pillow.

Chapter Twelve

John stood in Katey's doorway. She held the door open for a minute, studying him.

He didn't look right.

His eyes were glazed and he swayed in an odd manner. She took his hand, meaning to pull him across the threshold, but dropped it just as quickly. His hand was limp and cold, as if it had been waterlogged in a lake for days. His complexion was a pale, yellowy color, jaundiced. For a moment she wondered if maybe his drinking had finally taken its toll on his body. Yet that didn't seem to be it either.

"John," she said, gingerly taking his hand again. He pushed her aside and walked into the room. He stood swaying, as if the few seconds of energy had used up a whole slew of valuable resources.

He turned to her and spoke in a low, hard voice.

"Shut the door."

His eyes were now oddly huge, dark, seemingly penetrating right through her. She felt a shivery sense of excitement slither up her back.

"Shut the door now, bitch," he said firmly.

"Yes, Master," Katey said, nodding.

She walked over to the door and shut it. As she turned back toward him, he struck her on the face. Falling back with the force of it, she stumbled over the coffee table. Her breath was knocked out of her as she hit the floor. John towered over her, his eyes flashing.

"You will do everything I say," he said. Katey nodded, rubbing her cheek where a handprint was now throbbing to the surface.

"I can't hear you," John barked.

"Yes, Master," Katey said, crawling on her hands and knees toward him. She wrapped her arms around his legs.

"Yes, Master. I am ready and willing to obey your orders, Master," Katey said. She stretched out her tongue and ran it along the filthy line of his boots. John stood, watching her ass bob up down, her tongue swirling along his feet.

"Do that where it's going to do some good," John said, pulling her by the hair so that she was on her knees. He unzipped his pants with

The Birds and the Bees

one hand, clutching Katey by the head in the other. His cock was nearly hard already as his pants fell around his ankles. Katey took his cock into her mouth and started to suck, still hugging his knees. His cock too had that odd cold sensation.

"We have a lot of work to do today . . . a lot of work," John muttered as he pushed her head back and forth. Katey sucked hard and fast, wondering what the hell he was babbling about. Not only was he weirdly cold, he just plain tasted different. She wondered if maybe he had fucked his wife and that was her she was tasting. The thought of it made her warm between her legs, although she felt a twinge of jealousy. She knew, though, that the wifey didn't like to give head much these days, if she ever did at all. Wifey was still wrapped up in the kiddies.

John pulled on her hair so hard that she could feel it ripping from her scalp. Although part of her lamented the loss of her hair, the sensation was deliciously exquisite. Her cunt twitched while he rammed his cock into her mouth hard, pulling another section of hair from her head. She moaned and put a hand between her legs.

"Get your hands up where they belong, bitch," John ordered. A wave of delirium swept through her, the denial making her even more horny. She grabbed his ass as she knew he liked, digging her fingers in hard where his cheeks met.

He grabbed her ears as he fucked her, pulling on them so roughly that she thought they would come right off. Instead, he suddenly bucked so far into her that she swore he was right down her throat.

Hot, thick come poured down her.

She could feel it burning and she gagged, but he did not release his grip on her until the last drop was emptied out.

John staggered back until he flopped onto the couch, snatches of her hair still stuck in his fingers. Katey coughed, the come thick and strangely sweet in her throat.

As her breath returned to her, she felt lightheaded. A pulse throbbed through her, her body was humming. Her guts rumbled as she swallowed and she struggled to stand. John lay back on the couch, breathing heavily, his eyes glazed over again.

Katey coughed again, her body vibrating. She gasped for breath and felt as if something was stuck in her throat. It wiggled around and she fell back to her knees. She crawled over to John.

"Let's go," John said, standing up abruptly. He pulled his pants back up and buckled them. Katey hugged his knees, still coughing.

"Come on, we have things to do," he said, grabbing her hair. Katey stumbled to her feet, and they weaved their way out to his truck.

"Get in," he said, and no sooner had Katey

The Birds and the Bees

slammed the door than he gunned the engine and tore out of the driveway.

The tickle was odd in her throat, but there was nothing she could do but fumble under the seat and see if there was any booze to burn it away. She managed to dislodge several beer cans. A last she found a bottle with a bit of beer left in it. She held it up, trying to see how old and foul it might be. She coughed again. John didn't seem to give a shit that she was hacking her lungs out. He was driving fast, his face frozen, his eyes unblinking, as they careened to wherever it might be that they were going.

Katey unscrewed the bottle and drained the bitter contents. It was a foul thing, she had no idea what she was drinking. She coughed even more as the booze burned her throat. However, now as she coughed, whatever it was seemed to be growing looser. She leaned over her knees, feeling as though her ribs or her lungs might crack with every gasp of air she drew in between hacking fits.

One last cough sent the blockage into her lap with a splat. She stared in disbelief, gagging down her urge to puke.

It was a big sticky ball of something more than come. It was slimy and disgusting and worse than that, there were bees stuck in it.

Bees.

What the hell were bees doing in her throat?

Sèphera Girón

She nearly heaved again, and looked over at John.

He did not look well at all.

"Where are we going, honey?" she asked, scraping up the wad of grossness and flinging it out the window.

"Never you mind," he growled.

The truck swerved and rattled.

"Can we stop and get a drink? I just coughed up something foul."

Her stomach roiled.

"We aren't stopping." He reached over and grabbed the back of her head again. His touch instantly calmed her. He pulled her down.

"Suck my dick while I drive," he ordered. She fumbled with his zipper.

"But . . . I just . . ."

"Now, bitch!"

Katey obliged, now curious at how in the hell he could even get it up again.

The truck careened around corners, flying across potholes, thumping and scraping along dirt roads. Katey kept her head in his lap, knowing that he wasn't even feeling her, and she was just fine with that. He was on a mission, and she didn't know what it was, but she did know that he wasn't going to stop until he got there.

Katey thought about the lumpy thing that had been in her throat. What the hell had it been? Obviously it had been come, but how did the bees get into it?

The Birds and the Bees

The truck suddenly lurched to a halt. John flung open the door and would have stood up, except that Katey was still lying across his lap.

"Get up, bitch," he said, pushing her so hard she smashed her cheek against the window.

Katey staggered out of the car, watching John loping up a hill. She followed him, only stopping to spit out more of the foul aftertaste.

John reached the mouth of a cave, and after a moment's hesitation, entered it.

"Where are you going?" Katey asked as she ran after John into the cave. At last she caught up to him, and she clung to his cold clammy hand.

They walked in the dark through damp curves, more then once hitting a cold stone wall as they blindly followed the path. There was a faint noise. Katey couldn't place what it was until they got closer. Soon the sound filled her ears, filling her heart with terror. She knew that sound. Anyone would. It was the sound of hundreds of bees.

"John . . . we have to turn back," she cried, tugging on his arm.

"No," he said, finding her neck and gripping her hard. He pushed her in front of him.

"Don't make me go first," she sobbed. "Please, don't make me go first . . . I'm afraid of bees."

John grunted, his grip on her neck iron tight, a fist full of her hair in his hand.

The humming was louder still as the air grew

thicker. Katey gasped, trying not to cry in case a lone bee sought her out.

At last, they rounded one final corner.

Katey couldn't believe her eyes. The vision was indescribable.

There was a dim light, the glow of many candles mounted into the cave walls. Hundreds of bees were flying around, hanging in the air, an ebb and flow from one faraway wall.

Even in the dull light, Katey could see the entire side of the cavern was a nest. A bee hive. Lots of bee hives. A giant lump of honeycomb, swelling out from the wall, pregnant with thousands of humming bees.

"What is this place?" Katey asked. She instinctively scratched at her arms as she stared around. The bees hadn't noticed them yet, or if they did, they simply didn't care. There was work to be done, and they weren't going to stop their production chain because of visitors.

"John?" Katey tried to see John's face, tried to see what kind of expression he had. He was staring up at the giant hive, his eyes glowing, his mouth hanging open in some kind of half-dazed half grin.

"John?"

As if the spell were broken, John turned his eyes from the hive and looked at Katey.

"Be quiet. I am listening to my orders."

"What?"

"I have orders. I must obey," he said.

The Birds and the Bees

"Orders from who? You have an earpiece on?" she asked.

"I don't need an earpiece. I can hear what she tells me."

"Who, your wife?"

"No, the queen. All hail the queen." John dropped to his knees.

"Queen? In here? Are you nuts?" she asked. Then, thinking he might be switching from dominant to submissive, she grinned.

"Humble servant, you may rise," Katey said, sweeping her arms gracefully.

"Shhh . . . don't piss her off, man," John said, his face hidden on the ground.

"Piss *who* off?" Katey asked again impatiently.

"ME!"

The voice behind Katey echoed strangely, as if its owner was speaking through a filter. Upon turning, Katey had to refrain from screaming. Before her stood a sight that made her stomach lurch and her knees weak. She thought she might faint, and she wobbled, her fingers rubbing her temples.

The vision approached her, and it took Katey every fiber of her being not to run like crazy. The only thing that stopped her was all the bees. She knew, even before the news reports, that running away from a swarm of bees did no good.

This was more then a swarm in front of her,

though. This was a *person*, a woman apparently, covered head to toe with the quivering bodies of buzzing bees.

"Honor your Queen, Katey," the Queen commanded, raising her hand.

"How do I know you are my Queen?" Katey asked, hating herself even as the words slipped out. Who was she to backtalk to this freak?

"You know I am, Katey . . . You *know* I am," the woman behind the bees said almost urgently. Dark eyes peered out from behind her mask of bees.

Katey stood there, watching, as the woman raised her arms. The bees lifted off as easily as a cloak might have been whisked off a queen by her handmaidens. Naked, without her bees, a plumpish woman, a very pale plump woman, stood before Katey.

The woman's face was not pretty, even in the flattering darkness. She looked red-faced, splotchy even. Probably the result of so many bees dancing on her flesh. Her face not only was red and splotchy, it looked hard. Like she had done a lot of hard living before she had come to this cave.

The rest of her body was lumpy. Her stomach sagged, her thighs were huge, her ass was dimpled and layered. Her arms waddled when she moved them, as she did now.

"Katey . . ." The woman reached her hands toward Katey's face. Katey's heart was slam-

The Birds and the Bees

ming crazily against her chest, but what was she going to do if some whacked-out woman wanted to touch her face in a cave.

"Katey, don't be afraid. I called you here for a reason."

"I'm not afraid. Afraid of *what*? You?"

The lady laughed and clapped her hands.

"I like you, Katey. You are so damn spunky, yet so eager to please as well," The woman ran her hand along Katey's face. Katey relished the firm, yet gentle stroke. The woman caressed Katey's cheekbones and jawline. She ran her fingers along Katey's neck.

"Beautiful Katey . . . I know you will be happy to be part of this."

"Of what? I have to know what is what before I can make any promises."

"Let me show you, Katey."

The woman put her face close to Katey's, so close that Katey thought for sure she was going to kiss her, but she didn't. Instead she grabbed Katey by the hair, pulling her head back. Katey's breath hitched slightly.

"Oh . . . you like that?" the woman said. "You like it when someone pulls your hair like that?"

The woman slapped her with her other hand and turned away.

"You will only get pleasure when you please the Queen. Serve the Queen and you won't be sorry."

The Queen stood in front of Katey, her

breasts and tummy sagging. Katey stared at the large pendulous breasts, and reached for one.

"On your knees before you touch the Queen," the Queen ordered. Katey dropped to her knees. She reached up to touch the Queen's nipples.

"That's right, Katey. Please the Queen," the Queen sighed. Katey played with her nipples for a long time, turning them, tweaking them, taking them into her mouth and sucking loud and long on them. Every now and again she would look over to John, but he still remained on his knees, his face to the floor.

The Queen threw her head back and spread her legs. She grabbed Katie's hair and forced her between her legs. Katey was reluctant. This woman was strange and pungent. Yet as she buried her face into the woman's pussy, she was pleasantly surprised at the honey flavor and syrupy texture of her juices. Katey licked and suckled the Queen, enjoying the Queen's pleasurable movement almost as much as she was enjoying the endless streams of honey pouring from her hole. All women should taste so good, she decided.

The Queen bucked against Katie's face, pulling her hair and moaning deep in the back of her throat. Katey sucked faster, harder, twiddling and pinching nipples, slipping her finger up the Queen.

The Queen cried out, shuddering, as Katey felt her spasming, more honey flowing from

The Birds and the Bees

her, squirting from her, as if she were some kind of fountain. Honey trickled from her pussy and her nipples, so much so that Katey thought she would drown in it.

At last, the Queen was spent, and released her grip on Katey. Katey sank to the floor, her mouth and neck exhausted.

"Remove your clothes," the Queen commanded. The Queen was rubbing herself now, moving the honey along her own body in syrupy streams. She went over to a chair and sat in it, her legs spread, her fingers toying with herself.

"I want to see you," the Queen said. Katey started to protest, but then the Queen picked up a giant spear that had been lying beside her. John crawled over to the Queen, and sat at her feet, pulling a knife from his boot.

"I don't know you," Katey said.

"You will do as I command," the Queen said. "And don't worry, you will enjoy it as much as I do."

Katey slowly pulled off her own clothes. It was cold in this cave. Her nipples were hard, and she was amazed at just how wet she was when she pulled off her panties.

"Stand before me, so that I may be certain," the Queen mused. "Not a bad specimen, John. Not bad indeed, although I thought you were bringing someone a bit different."

"No, I thought this was the better bet. She has a submissive streak."

"Yes, I can see that," the Queen said with a lusty smile. She stood up, the wooden spear still in her hand.

"Tell me, young Katey . . . how do you like your life?"

"I don't know what you mean, my Queen."

"Are you bored? Are you ready for a change? Would you like to pay back all those assholes that ever did you wrong?"

Katey laughed cynically.

"Who wouldn't . . . man, payback time would fucking rock."

"Then you are in the right place, young lady. Come closer to me so that I may initiate you into my kingdom."

Chapter Thirteen

"So this is one of your hotshot parties," Tommy said, looking around the room. Gabrielle nodded. She had managed to convince Tommy to shower and put on fresh clothes finally. She sipped her drink, wondering how odd it was to drag someone who supposedly wanted to better his music career to a party that was a veritable who's who of players. It had been close to a nightmare, getting Tommy to get up and get dressed. She was shocked at his reluctance even though that was supposedly the whole reason he had come here. She chalked it up to nerves. Much like their sexual encounter. He must have just been tired and stressed out. Maybe he still was. Everyone reacted to stress differently, and he was a sensitive musician.

Still, she thought, it was weird that such a young man actually didn't want sex with the person he had supposedly so desired. She had tried to entice him again in the shower, but he had brushed her away. Now she stood here at this party, more frustrated than she had ever been before, wondering if she would ever get him "in the mood."

Gabrielle spied a producer and dragged Tommy toward him.

"Mr. Whitefield, I want to introduce you to a wonderful guitarist. He writes his own music." Gabrielle gushed on about Tommy, and the proper introductions were made. Gabrielle watched as Tommy schmoozed with ease with the producer. The conversation ended with the producer asking Tommy to send him a tape and slipping him a business card.

"See how easy it is when you have an in?" Gabrielle nudged.

Tommy sighed, staring at the card. "It's so corrupt, it makes me sick. How did music become such a commercial thing?"

"Music has always been commercial. It's just this is how it's done nowadays. Back in the old times, the musicians lived in the castles at the expense of the king, until he grew bored of them. Or they had benefactors. It's the same thing."

"Music is in the bones. It shouldn't be bought and sold like stocks." Tommy's face was flushed

The Birds and the Bees

and he finished another drink. He went over to the bar, and Gabrielle followed.

"Well, you are having a golden opportunity here, so just enjoy it."

"Right." Tommy threw back another scotch and looked around the room.

"You need to mellow out," Gabrielle said, touching his arm.

"Oh, I do, do I?" Tommy sneered. He looked at her and saw the concern in her face. His anger seemed to dissipate.

"You must think I'm some ungrateful hick," he said.

"No, I don't think that at all. I don't think anything except that you are obviously really fucked up right now. However, don't fuck things up because you feel out of place."

Tommy touched Gabrielle's cheek.

"I'm sorry," he said.

"Just chill out. No one likes these parties, but that's how things get done."

There was a loud crashing as a window imploded inward. People screamed and ran as dozens of black birds swarmed through the window like cockroaches emptying from a nest. The birds screeched and soared, flying into people, into their faces, into the food. They tore at people's faces, at their clothes. The floor was slick with blood as Tommy grabbed Gabrielle's hand and pulled her toward the door. Gabrielle's legs were frozen with fear as the nightmare scene unfolded.

She willed her legs to move, to follow Tommy. The scene was incredible. More birds flooded the room, until there was just the steady sound of screeching and flapping. Feathers flew, blood ran, as the birds viciously attacked.

Gabrielle found the strength to run, and adrenaline flowed through her. She followed Tommy out the door and into the street. Birds were everywhere, swarming the streets. Gabrielle and Tommy ran with their hands over their heads to ward off the attacking birds. They jumped over people who had already fallen in the streets. They ran through the maze of the downtown core and out toward the suburbs. The birds seemed to be heading into the downtown area, and the further away they got, the fewer birds there were. The streets were pandemonium as people flailed around in chaos.

Gabrielle led Tommy back toward her place, and they were able to get to her car. They climbed inside, birds beating against the windows. She fumbled with the keys, and at last the car turned over. It was hard going, getting out of the city, but at last they managed to make it to the outskirts. Gabrielle found a field and parked in it.

They sat, staring out into the darkness, smoking in fearful silence, watching the sky.

Tommy dozed off first.

The Birds and the Bees

As the morning sun beamed into the window, Gabrielle jerked awake. Her neck and shoulders were in agony. Slowly she opened her eyes and remembered where she was. In the car. She and Tommy were in the car, escaping a siege of birds.

Gabrielle turned toward Tommy. He wasn't there. His door was open and he wasn't there.

She looked out at the field, wondering if maybe he'd just gone to the bathroom. She waited a few minutes for him to come back, but he didn't.

Her heart beat wildly in her chest as she searched the sky. There were no birds around here. Of course. They were probably all in the city still. How she hoped they were gone.

Gabrielle cautiously opened her door and checked the ground as she stepped out. God knows, snakes might be next to go on a rampage. Fortunately, there seemed to be nothing on the ground.

She was afraid to call out his name, to draw attention to herself just in case there was something out there. The morning sun was already melting the dew from the grass. She stared at the meadow, and saw a trail of flattened grass. It wound its way across the field and toward the rolling hills. The tracks must be Tommy's. Tommy's or some creature's. She locked up the car and took her keys and purse. Her head pounded for want of a coffee, but there was no coffee to be had. She followed the tracks and discovered a cigarette butt. It was Tommy's. Satisfied, she continued on, very carefully and quietly, looking up continuously just in case there were more birds to come.

She came to the edge of the field, and now the trail was harder to follow. There wasn't as much grass, and so she had to really rely on instinct and random things she had learned from nature shows. Look for broken branches, trodden soil, ashes from cigarettes, a sneaker mark . . .

Why had he left her?

Now that her sleepy daze was wearing off, she started to get pissed off. What on earth had possessed him to take this little walk without waking her? Was he running away from her? And if so, where was he going?

The trail seemed to be dead now, and she was exhausted. She was hungry too, and in need of food and more importantly, coffee.

She stared up at the sky. What the hell was going on?

It was a nightmare. How on earth could birds burst into a party and take it over? What the hell was that all about?

She walked around the foot of the first hill a little longer, but now the trail was cold. Gone. He could have gone anywhere, anywhere for miles. He could have climbed any one of these hills, or wandered off to the park on the other side, or toward the creek, or through more end-

The Birds and the Bees

less fields. Wherever he had gone, he was not here and, she assumed, didn't want her to find him.

How she yearned to call out for him, but she was too afraid to call the birds. She knew they were there, somewhere. Could feel their presence more than she could feel Tommy. She wondered where they were watching her from.

It was creeping her out, and she decided to get back to the car. Back to the car and go home. She would get coffee and eat and see if he called her from anywhere. If she didn't hear from him by noon, she would come back and look for him.

The roads were deserted. Now Gabrielle knew what it must look like in those war-torn Third World countries. Garbage was strewn along the streets, windows were broken, there were piles of bloody rags every few feet. Now and again, there was a body, torn beyond recognition.

For the whole drive the radio announcer had tried to make sense of what was going on, but there was no explanation. What had started as random attacks by birds had turned into full-fledged chaos the night before. Speculations were numerous and bordering on the bizarre. The alignment of the planets, the greenhouse effect, pollution, migratory patterns gone awry, some kind of terrorist plan, mad scientists, the end of the world. It was all bizarre. It was all crazy. None of the theories made sense. How could anyone explain killer birds?

Gabrielle parked the car and scanned the skies. They were empty.

Silence.

Devoid of anything.

She ran from the car into her building.

Once inside her apartment, she slammed the door shut and locked it. Moving around as if in a dream, she checked her machine. Frantic messages from friends echoed back at her, but not a word from Tommy. She went to her computer and checked her e-mail. Strangely enough, among the endless lists and panicked messages, she found a note, with the heading FOR TOMMY.

The return sender was nobody she knew.

On impulse, she clicked it open.

Her body felt like it was filled with ice.

The e-mail was from his wife.

Dear Tommy

I understand why you had to go away for a while. You do whatever it takes to further your career. If that means staying with that woman you told me about, then I'll accept it. If you have to fuck your way to the big time, then that's what you have to. After all, you won't be the first, nor the last. In the meantime, remember that I am keeping your bed warm for you.

Love, Sheila

The Birds and the Bees

Gabrielle stared at the e-mail. There was an attachment with it. She opened it up and there was a j-peg of a naked woman, large breasts bared, her shaved cunt open for all to see. Gabrielle shook her head. As Gabrielle stared at the photo, trying to understand it, another e-mail pinged into her in box. It was another note for Tommy from the same address. She opened this one.

Dearest,
I am doing the best I can from my end to get money so we can get your dream off the ground. Between you fucking that reporter and me fucking the world, we are sure to go far. Here is the url for my new idea.
Love, Sheila

Gabrielle clicked on the url, and a whole Web page of the same naked woman popped up. The photos were grainy and amateurish, but the model had no shame. Obviously she had taken them on a digital camera and posted them on the Web. Gabrielle shook her head in amazement at the naive stupidity of such a feat. There was a message at the bottom of the screen.

"If you like what you see, you can join my club. Click here to find out how."

It was amazing. She wondered what Tommy would think of his wife, spread-eagled on the Net for the world to see. Ramming cucumbers up her twat, pulling her ass cheeks open. Gabrielle felt nauseous. In the meantime, she clicked back to the first message and reread both of them. Was it true? Was Tommy here because he was using Gabrielle to get ahead? She couldn't believe it.

Gabrielle started to shake. Tears welled up in her eyes as she tried to wrap her head around it. So he hadn't come to her for good. He had only come to Gabrielle to use her. He had no intention of staying. Or so these letters seemed to indicate.

Then again, the letters had been sent to *her*. Not to Tommy. Maybe the letters were just a scheme to piss her off so that she would throw Tommy out.

God, what a mess.

She should have known better.

The first tear fell, and with it came an avalanche of emotion. Anger and frustration, horror and fear all crashed and circled around her. What was she going to do? Tommy was missing. There was a plague of birds out there. Should she even bother looking for him? Had he just wandered off, or had he been led off? Was he really using her?

Yes, he had acted strange, but who knows how someone is supposed to act when he's just walked away from his wife. She remembered how fucked up her own breakup had been. The

The Birds and the Bees

vacillation, the roller coaster of emotions. The worry about the children.

The biggest fear of all, being alone.

And here she was, years later, still alone.

Alone.

Alone.

She heard a noise.

That noise.

That noise that filled her with all consuming dread. They were back. Sitting on her balcony rail. Flapping as they came back, landing and staring at her.

"What the hell do you want?" she cried out, bracing herself for them to smash through her window as they had at the party.

But they did not move.

They sat and stared.

Unblinking.

More of them came, still staring.

She wasn't alone.

She had the birds.

Tommy had heard a noise.

No, heard wasn't quite the word.

Felt.

A vibration was tingling through him, quivering hard enough that it had woken him from his uneasy sleep. He had sat up, startled, as the dawn broke over the horizon.

What a nightmare the night before had been. It couldn't have been real. There was no damn way. Yet here he was, in a car in the country.

The Birds and the Bees

own private hell deep within their bones. Katey would latch onto the bubble of pain, would prick it with her mind, would feel it wash across her. While the pain burst forth, her victim would stare at her, but only for a moment. Then the bees would leave her side and swarm the new host. If the victim was open to receiving the message of the bees, they would not die.

Instead, they would walk the path that she walked, finding their own special way to serve the Queen.

Katey existed now as a mass of quivering energy. All she wanted was to exist to serve her Queen.

There was no past. There was no future. There was just now. This moment. This moment of being, in which she passed along the message to those that could receive it.

The streets were filled with carnage. People ran and screamed, crazy with the mayhem. Bodies lay, in alleys, in doorways. The rags of beggars who would beg no more. Katey breathed it in. The blood of the fallen.

In the dream, she was climbing. Up along rocks and dirt, clumps of weeds tumbling under her touch. A sense of urgency consumed her. Her stomach filled with an ache, a sensation that she was going to be too late. Her fingernails ripped as she clawed at rocks, frantically kicking her feet to propel herself higher, faster, but she was still not moving as fast as she needed to be. The rocks felt like bubbles, the air like molasses. She feared she would arrive too late. The higher she climbed, the thicker the air became, cloying in her lungs. Gulping in more air, she found that if she kept her pace steady and sure, she made better time.

Higher and higher she climbed. The sense of urgency grew stronger. At last, she reached the top. On top of the highest rock, on top of the highest hill, there it was.

A nest.

The nest.

She climbed up the side of the nest. Inside, lay two sleeping forms. Children. Her children. Maternal love rushed through her and she reached out to touch them. Tears fell down her face. How she missed her children. Her heart ached as she crawled into the nest to stroke their backs.

The sky suddenly grew dark. Gabrielle looked up in time to see a giant feathered body appear before her. She reached for her children, but they had disappeared. In a panic she searched the nest, but there was no sign of them.

The bird screeched and she woke up.

Gabrielle had cried herself to sleep, but it didn't last long. She burst awake, angry and confused. This was not over. She was not going to give up this easily. There was a feeling in her stomach

The Birds and the Bees

that told her that Tommy hadn't gone anywhere. That he was still near the hillside somewhere.

Where would he have gone? Maybe he was just lost. Maybe he had gone to take a leak somewhere and wandered too far and she had driven off prematurely.

Her mind was a hazy mishmash. She knew she didn't make sense. She knew that she should be pissed off for thinking that he had left his wife for her, when the letters probably made more sense than anything at all that had happened lately. After all, there was no such thing as love at first sight. No such thing as jumping into a new relationship to find bliss and happily ever after.

It didn't happen. Not to her, for sure, and not to anyone she knew.

Everyone had an agenda. Admitted or not, everyone had their shit. It was like that song from *Evita* about love affairs and how everyone uses everyone for something.

He wanted to use her to get ahead. Maybe to piss off his wife. Maybe to better his existence.

And what had she wanted? Really wanted?

She wanted to wrap up his music in a bow and carry it around in her heart forever.

She laughed at the idea. Sure, his music was marvelous as well as his execution. But it was more than that.

She wanted more than a good song.

She wanted someone she could count on.

Someone who would hold her hand and say she was doing okay. Someone who would fuck her stupid as she fell asleep, and who would hold her when the nightmares came.

Someone she could look across the room at and think, "Wow, he has amazingly green eyes and he's all mine."

Was that so wrong?

Probably.

Then again, in all tragic tales, there was nothing so easy as love at first sight and happily ever after. There was always a hurdle to jump. A villain to fight. Love to be proven.

She smiled. Maybe she was going crazy. Or maybe this was a test. This might be the big test of what she was willing to go through to win the prize.

No matter what the consequences, she had to go back. She felt the humming in her gut strengthen as if in agreement. She had to go back to the hill and look for him.

Birds or no birds.

She drank a cup of coffee and threw together a sandwich. Then she tossed some fruit bars and a couple of cans of pop into her purse. She also took a flashlight, a knife, string, and a few other things. She had no idea why she was bringing them, but they couldn't hurt.

Once she got to the lobby, she realized her heart was slamming so hard in her chest that

The Birds and the Bees

she was forgetting to breathe. As she gulped in air, she realized that she felt truly alive. For the first time in ages, she wasn't walking mindlessly toward work or yet another party or club. She was going to find the man she loved, or thought she loved, or wanted to love.

She peered out the door of the lobby and didn't see the birds. She hoped that they still were huddled on her balcony.

The coast was clear, and she darted out to her car and slammed the door. As she started it up, the announcer was still babbling on in disbelief about the carnage the night before and how today, there was not a bird in sight.

Try my balcony, Gabrielle thought.

She didn't want to even look to see if the birds knew she had left. All she knew was that she had to get back to that field and see what happened to Tommy.

For better or for worse.

Till death did them part.

There were lots of cars on the road now, and people walked along the sidewalks, cautiously looking around. How quickly the city resumed its activities when the danger seemed past. She didn't think it was over at all. Not by a long shot.

And sure enough, the announcer was growing hysterical over another attack somewhere on the other side of the city. There was talk of calling in the Army. What good the Army would do against a plague of savage birds remained to be seen, except that, of course, they had lots of guns and bombs.

Wouldn't that be lovely?

Gabrielle could envision more carnage, death by bird and stray bullets. Buildings destroyed as machine gun fire hurtled into the air. But that wasn't her problem. Her problem now was finding Tommy.

She arrived back at the field, and drove along until she reached the hilly area where she had stopped before. There were trees, oddly devoid of birds. Bushes and long wild grass dotted the landscape. Even this daybreak felt odd. It was still quiet. Still untouched. She scanned the field, the trees, stared at the hills, but there was still no sign of Tommy.

She parked the car and got out, grabbing her supplies. Sweat was dripping from her brow, her shirt was already wet. She wiped her arm across her face, and briefly wondered what the hell she was doing.

But what else could she do?

Stay at home, watching TV reports on the latest wave of disaster? Wondering endlessly whatever became of Tommy? Watching for e-mail from Sheila?

Sheila.

She thought back to the naked pictures.

What the hell was that all about? Did she really think grainy photos of a gawky gap-toothed woman with sagging tummy and sagging

The Birds and the Bees

breasts was going to make her millions in Internet porn? Sure, there were a few people in the world that would look at anything, but the trend was, as it was everywhere, toward plastic perfection.

No one wanted real anymore. Not real music. Not real bodies. Age lines and stretch marks were to be hidden shamefully. Got a flabby gut? Get an electronic gadget for that washboard effect. Don't like lines around your eyes? Get a chemical peel. Laser surgery. Breasts too big? Chop them off. Breasts too small? Stuff balloons through your belly button.

It was no wonder women were fucked up. Body image alone was a nightmare. Their role in the world was even worse.

She was a mother who gave up her children. Sheila was a mother who had her child. She couldn't fault her that.

Sheila was dependent on Tommy because she had spent years raising that baby. That was her sole job, raising the baby and taking care of Tommy. And now, here was Gabrielle, ready to whisk Tommy away. Ready to take care of him financially as well as emotionally.

It must be a bit shocking for him. Maybe he had left the car to go for a walk to think it all over. Maybe he'd be just over a hill, lying in the sun with a piece of grass in his mouth, musing over what to do about the women in his life.

As she wandered along, her gut grew uneasy.

Sèphera Girón

Tommy was not waiting for her anywhere in a field. He didn't even know she had left or come back. He had not just gone on a walk to think.

There was something going on. She didn't know what it was or even how to prepare for it, but there was something going on.

Her body trembled. She could sense she was going in the right direction. At this point, she gave up all logical thinking and went with the urgency in her blood.

Approaching another hill, she heard something. She stopped.

It sounded like crying. Carefully and cautiously, she picked her way towards the sound.

At last, she came upon a strange sight. There were two little children sitting in the weeds, sobbing.

"What is wrong? Where is your mommy?" she asked them. They stopped crying and stared up at her with wide frightened eyes. They were filthy, and had obviously been roaming the hillside for a very long time.

"We lost our mommy," the little girl wailed. "She went inside and never came out."

"Inside?"

"Over there . . . she went over there and we're too scared . . ." The little boy cried.

Gabrielle knelt down to them, and they wrapped their little arms around her, sobbing all over again.

"How long has she been gone?"

The Birds and the Bees

"A long time," the girl said woefully.

"I'm so hungry," the boy cried.

Gabrielle rummaged through her purse and took out the fruit bars and juice. She opened them up for the children, who devoured them like animals.

"I'm so scared. I hope she didn't go away like Nigel did," the boy said.

"Nigel didn't go away . . . he's been watching us!" the little girl said indignantly.

"Nigel went away . . . he never came back."

"Who's Nigel?" Gabrielle asked.

"He's our brother who turned into an angel. He comes and talks to Mommy. He said Mommy is in trouble and we don't know what to do."

"Why don't you take me to where you lost your mommy?" Gabrielle said.

They stood up, and the children took her hand. They picked their way along the rocks, going higher into the hillside, until they came to the mouth of a cave.

"What are your names?" she asked them.

"I'm Deedee and this is Jimmy."

"Hi, Deedee and Jimmy. I'm Gabrielle."

"Gabrielle. What a weird name," Deedee said.

"I guess it is. But it's what my mother named me."

Gabrielle stood looking at the cave.

"Why did your mother go in there?"

"She was looking for the bees. They are everywhere, and she wanted to stop them before they got us again."

"Mommy said that if she could find the big nest, where the queen bee was, that she could make the bees go away and never hurt us again."

Gabrielle stared at the children. "Why did she bring you with her if she was doing something so dangerous? You know the bees are dangerous."

"She couldn't leave us alone. Eric went to school, and she couldn't leave us while she looked for the bees."

"What about your daddy? Do you have a daddy?"

"Daddy works all the time. He won't help Mommy with the bees. He laughs at her."

"Oh."

"The bees kept coming to our house, and they would crawl all over us. Mommy just wanted them gone. And now, Mommy's the one who's gone." Deedee's lip trembled. Gabrielle brushed the little girl's hair back from her face.

"I guess we have to go in if we want to find your mommy. And we'll all have to stay together this time."

Gabrielle watched as a few bees flew into the cave, flying slowly, heavy with pollen. Other bees, flying quicker, left the cave and soared out into the world.

Gabrielle's stomach heaved. She hated bees.

The Birds and the Bees

She hated the thought of the bees. And worst of all, she knew they were the killer bees. If they decided to attack, there would be nothing to do but let them.

Chapter Fourteen

Abraham stood behind the bakery, readying the large plastic bags of bread for the waiting birds. The sun was beaming down on him, making his dark skin glisten. He relished the warmth, but instinctively could sense a cool current underneath. The change of seasons that he had heard about.

One day soon, he would see snow. He would finally be able to walk in snow. Touch snow. Taste snow.

In the meantime, he surveyed the birds. Echoes of the news from TV and radio rattled around his head. He clicked his tongue.

"You birds disappoint me. I feed you every day, yet still you are not happy. What is it you are looking for?"

Sèphera Girón

The birds sat and stared, dotting the fences, standing on the ground, perching along the dumpsters. They warily watched and waited for Abraham to continue the morning ritual.

Abraham thought more about the coming winter. Birds migrated south for winter. That much he had learned on the Discovery Channel. But he also had learned that if you fed the birds, many did not leave. Some species were able to stand the cold and didn't migrate. He wondered about this immense number of black birds.

Were they hanging-around birds, or migrating birds? After the past few days, he knew they were carnivorous birds. Yet that didn't bother him.

He fiddled with the bags some more. A sensation rippled through him, giving him goose bumps.

Something didn't feel right to Abraham. It had nothing to do with the carnage of the night before. If there was one thing Abraham understood, it was random carnage. Or at least, what appeared to be random. There was always a deeper plan. There was always a pattern. A warning and a completion. It was just a matter of unraveling and interpreting it. The birds weren't after him. He fed him. They were part of him.

Again the rippling along his arms.

There was something disturbing.

Something beyond the carnivorous attacks

The Birds and the Bees

that had plagued the news. He had pretty much accepted the fact these birds were involved. Of course this particular flock was part of the swarm. He looked at them. At their war wounds. Some of them had gaps where feathers were missing and flesh showed through the black. Some of them still had spatters of blood. Bits of cloth stuck to their claws. Threads hanging from their beaks. More than one was missing an eye. More than one had lost a foot or a wing, and hopped along precariously but still with purpose.

Why did he feel like there was some sort of war being waged?

Why did he feel like there was no free land?

No land where there was no war?

Even in this so-called free land, there were rules. There were classes. There was that so-called glass ceiling that people like Abraham might hit and never get past. Even in the short time he had been here, he had started to realize that he might work his fingers to the bone, follow all the rules, and still might never get ahead.

Abraham dragged the bags and rustled around in them. This job was a good job. He was fed. He liked the people. He was grateful to be here. Whenever he felt despair or depression, he just thought back to the time when he was crawling through cracking dirt and jagged rocks, dying for water, watching for snakes, seeing a friend torn limb from limb, shuddering and spurting, screaming for help where there was no help but helplessness.

The birds watched and waited. A couple of them clicked and clacked in the back of their throats. There was something there. Something trembling just beneath the surface.

He wasn't sure why, but Abraham walked over to the first dumpster. There was a very strong sensation here. A scent. Something different. Not a derelict, not a wino, not an animal. Something different that was supposed to be here, for some reason.

Someone was here.

Abraham dropped the bags of bread and crept around the back of the dumpster. One of the birds cawed. It was not a warning cry. It was just like an "ahem" or a "check it out" kind of call.

"What is it?" Abraham asked the bird. It hopped off the fence and flew down to Abraham's shoulder. It chittered excitedly to Abraham.

"I don't know what you are saying," Abraham said, although he was only half right. In a very odd sort of way, he *did* know what the bird was saying to him. A wave of knowledge soared through him. He *knew*.

There is someone here. Someone who is supposed to be here. Someone who will change your life . . .

Abraham grinned. It was nonsense. Or at

The Birds and the Bees

least, the message was no doubt far from what he hoped it meant. The message would be interpreted at best as: "There is someone lurking behind you, watch out!"

The bird hopped from foot to foot as it perched on Abraham's shoulder. It spread its wings and shook and then picked at itself, muttering and chirping.

Abraham saw the bird was not alarmed at all, so maybe there was no harm here. He continued his way toward the dumpster. Behind it, the shadow of a person peeked out.

It was a girl. A skinny white girl, with wide frightened eyes.

"Don't hurt me!" she said, raising her hands.

"Don't hurt you? Why would I hurt you?" Abraham asked.

The girl huddled even further into a pile of rags and debris. The smell invaded Abraham's nostrils as her movement created a new waft of the pervasive stench that was chronic to this alley.

"Come on out of there. That's no place for a girl." Abraham reached his hand out toward her. The girl trembled and shook and refused to take it.

"How do I know . . . ?"

"What I want?" Abraham laughed. He spun around, holding his apron.

"I work here. I'm a baker. Why would I bother anyone where I work?"

The girl looked at him, at the whiteness of his uniform and the open back door of the bakery where so many delicious smells were wafting out.

"So, am I now in trouble for trespassing on your bakery property?"

Abraham laughed again and took her hand.

"This is not my property. I don't even know if the boss owns this property, really, if you want to get—how do you say it? Technical about such things?"

"That bakery sure smells good," the girl said, climbing out from behind the dumpster. She shook her knapsack, and bits of paper and a stuck piece of rotting something fell off it.

"Are you homeless?" Abraham asked. The bird on his shoulder shook its head and squawked.

"I did have a home. I'm looking for a new home. I guess I'm between homes." The girl said, kicking at the ground awkwardly.

Abraham nodded his head knowingly.

"Did the intruders come and burn down your house? Did they kill your parents?"

The girl looked in amazement at Abraham. "No."

"So your father beat you? You shamed the family?"

"No."

"You run away because they cannot feed you. You feel guilty they work so hard and can only

The Birds and the Bees

feed you while they themselves starve from the toil."

The girl shook her head again. Her face was growing red. "None of that."

"Then why did you run away?"

The girl stared off into space for a moment. When she looked back, her face was even more flushed. Abraham wondered if her face could explode, getting so red like that.

"You wouldn't believe it if I told you."

The bird screamed and fluttered and rose up from Abraham. It flew over to the fence and settled back in among the others. Several birds twittered and chirped at each other, as if discussing something.

"How about you have a seat right there." Abraham pointed to the rickety fire-escape stairs that were bolted into the bakery wall. "I'd better give these things their grub before all hell breaks loose."

Abraham tore open the large plastic bag of used bread. Upon seeing the action, the birds rose up in a mighty wave, with screeching and cawing. They hung in mid-flight, watching as Abraham reached into the bags and took out the bread. Many of them were already on the ground, scouting out lost crumbs. As the loaves were tossed to the birds, more and more of them arrived from the skies, descending on the back end of the bakery like a plague of locusts.

The girl watched warily. At one point she

stood, clutching the railing, looking as though she were readying to dart away. Abraham put his hand on her arm to calm her.

"Don't worry. The birds know the hand that feeds them. They will not turn on us."

"How do we know for sure they won't?"

"I know that I have been feeding them since I came here. They wait for me in the morning, they watch me leaving at night. They know I am the hunter, the provider, and it is easier for them that way. They would not hurt the provider unless there was a very good reason."

"Really?" The girl narrowed her eyes as she looked at the birds. "The birds would not hurt the provider?"

"Not for no reason. If they decided there was a threat, yes, they would. But there is no threat here."

The girl nodded. "Do you think it is possible to control them?"

Abraham watched the birds ravaging the bread. "Control them? You mean, commanding the flock?"

"Yes."

"I imagine if you had the right senses. The alpha bird perhaps?"

The girl stared at the birds again.

"I'm hungry," she whispered, putting her hand to her thin stomach.

"Of course you are. Come with me, we will both have breakfast."

The Birds and the Bees

Abraham led her into the bakery. He checked the ovens and said hi to Fred and Peter, who were putting the final touches on a rack of pastries. Abraham went out into the front and led the girl to a table.

"You might want to wash your hands and face a bit, in case the boss comes in," Abraham suggested, pointing to the bathroom.

"I bet I'm a mess. I've come a long way." She stood up and went into the bathroom.

Abraham made espresso and buttered two bagels. By the time he was finished, the girl was back. Her face was scrubbed clean, her hair combed. She was a nice-looking girl. But just a girl. Maybe back in his homeland, she would have been a good age for him. But here in the United States, a man in his twenties was not allowed by law to associate with a teenager. He knew that because the missionaries had told the tribe over and over again. It was a very important lesson to be drilled into their heads. Because if you broke the law, even accidentally, you could go to jail, or be sent back to Africa. And then, the struggle, the planning, it would all have been for nothing.

Abraham set the cup and plates in front of the girl.

"Here you are." He looked quizzically at her.

"Wendy," she said, reaching for a bagel. She ripped off a piece of it and crammed it into her mouth. "And you?"

"Abraham."

"Nice to meet you, Abraham."

Wendy wolfed down the bagel in a matter of seconds. Abraham got up and toasted her another.

"So tell me, Wendy. Why is it that you are between homes?"

"It's so weird, really. I mean . . . you'll think I'm crazy but I have to tell someone."

"Tell me then."

"It's like I was ordered to come here. Like there's some sort of purpose for me. I keep hearing voices in my head. I don't know if they belong to my animals, or if they are ghosts or what. But these voices, well, actually just one voice I call Blackie, kept telling me I had to leave. That there's something I'm supposed to be doing . . . but I don't know what it is."

"Voices in the head? Spirit guides?"

"I don't know. I just don't know. I don't even know if this is good or bad. I don't know." Wendy put her head in her hands and sighed. "There's more."

Abraham gave her another bagel and sat down again.

"What?"

"I think I can control the birds," she whispered. "That's crazy, isn't it?"

Abraham shook his head slowly.

"No. Not at all."

"I mean, I don't think it. I know it. I did it."

The Birds and the Bees

"Did what?"

Wendy sighed and took a sip of coffee. Her hands were shaking. "There was this guy, you see. I liked him. A lot. But he liked this other girl. And like, I got all jealous, and I told the birds to . . ."

"You had the birds attack someone?"

"She was a nasty bitch. She deserved it."

"Does anyone really deserve to die, Wendy?"

Wendy thought long and hard. When she looked up again, her eyes were hard and cold. "Yes. Lots of people deserve to die."

Abraham sighed and finished his bagel. "Who made you God to decide who gets to die?"

"I'm not God, but I know some people deserve to die. Some people just *should* die. They are sick. Sick in the mind. Sick in the body. Maybe they are draining society. Not contributing to it, you know. Maybe there are people sitting around collecting welfare. And for what? What meaning do they have in life? Maybe there are people trying to control other people. For what? A power trip?"

"Sounds like you are on a power trip."

"No. I may be young, but I've seen a few things. I've seen lazy people who think the world owes them a living. And that's fine if they don't bother anyone else. But if they bring children into the world, they should be doing everything they can to provide for them. And I don't mean color TVs and fancy-ass computers. I mean heat and food and shoes."

Abraham looked at Wendy. His eyes filled with tears. "I think most parents do the best they can. Really. You should be glad you have parents at all. Maybe you don't understand their . . . circumstances."

"How do you know I'm talking about my own parents?"

"Instinct, I guess."

"Well, you're right. I *am* pissed off at my parents. I don't understand why they sleep all day and talk on the Internet all night and dream about being rock stars and make my grandma feed us and clothe us. They always seem to have cigarettes and booze but heaven forbid I ever had clothes that weren't from Goodwill."

"Maybe they're drunks? Sick with the alcohol?"

"Maybe they are. Maybe they're just lazy. Two lazy-ass goofs who found each other."

"There might be more to the story than you know. Parents don't always tell their kids everything."

"All I know is that nobody cleans, nobody works, and there's never anything in the fridge but beer. I've been to other kids' houses. They have clean houses. They have food. They have working toilets and hot showers. They have shoes without holes and not a grandparent in sight."

The Birds and the Bees

Abraham sighed. "Maybe they are depressed. Maybe something happened."

"The only thing that happened was that Dad didn't become a rock star over night. But shit, man, I'm only fourteen and I know that very few people become rock stars. You have to get over it and move on. Why are my parents so fucking stupid?"

"I don't know, Wendy. I don't know if they are stupid. But I do know about dreams."

"What about you, Abraham? What is your dream?"

Abraham smiled. "I am living my dream. You speak of parents that are lazy. I saw my parents killed. My brothers became my parents, hundreds of us, left alone to wander the desert. We wandered for years. Our dream was a home. Peace. A better world. I came to United States to learn how to work and make money so I can go to school and then go back and help the brothers that didn't get out."

"Wow..." Wendy sipped her coffee as she considered this information. She grinned suddenly. "You are one of the Lost Boys! We learned about you in school. Our school raised money to help you come to America!"

Her face lit up, and she couldn't contain herself any longer. She jumped out of her chair and ran over to hug him.

"You are famous, Abraham. Well, maybe not

you personally, but your story is. I always thought it was such a cool story."

"A cool story, I don't think. A sad and exhausting one."

"But a happy ending! Look! You are here in America. You have a job and a home. You speak English wonderfully."

She stared at him longer. "No wonder you are so black. I mean, I don't mean to be rude or racist or nothing. I haven't seen many black people where I'm from and you are, like, really, really black."

Blackie.

Blackie, is that you?

"Was I supposed to meet you?" Wendy asked.

"I don't know," Abraham said, looking down at his hands. His mind was racing. He could feel her thoughts in his head, swarming rapidly through his mind before she even spoke. It was as if they had an electric connection. But he didn't know what it meant.

Soul mates?

She was fourteen. He was something in his twenties. He didn't know for sure how old he was, birthdays were unimportant in the quest for survival, but he knew the rules.

The rules about the Age of Consent.

Rules that he couldn't deny.

The electric connection was deep. Was animal. It hummed through his body, a gentle lull.

The Birds and the Bees

Abraham looked into Wendy's eyes, and he saw what he needed to see.

"Come with me," he said, reaching for her hand. She slipped her fingers along his, feeling his heat against her.

"Where are we going?" she asked.

"Out back. Just for a moment."

The sun was higher now and beamed down into the back alley. Most of the birds had fled. All that remained of the morning feast were a few crumbs and a couple of birds picking at them.

Abraham and Wendy stood on the back fire escape. Abraham looked up toward the sky, searching the clouds, the sun.

"Ah!" he said at last, pointing to a cloud bank. "So it is true."

Wendy squinted up into the direction he was pointing.

"What is true? I don't see anything but clouds."

"Over there, in that patch of clouds. There is a message."

Wendy looked up with a frown.

"A message in the cloud?"

"You know, from God. Like . . . hmmm . . . like when people read the bones, or the stones, or . . . like the teacups!"

"Divination." Wendy nodded. "You read clouds then?"

"Yes, sometimes. When I feel a calling, like I

did just now. You can find meaning in almost anything you know. A leaf. A wood knot. The sidewalk." Abraham pointed down to the ground.

Wendy kicked at a few rocks. "Divination in the sidewalk. Yeah, right."

"You don't have to believe me. It isn't really that the sidewalk truly carries the message. It is just that it allows your brain to form the pattern of the message that God is trying to send to you."

"So what is God saying to you today?" Wendy asked.

Abraham looked up at the sky. "He says you are here for a reason. You have a message for me. Hmm . . . maybe not a message. You are here to show me something or teach me something."

Abraham looked at her and grinned. "The little white girl is going to teach *me*?"

"Sounds like a come-on to me," Wendy said.

"Come-on?"

"You know, like you are . . . flirting with me."

Abraham shook his head. "Oh, no. *no*. I am not flirting. I cannot break the law, or they will send me back to Africa and I will be a disappointment to my brothers. No, this is something else."

"Like what?"

Abraham looked up again and pointed. "See. You are here. The birds are here. There is some-

The Birds and the Bees

thing. Some reason. You, me, and the birds. We are supposed to do something."

"Like what? Destroy the weak and the sick and those that piss us off?" Wendy sneered.

"Maybe. Survival of the fittest, you know." Abraham grinned, his teeth very white. "I have survived much. Maybe it is my turn to be the boss man. And maybe you are supposed to be the boss woman."

"That's nuts. Why us? Who are we?"

"God works in mysterious ways. He gave us the closeness to the birds. There is much evil coming. Much evil. We will need weapons to fight off the mass destruction."

"Oh, you think Armageddon is upon us?"

"I think there is something coming. Something big. And we'd better be ready for it."

"So how do we do that?"

"We practice. Call the birds, Wendy. Call them without benefit of food and see what happens."

Wendy closed her eyes. She thought of Blackie and Blackie's voice.

Where are you?

I am here.

Wendy smiled. Blackie was still with her. Still in her mind.

What do I do now?

Whatever you want.

She imagined the birds. Imagined them winging their way toward her. Imagined the fluttering of feathers, the screeching. She imagined them standing before her, row after row, awaiting their next order.

When she opened her eyes, she covered her mouth in shock. Before her stood row after row of birds. Their beady eyes stared at her. Cold black eyes. Long pointed beaks. They watched and waited for her to give a command.

"What do we want with the birds, Abraham?" Wendy finally said. Abraham stood silently, his mind racing.

The new land. The new order.

Did he really have to work two jobs to try to come up with money for an education? Or could he find himself in a new position of power by weeding out the sick and the poor and the stupid?

Wasn't it time for a new world order?

A new human world order.

If they had the army of birds, the laws meant nothing.

Abraham looked over at Wendy, at her eyes glistening with tears, at her hair blowing in the breeze of a thousand flapping wings as the birds took flight at her silent command.

He felt a stirring within himself that he had never felt before. A heady sense of power bubbled up within him. And with it came an incredible sense of lust and longing that trembled in his blood. He reached over to Wendy and kissed her on the lips. Shocked, she started to

The Birds and the Bees

push him away, but as she kissed him, she felt the electric rush pulse stronger through them. They were pure energy. Strong and omnipotent. They could have power, create a new city with their legion of birds. They could weed out the sick, the stupid, the weak. They could weed out the leeches of society.

Wendy touched her tongue against Abraham's, and he responded lustily. They mouthed each other a moment more.

He stopped kissing her, and stepped back, his dark eyes shining.

"My angel. You are the reason I survived as I did. We can create a most wonderful future," sighed Abraham.

"We can create a wonderful world." Wendy grinned.

Chapter Fifteen

The children led Gabrielle into the cave. It was cold and dark even with the glow of the flashlight.

"Where did you last see your mommy?" she asked, shining the flashlight over the area where the frankincense had been burning.

"She went down that way." Deedee pointed. Gabrielle swung the light down the tunnel. In the air, she saw a couple of bees winging their way deeper into the cave.

"And she never came back," Gabrielle mused.

Part of her screamed. *Run! Run away now! Call the cops! Get the hell out!*

But where were the cops? After last night, there would be no cops to drag to a cave to search for a missing woman. Besides, Tommy might be here somewhere as well. And if the woman and/or Tommy were in some kind of trouble, every minute would count.

Gabrielle stopped for a moment, and took the knife out of her bag and examined it. She watched the blade glint in the half-light. She wished she had a bigger knife. On the other hand, she wasn't even certain she could use a knife in any meaningful fashion. She had never had to fight anything with a knife before. But times were changing. Changing fast.

"Follow me," she said to the children. "Let's see what we've got."

Gabrielle and the children crept along the tunnel.

They quietly wandered down the deep sloping curves of the cave until they saw the glow of a light.

When they turned the corner, Gabrielle was speechless.

There were so many people moving around, yet they made very little noise. Certainly no chattering or bantering. Back and forth they went, in repetitive patterns like machines. In the dim light it was hard to make out what their movements consisted of, what it was that they were doing.

Some of the movements were obvious gestures, such as lighting candles, piling stones, digging in the dirt, carving in the wall. The peo-

The Birds and the Bees

ple moved robotically. Scooping and pouring and layering.

Others just sat on the floor staring.

Around them, bees buzzed, weaving among and lighting on the humans with harmonious energy. Some of the people were covered with bees, apparently unaware of them as they walked about their business. People lay passively on the floor in fetal positions, while others layered a sticky film onto them. There were shadowy movements in the pockets of the wall. Giant honeycombs hid where arms and legs intertwined, and rhythmic movements shook the jellylike substance.

"There's Mommy!" Deedee pointed. Gabrielle followed her finger and gasped. A woman was stuck into the side of the wall, covered in the fine white film. She appeared to be sleeping. Deedee ran over to the woman.

"Mommy! Mommy!" Deedee cried, reaching out toward Mary Anne. Gabrielle ran after her, and caught her. She held the tiny child snugly in her arms.

"Don't touch her, honey. Not yet," Gabrielle whispered into the child's ear.

"I miss Mommy," Deedee said, reaching for her mother, tears streaking down her face.

Gabrielle walked right up to the odd sack of a woman and knelt down beside her. She studied Mary Anne, or at least, what she could see of her. There was no way to tell if the woman was alive or dead. Half curled, sloped into the wall, the woman cupped something in her hands. Gabrielle pressed closer to see it better, craning her neck, jiggling her flashlight on it. A bee sat in Mary Anne's palm.

"Uh . . . Gabrielle . . ." Jimmy whispered, tugging at her arm. Gabrielle turned to look at him, and then saw what he was trying to tell her.

Their entrance had not gone unnoticed. The entire room was watching them. The steady noise of the room had stopped. All eyes were on her and the children. Her heart pounded painfully against her chest.

She wasn't doing anything wrong, was she? Was she really?

There weren't any Keep Out signs anywhere.

"What is this place?" she asked the nearest man, hating how her voice trembled. He was a young man, with tousled hair and a lot of tattoos. He looked at her with unfocused eyes, not understanding her. His arm twitched now and again as Gabrielle waited for an answer.

People who had been resting on the floor stood up. Others who had been touching and fondling each other in the pockets of the walls peered out.

The candles flickered, and the clammy coldness of the cave seeped into her bones. In the air was a sense of suspended animation. A dwindling diminuendo before the final cascading crescendo. A smell of sweetness tickled her

The Birds and the Bees

nose, while an undercurrent of something rotten heaved in her stomach. The more the people moved around, the more foul the smell became, as if it were seeping from the very pores of the people themselves.

Gabrielle instinctively took the children into her arms and stepped back.

"Where am I?" she asked. There was still no reply. The people slowly shuffled toward them, lumbering like zombies in a multitude of movies.

"Hey, I didn't mean to interrupt. These children, they are just looking. . . ."

Gabrielle fumbled with her bag and drew up the knife. She held it in front of her, its long silver blade catching the reflection of hundreds of flickering candles. Large dark eyes followed the blade as she sliced the air.

"The children just want their mother," she said firmly.

"Mommy!" Deedee wailed, staring over at her mother. Mary Anne stirred a bit, her foot pressing against the gelatinous film.

"She's alive!" Gabrielle gasped.

Deedee clutched Gabrielle's leg. "Help my mommy."

A man hobbled closer to Gabrielle. He touched her arm, his mouth open in a drooling leer.

"Get away from me," she shouted, raising the

knife. "I'm not hurting anyone. I'm just trying to help."

The man recoiled from the knife and slowly shuffled back in among the others, who muttered among themselves. Gabrielle looked over at Mary Anne, who had raised her head at the sound of her child's voice. She had realized she was stuck in a wall of gunk. Pushing against it, Mary Anne was unable to break through the mucusy membrane. Her movements grew more spastic as she fought the gluey goo.

Gabrielle slowly moved back toward the woman, keeping her eyes on the people surrounding her. She pressed the knife against Mary Anne's filmy sack. The blade sank in, but didn't slice it open.

Mary Anne squirmed, her eyes open, her hand reaching out toward Deedee and Jimmy. They touched her, pushing their little fingers through the sticky jelly. Gabrielle didn't stop them as they pulled and dug, trying to free their mother. Gabrielle kept her eyes on the scene around her, making certain that no one snuck up on her while she wasn't looking.

Then she saw him.

He was sitting on a rock, staring into space, slightly apart from the others. Gabrielle stifled a cry and dropped the knife.

"Oh, my God!"

Gabrielle fell to her knees, retrieving the knife, and moved slowly toward Tommy, the

The Birds and the Bees

inhabitants of the cave warily watching her. She crept toward him, inch by inch. He sat, rocking back and forth, staring at nothing in the flickering candlelight.

"Tommy!" she said loudly as she touched his arm. He did not respond. In fact, she could now see that he was singing to himself. A weird little nursery rhyme.

"'Round and 'round..." he muttered.

"Tommy, I'm here for you," she said, shaking him. He stirred a bit and then looked at her. He blinked a few times, as if coming out of a deep sleep.

"Gabrielle?" he whispered. Startled, he looked around the room. "Where am I?"

"Tommy, I have to get you out of here...."

The crowd around them rippled, and there was a low buzzing as they stepped aside to let someone through.

Someone or something?

Gabrielle had never seen such a hideous sight in her life.

She thought it might be a woman. Was it a woman? Was it some deformity?

The monstrosity stepped forward. Her body was a woman's, with strange black and yellow fur patterning sprouting in places. Huge breasts hung heavily, large liquid drops leaking from curiously pointed sharp nipples. Her stomach and hips were large and round, her legs heavy and furry. Crawling beside her was a young naked woman who wrapped herself around her leg and looked up at Gabrielle with round dark eyes. The younger woman's skinny body was covered in red welts and sticky liquids. Her movements were serpentine, barely human, and her stare sent shivers up Gabrielle's spine.

Gabrielle's gaze went from the strange waif weaving around the monstrosity's legs and back up to the monstrosity's hideous face.

Her eyes were huge and black, her face a puffy mishmash of flesh and fur. When she opened her mouth, a few bees flew out. Her voice sounded as if it had gone through some kind of machine. It had a hollow buzzing quality to it.

"Leave him," the Queen Bee commanded, pointing at Tommy, who was shivering with cold and trying to stand.

"I want to take him with me. He doesn't belong here." Gabrielle said.

"He is part of me now," the Queen said, drawing closer. She raised her hand and instantly, Tommy's gaze followed her fingers. The Queen purred, running her hands through his ringlets.

"He is mine. They are mine. All to do my bidding."

"I don't care about the others, just let him go."

The Queen stood behind Tommy, running her hands along his chest, pulling aside the torn shreds of shirt, nuzzling her face into the crook of his neck. She darted her tongue out. It was

The Birds and the Bees

long and black, like the proboscis on a fly. The tongue wound around his neck, along his ear, darting along his eyelids and nose. Tommy's eyes rolled back. The Queen toyed with his nipples, tweaking them.

"You have many other men here. Many handsome men. Why can't I have him back?" Gabrielle pleaded, still clutching the knife.

"Because I want all the men. All the women. Everyone must serve me and only me." The Queen Bee stepped away from Tommy and he wavered, as if he would fall.

"Serve you for what? Who are you?"

"I am Armina. This is my army."

"Army for what?" Gabrielle stared around the room at all the people. Now that her eyes were adjusting to the light better, she could see that many were in a similar state of metamorphosis as Armina. Most of the people here were naked men, and what she had mistaken for zombielike stares were penetrating fixations by large black pupilless eyes. They stood, whispering among themselves, slowly moving around. Many returned to the work they had been doing, whether it was building up the hive, sorting the honey, lighting the candles, or some other small repetitive task.

Some sat and stared at nothing, rocking back and forth much like Tommy had been. But there was still a circle of more aggressive-looking men standing around, holding sticks and rocks, and Gabrielle expected they were Armina's guards.

"Armina . . . I have no interest in disturbing whatever it is you are doing here. It looks like a very interesting . . . um . . . commune . . . I'm sure you have your reasons, religious or otherwise. I only stumbled in here because the children need their mother and I need my boyfriend."

Armina laughed loud and long.

"He is not your boyfriend. If he had been true to his love, to his heart, he would never have heard my call. He would never have wandered through the fields and darkness to find what tickled his heart. There would have been no gap in his love for you for me to get through if he truly loved you."

Gabrielle stared at Tommy, the knife clattering from her hand and onto the ground.

"That's not true . . ."

"Oh, but it is, Gabrielle."

Gabrielle jerked her head back toward Armina in stunned disbelief.

"Yes, that is your name. I know you. I remember you. I remember you in school."

"School?"

"You were a bookworm, an outsider, much like me. You were an outsider 'cause you chose to be. You had the looks, the intellect, the mother love, to be part of the crowd. But you chose solitude. You had your reasons."

The Birds and the Bees

Gabrielle shook her head and tried to see Armina beneath the change.

She thought back years and years. Back to being a child, catching bees in jelly jars in the clover fields. Back to grade school, where people used to bring in things like robin eggs and crow feathers for show and tell. Back to when she was a gawky little girl, more in tune with nature and the birds singing outside the classroom than she was with whatever the teacher was droning on about inside. Back to a time when her grandmother used to listen to her problems, the only one who ever understood her, until she died suddenly. Back to the funeral where her grandmother was mourned. Back to the cafeteria, sitting alone. Who else was alone?

Then she saw her in her mind's eye.

Armina.

Amy.

The poor little girl from the other side of the tracks. The girl whose mother's life fueled the town gossip and who never had a real father. The little girl who ate alone and ate often.

Gabrielle had watched the redheaded girl often from her own corner in the lunchroom. Watched the girl scarf down her own meager sandwich and then go through the garbage when she thought no one was looking. Amy would rummage, pulling out half-eaten twinkies and cupcakes, half-empty bags of chips. She would smuggle the goodies into her pockets and wolf them down when she thought no one was looking. And no one was.

No one ever looked at Amy. Except Gabrielle.

No one could understand how Amy grew so large so quickly, except Gabrielle.

No one saw Amy sit in the corner of the library, examining her loot, stuffing her face quickly and efficiently before anyone caught her.

No one heard the muffled sounds of chewing and crying and understood what it was except Gabrielle.

The only one who could have explained Amy's sorrow to anyone had been Gabrielle, but what was she to do?

She was a child herself.

A sad lonely child who wasn't as bad off as Amy, who had a prettier face, but still a child who was shy. A child who was afraid to talk to others, for others often did not know what she was trying to say.

Gabrielle would speak of ideas and places she had read about in books, while her peers would be throwing balls around and watching TV. They thought she was a geek and a nerd at the best of times, and at the worst, she found that more and more often, it was a struggle just to say hello to anyone at all in the morning. No one noticed. No one noticed because Gabrielle was invisible. Almost as invisible as Amy had been.

The Birds and the Bees

"I never chose solitude. I was shunned. Nobody liked me," Gabrielle protested.

"Nonsense. I can read you like the books you read, Gabrielle. You always wanted mind expansion. You always thought the universe was so big and that there was a reason for everything. You have made yourself crazy trying to figure it out. You lost your marriage and your children in your useless quest for meaning."

"You are the crazy one!" Gabrielle sputtered, throwing her hands out at Armina.

"No, I'm not. You have relentlessly chased a dream that doesn't exist. There is no yin and yang. There is no cosmic answer. There are no whys or hows or wherefores. There are no soul mates. There is no heaven. There is only now."

"So now you think you are the Almighty Creator, the Master of all the answers?" Gabrielle asked.

"I am *a* creator. There are always creators. There will always be the strong and the weak. I may have been weak once, but I will never be weak again. I have spent a lifetime building my energy, and now I am building my empire. Once I am ready, I will control all."

The Queen stared at Gabrielle with her huge multilayered eyes. A sharp jab of pain seared through Gabrielle's brain. She sank to her knees clutching her head.

"*No*, get out of my head."

Sèphera Girón

"Join us, Gabrielle. Stop fighting, for you can't win."

"No! I won't be part of this. I won't."

The buzzing in Gabrielle's head grew stronger, blinding her with a glowing light. She writhed on the ground, kicking her feet and screaming. The Queen stood and stared, a slow smile creeping along her lips.

Suddenly the Queen was knocked to the ground.

Deedee and Jimmy were pummeling her. Deedee held the knife and pointed it at Armina's face.

"Let our mommy go!" they cried, kicking at the fallen woman. The noise in Gabrielle's head stopped and as she struggled to stand up, she was grabbed from behind and thrown over the strong shoulder of a man. She struggled against the strong embrace, but he held her firmly. As the man made his way toward the tunnel, she realized it was Tommy.

"The children," Gabrielle cried out, clawing the air.

"Shhh . . ." Tommy said. "We have to get out of here."

He ran carefully and quietly while Gabrielle marveled at his sheer stubborn strength.

Once around the corner from the hive, Tommy carefully put Gabrielle down.

"Can you walk?"

The Birds and the Bees

Gabrielle pushed her feet against the ground and wriggled her ankles.

"I'm fine."

Shouts echoed down the cavern as well as the sound of running.

"We'd better get moving."

Gabrielle and Tommy ran the rest of the way out of the winding curves of the cave.

"We have to get the children," Gabrielle panted as she followed Tommy's long quick strides.

"We will, Gabrielle. We'll get help and come back for them. I promise."

They broke out into the sunlight, blinded momentarily. As their eyes adjusted, they tore down the hillside, darting along the bushes and trees until they reached the car. A cloud of bees swooped out of the cave and angrily bore down on them.

"Hurry!" Tommy cried as Gabrielle fumbled with the keys. At last her shaking fingers were able to unlock the passenger side of the car. She dove across the seat and Tommy slid in after her, slamming the door just as the bees descended. The car gears ground and heaved as bees swarmed underneath, making their way through the motor.

"Shut the vents!" she cried.

Tommy slapped down all the little vent covers as Gabrielle put the car into drive. It roared and grumbled as bees were churned in the gears. A few made their way through the vents and attacked Tommy. He swatted at them, smashing them time and again with anything he could find. Coffee cups, tapes, CDs, pens.

Gabrielle started to drive, but the windshield was thick with bees. She put her wipers on, and the bees were smeared away, to be replaced by more bees. As Gabrielle peered through tiny spots where she could see, she drove faster.

"I hope to God there's no one else around here!" she shouted. Tommy nodded, decapitating dazed bees with a CD case.

Gabrielle drove, fishtailing down the hillside until she thumped onto the road. As she picked up speed and kept the windshield wipers on, the bees lost their grip.

Before long, the car was speeding down the highway, heading for the city, the bees falling behind them.

Gabrielle was shaking, her knuckles white as she gripped the steering wheel.

"What the hell was that all about?" she finally sputtered.

"I don't know," Tommy said, turning to look behind them.

"I thought I lost you," Gabrielle said.

They drove on, the miles soaring by.

"Why did you leave?" she asked.

Tommy gazed out at the highway and furrowed his brow. "I don't really remember much of what happened at all."

The Birds and the Bees

He looked down at his clothes, or what was left of his clothes. There were smears and rips all over him. His body was covered in scratches and stickiness. He touched some of the stickiness and held it up to the light.

"I don't understand any of this," he said.

"This is a fucking nightmare," Gabrielle said, staring at the chaos in front of her as they entered the city.

"Oh, my God, now what?"

Tanks were rolling down the road. Military men marched down the streets, rifles ready. People ran screaming, others walked quickly, some just stood dazed. The smell of gunfire hung heavy in the smoggy air. There were no birds, no bees in sight. Just people. Hysterical people, pushing and shouting. Stunned people, walking slowly. People on bikes and scooters, carrying bags, wearing big hats and sunglasses.

A few windows were broken in the shops, glass lying shattered on the ground, sparkling in the sunlight. Garbage was strewn, cans on their sides. Parked cars showed evidence of random carnage. Horns honked now and again as a frantic biker skipped from sidewalk to road.

"I've never seen a tank before," Gabrielle said.

"Me neither. Not one up close."

They edged the car along in the traffic, watching for any sign of danger. The closer they got to Gabrielle's place, the more an eerie calm settled over them.

"Maybe the Army scared the birds away," she said. "Or got them all, or something."

"You think we would all be so lucky? To be rid of those birds so fast? And what about the bees? I think we know how that one is going to go."

"We know where the Queen Bee is! We can lead the Army to the Queen Bee and destroy the hive. Then the swarming of the bees will stop."

"But what about all the people she has in there? They aren't all killers. They are like me, lured there, until they change."

"How did she get you there?"

"I don't know. It's all like a dream. It was just a yearning to go where she was or something. She somehow called me and I followed."

"You see, and you are here now. You didn't have to stay there. We have to get the other people out before they are trapped too!"

"And how the hell are we going to do that? If we go to the Army, they'll just swarm in. What are we going to do?"

"I don't know. We'll get supplies at my place and figure it out."

They parked the car. The street and sidewalk were empty. Not a person was around. No cars, no bicycles. The neighborhood was a ghost town.

They ran from the car to the building. No one was in the hallways. Gabrielle pushed the ele-

The Birds and the Bees

vator button, and Tommy put his hand over hers.

"Do you really want to take the elevator when there's so much crazy shit going on?"

Gabrielle nodded in agreement.

"Over here." Gabrielle led him to the stairwell, and they climbed flight after flight until they reached her landing.

At last they were in the apartment. Gabrielle bolted the door and leaned back against it, panting and sweating. She stared at Tommy.

"Holy fuck, Tommy . . . what are we going to do?"

She wiped her brow with her hand, leaving more dirt smeared across it. Tommy paced back and forth.

"I don't know . . . shit, man. I don't know."

Gabrielle stared down at herself and then at Tommy. She lifted her arm and sniffed.

"Whoah, we need to change big-time."

She took his hand.

"Let's talk in the shower."

They peeled off their clothes, and Gabrielle turned on the shower. She stepped in first, letting the hot spray hit her. It felt so good, the water pounding against her flesh. She wished she could stand under there forever, feeling the soothing patter of the water, and never come out.

Pulling the shower curtain aside, Tommy stepped in carefully, and she stood aside to let him feel the soothing spray. He carefully pulled the curtain shut again.

They both stood there, eyes shut, sharing the water, letting it run along them, washing away the grime of the cave, the stickiness of the honey, the musky scent of fear.

Gabrielle took the sponge and poured soap on it and scrubbed it along Tommy's back. The white lather collected up the stubborn honey and bits of blackness. A scent of lavender filled the air, and they breathed its sweetness.

Tommy turned to face her and took her face in his hands. He gently pressed his lips against hers, rubbing them softly against each other. Gabrielle sighed and wrapped her arms around him, pulling his slippery soft body against hers. She held him tightly, savoring the feeling, wishing that they could stand here in the shower forever and not ever have to see birds or bees or even people again.

Tommy ran his hands along her body and cupped her ass in his hands, holding her close. She held him tighter and they rocked back and forth, eyes shut in exhaustion.

Suddenly there was a crash from the other room that jolted them back to their senses.

"What the hell was that?" Gabrielle cried, shutting off the shower.

"I don't know!" Tommy said, pulling the curtain open. He grabbed a towel off the hook. "Wait here."

The Birds and the Bees

Tommy wrapped the towel around himself and grabbed the toilet plunger as he left the bathroom. Gabrielle took another towel and wrapped it around herself. They made their way into the living room. Gabrielle heard another crash from the balcony.

"Oh, no!" She cried, pointing at the open balcony door.

"I bet they came in!"

"Who?" asked Tommy.

"The birds . . . the damnable birds that are always there. Somehow they got the door open. . . ."

"God." Tommy crept along the wall towards the door. There was another rattling from the balcony. He reached out to slide the door shut as a woman jumped into the room.

She pushed at Tommy, knocking him off balance and over the sofa, where he fell onto the floor. The woman charged at Gabrielle and tackled her, screaming and clawing at her.

The woman and Gabrielle wrestled and punched and rolled along the floor. Tommy pulled himself back up and found the plunger. He raised the plunger, was about to strike, and then stopped.

"Sheila!" he cried out. The plunger slid from his hand. "Sheila, what are you doing!"

He reached out and pulled Sheila off Gabrielle. The two women stood staring at each other warily.

"Stay the fuck away from my husband, you filthy disgusting whore!" Sheila screamed.

"He came to me."

"You fucking skank. Can't get your own man, you have to steal someone else's."

"I didn't steal anyone. He came to me with his own free will. Think about that one."

Sheila's fist flew out and punched Gabrielle across the jaw. Blood poured out of Gabrielle's mouth and she went to hit Sheila back, but Tommy held her arm.

"Stop it now," he said. "Christ, I sure as hell am not worth fighting for."

"You ran away from me. You and Wendy both left me. How could you?" Sheila cried.

"I didn't take Wendy. I left her with you."

"You lying asshole. You've always been a liar. You fucking prick. Where is my daughter?"

"I don't know, Sheila. I don't know what you are talking about."

Sheila's lip trembled and her eyes glossed with tears.

"Why did you leave me, Tommy? We never even discussed it. You just up and left."

"I needed to think, Sheila. I need to think."

Sheila took Tommy's hand and kissed it.

"I love you, Tommy. Please come back home. We can make things better. I promise."

"I love you too, Sheila. But I'm so confused." Tommy's eyes welled up with tears. Sheila hugged him, held him, kissing him along the

The Birds and the Bees

neck. Gabrielle sat down wearily on the couch, watching them. Her stomach knotted, rage boiled through her blood.

How dare he? How dare he make her look like a whore, when it was he who had pursued her? He was the one who'd kept the interest going, playing dangerous games in e-mail and messenger. Now he was the innocent while Gabrielle took the rap? How dare he?

"Tommy, why didn't you answer my e-mail? Didn't you see how I'm going to make us lots of money?" she asked, kissing his naked chest.

"What e-mail?"

"About me starting the porn site."

"You are so clever," Tommy said, kissing the top of her head.

Gabrielle's fingers clenched. What a bastard. What a bitch.

How dare they drag her into their twisted little bullshit head games?

"Tommy, you must come away with me now," Sheila said.

Tommy shook his head.

"I'm not ready. I have some things to do, and I need to think."

"What is there to think about? The new world order is here," Sheila said, suddenly standing straight, her hand clutching Tommy by the balls. "We have to be ready for the new world order. We have been called."

Sheila's eyes grew dark and large until there

were no pupils left. Where her breasts bulged prettily in her T-shirt, great streams of liquid seeped out. Her crotch was soaked and dripping onto the floor.

"Let go, Sheila," Tommy said quietly. Sheila's hands squeezed tighter, and her voice grew lower.

"You must come with me now, Tommy, before all is lost."

Gabrielle watched Sheila twisting Tommy's balls, anger fueling her further. There had to be something she could do. Some way to stop the bitch, but if she made any movement, Sheila would hurt Tommy more.

All Gabrielle wanted in that moment was for Sheila to die.

Stop it, you fucking bitch, just die already.

A great wind swept through the apartment.

"The time is now, Tommy, come." Sheila started walking, pulling Tommy by the balls toward the front door. At that moment, a huge black bird soared through the open balcony door and landed on Sheila's head. Giant claws ripped at Sheila's scalp as she screamed. She released her grip on Tommy's balls as she swatted at the bird. Three more birds flew in for attack, and soon there were too many birds to count, pecking and clawing at Sheila.

Tommy and Gabrielle ran for the bedroom as Sheila writhed on the ground. Claws ripped at her face, piercing her eyes until they were a

The Birds and the Bees

bloody pulp, her nose just a mashed mess of meat.

"Help me!" Sheila cried as her throat was torn open. A gush of blood flooded the birds, spraying their wings with crimson drops. They squawked, a flurry of flapping feathers.

"Sheila..." Tommy moaned, sinking down on the bed as he heard the last of the crows fly away. "Christ... I didn't even try to help her."

"What could you have done?" Gabrielle asked. "Nothing! That's what. There wasn't a damn thing for you to do about it. Besides, did you look at her face? How she sort of... changed before our very eyes?"

"Something was really wrong with her." Tommy nodded. "It was like... she was being controlled or something."

"Like you were."

"Do you think it was the Queen Bee?"

"I'm sure it was. Did you see her eyes? And she started leaking that honey crap all over the place."

"Sheila!" Tommy sobbed as the realization that his wife was dead flooded him. "God, I loved her."

Gabrielle watched him cry.

She felt nothing.

She was numb.

Ice.

She wanted to feel sad for him that his wife was dead, or so they thought. They hadn't actually opened the door yet to check. But she was still outraged at how the minute Sheila appeared, it was as if Gabrielle had never existed at all.

She wondered what he felt for her, if anything. Or had he just been using her to make his wife jealous? She stared at him, thinking back to when she first heard him play.

How stupid she had been to get so tangled up in this mess. She knew better. She knew way better than to get involved with someone not yet divorced, unless it was just for a fun fling. She didn't know what her expectations had been, but they had involved some sort of future. And he had led her to believe, in endless e-mails and messages, that he had envisioned a future together too.

She expected that now he would want a future with her because he had no wife. Gabrielle would never know the truth about why he was here. She would never be able to figure out if he really had loved her, or if it had been just a game.

"What did she mean?" Tommy sobbed.

"Huh?" Gabrielle realized Tommy was talking to her.

"About Wendy? What did she mean Wendy was gone?"

"I don't know. Maybe she was lying. So that you would go to her."

"She wouldn't lie about Wendy."

The Birds and the Bees

"Why not? She broke into my apartment and tried to kill me. Why wouldn't she say anything at all to try to entice you back to her?"

"She wouldn't..."

"She wasn't herself. You said so. So don't worry about Wendy. She's a big girl, I'm sure she's fine."

"There's no noise out there."

"I know. Do you think we should look now?"

They cracked open the door and peered out. Feathers and blood and bits of flesh and scraps of clothing were strewn around the room. The birds seemed to be gone. Gabrielle felt bile rise in her throat as Tommy vomited all over the rug.

"Sheila..." he croaked, heading for the bathroom to puke again.

Gabrielle looked around the living room of devastation. All the birds were gone. She looked at the balcony. The railings were full of the birds, sitting and staring at her. She slammed the door shut.

"Tommy, we have to get out of here," she said, running back into the bedroom. Hurriedly, she rummaged through her dresser, tossing clothes and underwear around until she found something to wear. She went through Tommy's knapsack until she found him a shirt and jeans to put on. Tugging her T-shirt on, she tossed Tommy's clothes into the bathroom.

"Put these on!" she cried. "Hurry."

Sèphera Girón

Tommy finished retching, and she heard the toilet flush and the sound of running water.

How the hell were they going to get those children out? And everyone else?

She picked up the phone, but the line was dead.

Outside, she could hear the rumble of tanks and the odd ricochet of gunfire.

Was there a way to flag down someone to tell them of the cave?

Would they believe her?

Would they just go in and blow up everyone?

"Hurry up, Tommy!" she screamed.

She grabbed her knapsack and dumped knives into it. She searched the kitchen and found more bug spray, candles, matches, the fire extinguisher. Her mind spun wildly, and she couldn't get focused.

How do you kill bees? Killer bees? Half-human bees?

She had no frankincense to hypnotize them.

What else would hypnotize bees?

She caught sight of the tape deck sitting on her coffee table.

Music?

Did bees get hypnotized by music? Or was that only savage beasts? The Queen Bee was half human. Maybe she was soothable?

Gabrielle felt as though her mind had truly snapped as she flung cassettes and CDs into the overfull knapsack and checked the tape deck for

The Birds and the Bees

batteries. Yes, there were batteries in there.

Then her glance fell on Tommy's guitar. They would take that too. Maybe he could hypnotize the Queen with music long enough for Gabrielle to get the kids out.

It was ludicrous.

"Hurry up!" Gabrielle screamed again, slipping on bloody bits of Sheila as she grabbed the guitar.

Tommy finally emerged from the bathroom, shaking and pale. He stared at Gabrielle.

"What the hell are you doing?"

"If we can't kill them, we'll hypnotize them. But first, we'll try to get the Army to listen."

"Yeah, like the Army is going to listen to us!"

"They might. We don't know that. They just might, you know. They are here to destroy the plagues."

"A fine job they are doing too . . ." Tommy said, his voice quivering as he tried not to look at Sheila.

"Let's go."

Chapter Sixteen

Back in the hive, Armina looked at her busy bees.

"Keep working. Keep building, my sweets. More are coming all the time."

The cave was very crowded with so many people. Many of them new, walking, lifting, lighting, scooping, digging, carving, piling. All working in sync to create a huge new honeycomb. All working at their designated jobs.

Katey held a glass of nectar out for Armina.

"Here you are, Mistress," she said, nodding her head. Armina took the glass and held it up to the light. The liquid was a golden color.

"Perfect," Armina said as she took a sip. "Absolutely perfect."

"Is there anything else I can do for you, Mistress?" Katey asked.

"You can rub my back. I'm so itchy these days."

Katey nodded and proceeded to rub Armina's back. It was a tangle of yellow and black fur, and the buds of wings were beginning to grow. Armina's arms and fingers were black and beetlelike, her nails long and sharp. As Katey's hands prodded and probed Armina, she noticed that there was a very sharp point at the end of her tailbone.

"Your stinger is growing in nicely," Katey told her.

"I hope so, 'cause I'm looking forward to using it. There are a few people I'm hoping to get. That bitch Gabrielle for one."

"Why do you have it in for her so bad?"

"I just do. I hate to see waste. She has had so many good opportunities in her life, and she has thrown them all away. It pisses me off no end."

Armina shut her eyes.

"They are coming back. I can feel Tommy. And he can feel me too, calling him, as I called him before. It wasn't hard to sway him. He is so weak. But then, most men are, aren't they?"

Armina laughed. Katey shrugged and looked over at John, who was building a sticky nest around his sleeping children. Katey looked over at Mary Anne, who had finally come out of her

The Birds and the Bees

own hidey-hole and was sitting on a rock amid all the business. She held a bee in her hand, and was talking to it.

"Mary Anne is nuts," Katey said, staring at the rocking woman.

"Yes and no. I had to make her believe that bee was her dead son. It keeps her from really seeing him."

"She can't see her dead son."

"Yes, she can. And so can the children. He is here, trying to figure out how to help them. But I am stronger than any spirit." Armina smiled slyly and stuck out her tongue to taste a piece of honeycomb on the wall beside her.

"When will you be finished recruiting? This place is getting really full."

"I will never be finished. We finish building up this cave and then expand outwards into the hillside. We will never stop until we have control of the world."

"And then what?"

"Then I am Queen of the world."

Katey nodded, finishing the massage.

"And a beautiful Queen you will be," Katey said, coming around to the front of Armina. She kneeled on the floor before her and placed her head in the Queen's lap.

"I am proud to be your servant," Katey said. The Queen ran her long tongue along Katey's face and down the girl's back. She tasted wonderful, and now that she had a moment, the Queen decided to take some time to play.

"Nigel . . . I can't hear you in here. There is too much noise," Mary Anne said to the tiny bee in her hand. The bee crawled and fluttered, tiny black legs creeping along her palm.

Mary Anne looked over at John, who was pulling wads of goo over her other children. She hoped that Eric was safe somewhere. That maybe another parent had taken him in when it was discovered his parents and siblings were missing. She felt like such a bad mother. How could she lose four children like this?

Tears welled up into her eyes, and she touched a finger to the tiny bee in her hand.

"What should I do, Nigel?" she asked the bee. "What do I do now?"

She held the bee up, staring at it, trying to feel its mind, as she always felt Nigel in her head. But it wasn't there.

Mary Anne looked around the room. Everyone was so busy, doing some assigned task or another, and here she sat, talking to a bee that was her dead son.

She couldn't hear him. She had to hear him. She needed to know what to do. How to help her children away from the clutches of her husband.

She slowly stood up and carefully, cautiously, worked her way toward the cave entrance. The

The Birds and the Bees

Queen was occupied with that slave girl. She wouldn't notice her not working with the others.

Mary Anne slipped out of the busy room and headed down the tunnel. She hadn't gotten very far when a huge pain shot through her head.

She took a step backward, and the pain went away. But when she took a step forward, the pain began again.

This must be as far as she could get.

She sat down in the dark, leaning against the cold dank wall of the cave. She touched the little bee in her hand.

"Nigel . . . what do I do now?"

There was a ripple in the air, and then she felt him. Felt his presence, in her bones, in her head. Felt him as she had always felt him, and tears of joy ran down her cheeks.

"You are here, baby!" She laughed, reaching into the air at nothing.

"Mommy," the voice said. "Be ready. The end is near."

"Nigel?" she said, but she knew he was already gone.

The bee buzzed in her hand and stung her. She stood up and went back into the hive.

Gabrielle and Tommy crept into the cave, knives in their hands, Tommy clutching his guitar. They hadn't said a word the whole drive up. It all seemed a ludicrous and useless game.

On the way, they had tried several times to tell soldiers where they were headed, but the soldiers seemed to not take them seriously.

"Do you know how many people today have told us where to find the hive? Or the nest? If we followed every hunch, we'd be so split up we'd be no good to anyone," one of the kinder ones had explained.

Now, here they were, facing the dreaded hive, alone.

"Why are we here again?" Tommy asked. "Why don't we run for our lives?"

"Wouldn't you want someone to save your child if she was in that hellhole? Wouldn't you want someone to save you? Oh, yeah, that's right. I *did*," Gabrielle sneered, still bitter over the business with Sheila.

"Stop being such a bitch."

"Hey, I wasn't the one leading you around by the balls."

"Oh, no?"

Tommy glared at her and stopped himself from saying anything more.

They rounded the corner and beheld the bustling hive once more.

"Christ," Tommy said, staring at the huge honeycombs dripping from the walls and ceilings.

"Amazing."

They hadn't been gone that long, but the work that had been completed in their absence was

The Birds and the Bees

incredible. The entire cavern was a golden palace.

"Now, let's find the Queen and get the hell out of here," Gabrielle said.

Armina wasn't hard to spot, sitting on a high rock, which had a large stone throne, watching her drones work. Katey was curled up at her feet. Armina's giant black bug eyes turned to focus on the intruders.

"You've seen the error of your ways and have come to join the party," the Queen said to them.

"Yes," Gabrielle said, bowing to her. "We have come to pay you an homage and beg you to let us be part of your Army."

"An homage?"

Tommy held up his guitar. "I want to sing for you."

The Queen nodded. "So sing then."

"You won't hear me from there."

"Then climb on up." Armina waved at the rocks leading up to her high seat. Tommy started to climb, and Gabrielle helped him, juggling the guitar and bags.

When Tommy reached the rock, he bowed his head to Armina. Gabrielle stood beside him, smiling too wide.

"I . . . I just want to sing you a song," he said nervously. He looked over at Gabrielle, who hit play on the tape deck. It was a slow, rhythmic song that Tommy had recorded a few months ago. He played along to it, and his throaty voice filled the cavern. Armina watched, feeling the music tickle her bones. She watched Tommy sing and play, marveling at how his fingers danced along the strings, at the amazing way he tweaked the music from both his throat and the ax.

Gabrielle watched the cavern. Everyone had stopped working and was watching Tommy. As one song led into another and then another after that, she could feel the relaxation in the air. Many of the bee people started to doze off. The Queen herself was growing glassy-eyed and her head nodded now and again.

Slowly, so very slowly, Gabrielle reached into her knapsack and grabbed one of the large cans of wasp killer. Carefully, she pulled it out. Slowly. So slowly so that her movement was more like her slowly dancing to the seductive beat of the music.

She had the can in her trembling fingers, a knife in her belt. She looked at the Queen. She looked at the drones. She saw where the sleeping children lay. She looked at Tommy.

He sang softly.

Gabrielle pulled out the can and sprayed the Queen in the eyes.

The Queen screamed, rubbing her face. Chaos ensured and Gabrielle pulled out the knife and lunged at the Queen, plunging the knife into her over and over.

The Queen pushed her off and leaped onto

The Birds and the Bees

Tommy. They toppled off the perch and landed with a huge thud onto the stone cave floor. Tommy moaned from beneath the huge heavy Queen. She pushed herself up so that she was straddling him and wrapped his hair between her hands, smashing his head against the floor. Armina pulled him up, one last time, looking into his eyes. He moaned weakly.

"You bastard," Armina hissed. "You are all lying bastards."

Armina drove her stinger deep into his heart.

Tommy screamed trying to push her off him, but the blood poured out quickly from his gaping wound as she continued to grind deep into him. Gabrielle dove off the perch and toppled the Queen from Tommy. They rolled around the floor, but the Queen was much larger then Gabrielle. The Queen buzzed angrily, trying to navigate her stinger to a spot on Gabrielle, but Gabrielle kept slipping away. Mary Anne watched from her corner, and as she saw some of the more changed drones head toward Gabrielle, she charged in.

Mary Anne dived on the Queen as Gabrielle kicked and punched. The Queen picked up Mary Anne and threw her so hard she bounced off a rock. Gabrielle ran over to her bag and pulled out the fire extinguisher. As Armina towered over Mary Anne, Gabrielle shot a jet of foam at Armina.

Armina turned to face Gabrielle, and Mary Anne tackled her.

Several drones grabbed the women and pinned them back, while Armina picked herself up.

"You bitch. Look what you've done," Armina screamed, pointing to Tommy, who lay dying with blood gushing from his body in a crimson stream.

"Let the children go!" Gabrielle cried.

"Let the children go?" The Queen smirked. "The children? Which children might those be? Hers?" Armina nodded towards Mary Anne.

"Or perhaps, they are yours!" Armina laughed, pointing to a honeycomb very high up.

Inside Gabrielle could see the vague forms of two children. Her children.

Gabrielle gasped and rage flooded her. She struggled against the drones, but they dragged her far from the Queen.

"You bitch!" Gabrielle cried. "How dare you?"

"Nigel!" Mary Anne screamed. "For God's sake, help us now!"

"No one can hear you." Armina laughed. "Who is going to come for you? No one knows, no one believes this place exists except those that are meant to. I made sure of that!"

No.

Not my children.

Armina stretched her sickly arms out and from behind her, wings unfurled.

The Birds and the Bees

The Queen flickered the newly born wings quickly, and soon she was in the air, heading for the pocket where Gabrielle's children lay embedded.

"*No!*" Gabrielle screamed. "Leave them alone! They have done nothing to you!"

A hard smack hit Gabrielle across the face. It was Katey.

"Leave my Queen alone," Katey screamed. "You came here uninvited, now deal with it."

"Fuck you!" Gabrielle pushed Katey. John ran over and jumped on Gabrielle. Mary Anne tackled John. The four rolled and punched and screamed at each other, while the Queen flew around, inspecting the new honeycomb, on her way up to the pod where Gabrielle's children lay.

The rest of the hive watched the scene unfold. Some of them stopped watching and went back to work.

Mary Anne found two of the knives that were scattered on the ground, and ran up behind Katey. She shoved one knife into the skinny girl's back, and jumped against her so that she fell onto her with all her strength. Katey screamed.

The scream reached the ears of Armina.

"*No!*" cried Armina. "Not her!"

"See how it feels, bitch!" Gabrielle cried from beneath John, whose hands were tight around her throat. "Let our children go!"

"Never!" Armina cried.

Mary Anne ran for John, and was about to leap onto him as well when a drone caught her and held her back. John turned to face her, and stood up, eyes glowing.

"You bastard. You deserve to die!" Mary Anne screamed at him. He dripped long streams of goo from his mouth and nose, and his eyes were large and buglike. Gabrielle pulled herself up, gasping for air, rubbing her throat. She threw herself at John, knocking him forward. He fell against a rock, hitting his head.

A gust of cold air invaded the cave.

For a moment, everything stopped.

And then, there were birds.

Huge black birds soared toward Armina, pecking at her wings, tearing at her nails, ripping her fur off in clumps. Armina fell back to the earth with a crash.

The spell was broken and pandemonium ensued as people looked around themselves, seeing where they were, what they were becoming.

The birds savagely attacked the Queen, descending on her like rabid animals. Swarms of bees soared out in retaliation, stinging the birds. Birds covered with bees fell to the ground, while more birds snapped and destroyed. The Queen's screams were lost in the caws of the birds as they tore her, piece by piece. Bits of the Queen were flung everywhere. Wings were pulled out, her stinger was ripped apart. As the Queen was shredded, the bees lost

The Birds and the Bees

their instinct and one by one, fell in mid-flight to a paralysis on the ground.

The birds covered the Queen, chewing and pulling at her body parts. In no time at all, it was as if the Queen had never existed.

The birds swirled around the cave in a wave, and then were gone.

A stunned silence filled the cave as people looked at themselves and each other. The Queen was nothing. A few people lay on the ground. Hurt. Dying. Dead.

"Daddy?"

Wendy and Abraham stood in the entrance to the cavern. Wendy ran over to Tommy's body.

"Oh, Daddy, I got here as quick as I could . . . and now . . ." She held her father's limp hand. She looked up at Abraham.

"We were too late."

"I'm sorry, Wendy. We did our best." Abraham wrapped his arm around her as she sobbed.

As people slowly came out of their daze, they realized they were free. They stared at each other, murmuring and muttering. They hugged their loved ones. Many walked and ran from the cave. Many stood around stunned, as if they couldn't digest what had happened at all.

Gabrielle climbed up the honeycomb and into the pocket where her children sat. They hugged her tearfully.

"We were so scared, Mommy."

"I know, honey. So was I," Gabrielle said, soothing them.

"I wanna go home," the girl said.

"Me too," said Gabrielle.

Carefully, they climbed back down the hive.

Mary Anne hugged her own children and led them toward the entrance. Soon they were joined by Gabrielle and her children.

Dawn bathed the land with warm orange light.

"It feels so good to breathe," Mary Anne sighed, her arms around her children.

A steady stream of people emerged from the cave and wandered out across the fields, down the hills, toward the roads.

A huge black bird sat on a nearby rock.

Mary Anne dropped her arms from her children and walked over to it.

"Nigel?"

Mommy.

"Nigel, you saved us all." Mary Anne sank to her knees, sobbing. Abraham spotted Mary Anne and stood beside her. He looked at the hillside and the trees, heavy with a sea of black bodies. The birds stood silently watching.

Waiting.

"We have to send the birds back now. Their job here is done," he said.

"Send them back?"

"To the other side."

Mary Anne shook her head.

The Birds and the Bees

"What are you talking about?"

"They are messengers from the other side. They were here for a purpose. Maybe misused. Maybe not. It is not for us to judge. What is done is done."

"I don't understand you."

"I know now what my purpose has been all along. To help stop this . . . this new war. And now that the birds have destroyed the bees, we must send them back so that they don't get lost on this side and fall into destructive hands," Abraham said.

Gabrielle narrowed her eyes at the birds.

"I think that they can read our minds," Gabrielle said warily.

"Some people can communicate with animals. Some say the black birds are tricksters. Maybe they will do what you say, maybe they won't. That is why we must make sure they get back to the creator as soon as possible."

"How on earth do we do that?"

"We pray. We give thanks. We give thanks for what we have. That we have survived. We give sorrow for those who did not make it." He turned to face the survivors who watched him. "Hold hands."

Mary Anne, Gabrielle, the children, and several others clasped hands, watching Abraham.

Abraham spoke in his native tongue. He felt a flood of words and energy bathe him, and in it, he knew he was right. He knew what his purpose had been all along. Why he had survived the travails of his childhood. Why he had been brought to this new land. He prayed to his God. He thanked his God. Tears of joy flooded him. How he loved this new land, and these people. These people that looked to him for guidance.

"Nigel . . . we thank you, you are free to go," Abraham said in English. The biggest black bird circled up and was gone.

Mary Anne watched it disappear into the sky, tears streaming down her face. "Good-bye, Nigel. I love you," she whispered.

"Blackie, we thank you, you are free to go," Abraham said. Another bird took flight, and they watched until he too disappeared.

"Carmina, we thank you. You are free to go." Abraham looked over at Gabrielle.

"Grandmother?" she gasped.

"Yes, your grandmother."

"Oh my . . ." Gabrielle was speechless as she watched the strong-winged bird fly up into the sky. Tears filled her eyes. All along, it had been her grandmother, trying to protect her. Her stomach was in knots.

"All of you, all of you wonderful brave souls, you are free to go back to your creator."

A huge wind blew up. The sky grew dark and stormy. A cloud hung low, rolling and turning. The sky opened up and a bright light appeared. Hundreds of birds circled and swirled and

The Birds and the Bees

screamed as they flew up and up toward the light.

As the sky closed again, thunder rolled and lightning flashed and then, in moments, the sky was clear once more.

The people watched in stunned disbelief. They stared at each other in silence, and then they all hugged each other. Tears flowed and one by one, they broke the circle and wandered off, trying to remember the life they had had before.

Gabrielle started the car. She had her kids and Wendy and Abraham as passengers. Her thoughts strayed to Tommy, but she stopped them. There was too much to think about. Too many regrets. Too many foolish chances where she had almost lost herself. She took a deep breath.

"God, how I hope that really is the end."

She flipped on the radio. There was a lot of static and crackling as she twirled the dials to find a station that worked.

At last, she tuned in the hysterical voice of an announcer.

"A plane has just hit the World Trade Center. . . ."

A new sorrow will fill the land. But man will persevere. In times of trouble, true human courage will take hold. Sides will be taken, humanity will question itself again and again.

And in the end, there will be survival of the fittest.

Sèphera Girón
House of Pain

The house looks so normal. Just a charming home in a small town--perfect for a young couple starting out together. But this house was built on the site of an unspeakable series of murders, butchery so savage that the brick walls of the basement seemed to flow with blood. Tony was just a boy then but he stood and watched as the notorious house was demolished. Now he's a man, and he's brought his beautiful young wife with him to live in the new house built on the site, without telling her of its hideous secret. Still the nightmares come to her, visions of horror, suffering and perversion, drawing her down to the basement, to a dank tunnel that lies beyond a wall. What calls to her from inside the tunnel? What waits in the darkness to be unleashed?

___4907-4 $5.99 US/$6.99 CAN

Dorchester Publishing Co., Inc.
P.O. Box 6640
Wayne, PA 19087-8640

Please add $2.50 for shipping and handling for the first book and $.75 for each book thereafter. NY and PA residents, please add appropriate sales tax. No cash, stamps, or C.O.D.s. All orders shipped within 6 weeks via postal service book rate. Canadian orders require $2.50 extra postage and must be paid in U.S. dollars through a U.S. banking facility.

Name_____
Address_____
City_____ State _____ Zip _____
I have enclosed $_____ in payment for the checked book(s).
Payment <u>must</u> accompany all orders. ❏ Please send a free catalog.
CHECK OUT OUR WEBSITE! www.dorchesterpub.com

ATTENTION BOOK LOVERS!

Can't get enough
of your favorite HORROR?

Call **1-800-481-9191** to:

— order books —
— receive a **FREE** catalog —
— join our book clubs to **SAVE 20%**! —

Open Mon.-Fri. 10 AM-9 PM EST

Visit
www.dorchesterpub.com
for special offers and inside
information on the authors you love.

We accept Visa, MasterCard or Discover®.